Simon helped her up ⬚⬚⬚⬚⬚⬚⬚
before he mounted the horse and sat behind
her, putting his arms around her and holding
on to the reins. "We leave now."

"What do you mean by this? Where are you taking me?"

Simon's hands came to rest around her waist, anchoring her to him. "Somewhere nearby and where you can take shelter for the night—Trebarr Castle."

Elowen tried to put a little space between them so that she wasn't leaning back against the man. "Trebarr Castle?"

"Does that worry you?" He leaned forward, his hard body meeting the back of hers, sending a frisson through her, his low voice a caress against her ear. "Or mayhap that angers you?"

"Anger me? No, of course not." She sighed. "I am indebted to you for coming to my aid, Simon. I would not be so churlish to mind that you are taking me to Trebarr Castle."

He chuckled softly. "The Elowen Bawden of old would certainly have minded breaching enemy lines."

"Yes, but I am no longer that impulsive and rather foolish maiden."

"Shame, for I rather liked her impertinent tongue. Whatever happened?"

STRANDED WITH HER FORBIDDEN KNIGHT

MELISSA OLIVER

HISTORICAL

Harlequin®
HISTORICAL

ISBN-13: 978-1-335-59629-1

Stranded with Her Forbidden Knight

Recycling programs for this product may not exist in your area.

Harlequin Enterprises ULC
22 Adelaide St. West, 41st Floor
Toronto, Ontario M5H 4E3, Canada
www.Harlequin.com

Printed in U.S.A.

Melissa Oliver is from southwest London, where she writes sweeping historical romance, and is the winner of the Romantic Novelists' Association's 2020 Joan Hessayon Award for new writers for her debut, *The Rebel Heiress and the Knight*.

For more information, visit www.melissaoliverauthor.com.

Follow Melissa on:
Instagram: @MelissaOliverAuthor
Twitter: @MelissaOAuthor
Facebook: MelissaOliverAuthor

Visit the Author Profile page
at Harlequin.com.

True love conquers all obstacles,
defies all storms and deepens its colors
with the passage of time.

I dedicate this book to Jack for always
being there for me. x

Prologue

West Cornwall,
1342

That fateful day had started just the same way as the one before. Yet, it would end like no other. It would end with a tragedy that would change their lives forever.

It had begun as it always had. With two families that despised one another. Two families that each desired the downfall of the other. Just two powerful Cornish families...

Indeed, the enmity between the Trebarrs and Bawdens was as strong and fierce as the waves that frothed and crashed against the cliff, splattering high up in the sky. Even on this mundane of days when the sea was calm and the sky was clear, with only the lightest of breezes rippling through the long, tall grasses dotted around the top of the jagged coastline in the western most point of Simon's beloved Cornwall.

Yet, *she* would have it said that it was hers—*her* beloved western Cornwall. In truth, all of Elowen Bawden's kin would have been of the same mind. As though the Trebarrs could not also trace their lineage back to a time before the Norman conquest. As though the Trebarrs did not also lay claim to their land, their tinnery, their family name, their honour. No, the Bawdens deemed them somehow to be less than they and why? Well, because they believed the Trebarrs to be betraying their Cornish traditions. And that they were once merchants, traders in fine cattle from Brittany, who eventually settled in Cornwall as many old Cornish families did.

It was jealousy and resentment that fuelled the Bawdens' anger, yet the Trebarrs could hardly be at fault for that. Despite all his faults, Simon's father looked ahead to the future prosperity of their kin instead of constantly looking back. It was nothing more than resentment. The Bawdens resented the fact that Edward of Woodstock, the first Duke of Cornwall, The Black Prince, himself, had given his favour to the Trebarrs and bestowed land that once belonged to the Bawdens along with an old tinnery. Jealousy indeed…

Yet, on that fateful day as Simon approached the edge of the cliff and stumbled upon a lone figure—a girl, or rather a young woman—he had no inclination of what might then unfold and unravel soon after. All Simon had wanted was to gratify his curiosity as to the identity of the interloper, which had then been gratified forthwith, as soon as the girl pulled down the hood of her embroidered woollen cape.

It was *her*.

Just as he'd suspected.

It was Elowen Bawden standing tall and proud with her head thrown back, her eyes shut tightly, breathing the salty sea air into her chest. God, but she looked magnificent, despite the fact that she stood on Trebarr land. For a moment, though, Simon watched her from afar, mesmerised by her famously unusual hair, plaited long and slung over one shoulder. The colour, so fair, so pale, that it almost blinded with its unruly silvery pale brilliance.

Simon gave his head a shake, clearing his mind from his musings, and reminded himself of his duty.

'Well, well, well,' he said out loud, breaking whatever solitude Elowen Bawden had been savouring here. 'Trespassing on Trebarr land, I see.'

She turned on her heel, her long woollen cape flapping around her, evidently annoyed at being disturbed in such a manner. 'If you could "see" anything at all, then you would know that this land is not in any way yours, Trebarr.'

God, but how he hated the haughty, imperious manner that the girl used to address him—a clipped tone that could crack even the hardiest of findings in the mines. 'Oh, and how would you surmise that, Mistress Bawden?'

'Quite easily, Trebarr.'

'Even when the prince of this kingdom, the county's own duke, has decreed it so? The very land you stand on belongs to the Trebarrs and no other.'

She lifted a shoulder and dropped it nonchalantly. 'The king himself could decree it and I would still not accept it so.'

'Then it is a good thing that it has little to do with the likes of you! And by the by, what you just said is treason.'

'I am sorry but should I care?'

Simon took a step towards her. 'Yes, for silly girls who are found guilty of such crimes against the Crown are thrown off the cliff to the depths of the sea.'

Elowen actually rolled her eyes. Rolled those bored dark brown eyes that seemed to see right through him. Indeed, she had taken his measure and knew that he was nothing more than a second son who had to make his way in the world. Not that she cared either way about a Trebarr. As he cared little about Elowen or her kin. But by God her cool appraisal stung. As did her indifference. No wonder the girl was known as the Ice Maiden. And it was at moments like this that Simon felt the need to ruffle her a little. Just to make her feel a little unsettled and discomposed as he did. Especially while she just stood there belligerent and unfazed at being alone with him on Trebarr land.

'And you would do that, eh? Throw me off the edge and into the sea?' He knew that she was goading him intentionally, but Elowen Bawden always managed to get under his skin whenever they met. Which was not just the handful of times the Trebarrs had been forced to endure the Bawdens' company at formal banquets held for all local Cornish nobility. No, Simon had encountered the termagant whenever she trailed after her twin brother, Hedyn, and followed wherever he led, usually trespassing on Trebarr land, as she had today.

Yet, there was another time, one that was burnt into his memory, when Simon had watched in fascination as she came out of the sea after a swim and how it had managed to stir an unwanted emotion in his chest for a maid who always seemed to plague him, as she was wont of doing now.

'Don't tempt me.' Simon knew that he'd used the wrong words the moment he'd said them. Indeed, he'd blundered badly as all sorts of temptations filled his head. And every one included the icy maiden standing in front of him.

'I wouldn't dream of doing anything that might tempt you, Trebarr. Not even to commit a misdeed such as that.' She lifted her head, her brown eyes glittering with mirth.

'You enjoy provoking me, Elowen,' he whispered, taking another step towards her.

'I admit that I do, Simon.' She shrugged. 'It's just so easy to do.'

'Well, why not save it for another?' He lifted her chin up with his finger and thumb so that her eyes met his. 'Such as the man you'll soon be wed to.'

He took in her small gasp, her brows knitting in the middle, and smiled, knowing that he'd given her some of her own teasing provocation.

'That is not your concern, Trebarr.'

'No, it's not but it might be for your intended. And you would not want to add any further concerns to a man who is so much older than your own father. Why, he could be your grandsire.' He tapped his chin with his fingertips. 'Tell me again, Elowen, but are his son and daughter not older than you as well?'

Somehow, she had managed to mask her annoyance as she raised a brow and gave him a disdainful glare. Her voice, however, was still as cool and indifferent as usual. As though they were discussing the weather. 'I believe that that, too, is none of your concern, Trebarr.'

'Always so composed. Always so aloof. I wonder if Philip of Hanford knows that he is soon to be wed to a young maiden known to possess such an icy heart.'

'And what would you know of my heart or what I

might possess?' It was then that she pulled away. The flicker of anger that sparked in her eyes, which was just as quickly extinguished, made him wonder whether he'd imagined it all along.

'I would never assume to know that, nor would I want to.' He looked away in disgust. 'But I do know that might be the reason you remind me so much of Morvoren, the sea maiden with the cold heart. Now go, Elowen. You don't belong here.'

'Devil take you, Simon!' she said as she turned to leave, taking a step away from him. But Elowen Bawden took a wrong step, as the ground beneath her feet, unsteady and uneven, made her stumble backwards.

Her desperate scream went through him as he watched Elowen flapping her arms about her as she fell. Without another thought, Simon threw himself at her, able to grasp her before she plummeted down to her inevitable death. 'I have you. Hush now, I have you.'

It was the first time that he'd held Elowen Bawden in his arms. Her shivering body folded into his; her scent, cool and distinctive, wrapped around him. Simon ran his fingers up and down her spine, trying to soothe her, nestling his face into that unusual silvery pale hair, inhaling deeply.

He had never been this close to her. He'd never touched her and nor would he be allowed to again. Not that he'd ever wanted to. Well, that wasn't quite true but Simon needed to remind himself of who this maid was. And yet, it was Elowen Bawden who came to that realisation first.

'You saved my life.' She tilted her head back, a ghost of a smile hovering at her lips. 'I admit that I cannot quite believe it.'

'Can you not?' His voice was low and raspy, even to his own ears. This close to Elowen Bawden, Simon was unable to think as he should, as he surely must, because he had the sudden urge to press his mouth to hers just so that he could taste her. His curiosity to know more about her was becoming a little overwhelming.

Elowen shook her head. 'In truth, I had thought you'd welcome my demise and believed it to be a justified penance for such treasonous beliefs.'

'You cannot believe such a thing. Not even of me,' he muttered hoarsely.

Her lips curled into a soft smile. 'Either way, I thank you.'

'You are welcome.'

Instead of pulling away, they both stayed as they were, watching one another, curious and unyielding. In truth, Simon felt reluctant to let her go just then. What he actually wanted was to savour this moment, knowing it would never happen again. Elowen would never allow it. Besides, she was destined to marry another. And a good thing too.

But for now… For now, they had this moment…

His eyes dropped to her lips and he dipped his head down lower until there was little separating them. He noticed her lick her lips, the air around them stilling as though time had slowed, drowning out everything except for the beating of his heart.

'Let. Go. Of my sister!'

Of course, it was at that precise moment that Elowen Bawden's hot-tempered twin, Hedyn, had to come upon them. Simon would have laughed at his bad luck, had it not been for the realisation that the situation could get more unpleasant if he didn't attempt to smooth things over. After all, had Simon a sister, he would have felt just as angry to discover her in the arms of a Bawden.

'Did you hear what I said?'

'Good morrow, Hedyn. I am glad that you're here, for you can escort your sister home.' Simon dropped his arms to his sides and took a step away from Elowen. 'In truth, you have arrived just in time to do so.'

'It seems that I have.' The young man drew out his sword from its scabbard and pointed it at him. 'But I should cut you from here to here for even laying your filthy hands on her.'

Simon held his hands in the air and moved cautiously towards him. 'Come now, I do not want any trouble.'

'Then you should have thought of that before you touched my sister.' He spat. 'You dare dishonour her in such a manner!'

'Stop it, Hedyn. No such dishonour was made.'

'You would take his side in it, Elowen? A Trebarr?' he cried in outrage.

'No, never. But I… I was about to fall off the edge of the cliff, and Simon Trebarr grabbed my hand and pulled me against him. That is all that you have seen here. Nothing more, I assure you.'

'And yet I am not assured.' Hedyn Bawden strode closer, his pale, almost white, hair the same shade as his sister's. 'For it does not in any manner explain why you would be alone with a Trebarr, Elowen.'

'I… I was not.'

'Why are you even here on this land with such a worthless nobody, Elowen? Why would I find you alone with this Trebarr filth?'

'Enough!' Simon roared. 'Enough of your insults, and especially after the assistance I have given to your sister. Now, take her by the hand and go, Bawden. Go!'

'Do not ever presume to command me.'

'I shall do precisely what I like on Trebarr land. This is your final warning, Bawden. Go. Now.'

Elowen had the good sense to move towards her brother, taking him by the hand and attempting to pull him away from this situation that was rapidly becoming more and more fractious.

'That's right. Go, leave and never dare insult me again!'

Simon knew that he should not allow the Bawden heir to rouse his anger but unlike his sister, who intrigued him with her air of cool, calm detachment, Hedyn Bawden was a seething, angry coil of instability waiting to explode at any minute. And Simon would not put up with him casting aspersions on his family's name and honour. It was unacceptable. The younger man was nothing more than a petulant fool, but a dangerous one at that.

'Oh, I dare…' The man sneered. 'Because it is *you* insulting me, Trebarr, when you touched my sister!'

'Stop it, Hedyn. *Please.*'

The younger man turned to face his sister, his features softening. 'He was holding you, Elowen.'

'If he hadn't, I would have perished.' She spoke so gently, resting her hand on his arm, evidently trying to soothe her brother's torrent of rage bubbling under the surface, as one would an injured wild animal lashing out. 'Can you see?'

'Not *him*.' Hedyn shook his head, his features contorted in anguish as he cupped her face. A wordless exchange passed between the twins, an understanding that only those with such close bonds as the pair in front of Simon obviously had. A secret language that only they shared. A silent war, a clash of beliefs. Because in truth, Hedyn Bawden must have sensed the truth of what would have happened had he not appeared when he had, despite what his sister was trying to tell him. That Simon would have kissed Elowen and she would likely have allowed it.

'Let *him* not be the one,' he pleaded with her. 'He's a Trebarr, Elowen. He should not even breathe the same air as you.'

But this was more than Simon could tolerate. He had just about enough of both of them in truth. 'Ah, but it is Trebarr air that you breathe.'

It was a flippant nothing of a remark but in hindsight one that Simon should not have made, knowing the mood and temper Hedyn Bawden was in.

The younger man spun around and lifted the sword he'd been holding and pointed it straight at Simon, the tension once again mounting between them. 'What did you say?'

'I believe you heard, Bawden, but I shall repeat myself just so you manage to understand me. This air, the very air that you and especially Elowen are breathing, is Trebarr air. Ours, *mine*.'

'You are nothing but an opportunist reprobate, like all your damn family. And what do you mean, *especially* Elowen?'

'I believe that you know.'

Elowen turned to him and scowled. 'Stop it, Simon!'

'*Simon*, eh?' Hedyn grimaced at his sister. 'When did

you begin such familiarity with a Trebarr? Calling him by his given name. And what the hell does he mean, that I should know? Know what, Elowen?'

'Nothing, he means nothing. Please, let us just go back home.'

'No, I want to know what he means.'

'Listen to your sister, Bawden.'

But the man ignored both of them. 'Are you insinuating that there is some attachment between you and Elowen? Or mayhap you were about to take advantage of my sister in this remote place? Either way, I cannot fathom why she would protect you.'

'Because it is not true.'

'I do not believe you, Trebarr!'

'I care not what you believe, Bawden!'

Hedyn took a step towards him. 'You are to keep away from her, do you understand?' Hedyn barked, trying again to get a rise out of him. 'Or would you prefer that I make you understand?'

Simon blew out frustrated air from his mouth and shook his head. 'Just go. Go before you make yourself look even more ridiculous than you already do.'

'Ridiculous? You believe that I am ridiculous for looking out for my sister's honour?' The anger he'd been holding on to finally snapped. Simon had to end this discourse before it grew out of hand.

'You're beginning to bore me, Bawden. And your sister's honour is just as it was before you came to all sorts of ill-begotten conclusions. Now, go and leave me in peace.' With that, Simon turned his back on the man, hoping that it would finally put an end to this nonsensical interlude.

He sadly had no such good fortune, for the moment his back was turned, Hedyn came lunging at him, his sister screaming for her brother to stop.

Simon would have agreed with Elowen but knew that the younger man was now beyond all sense and reason, seeing this whole exchange as a slight on him and his family. As always, making everything about the Bawden name.

Simon spun around, drawing out his sword from its scabbard, just in time to strike out a defensive move. He'd have had a blade stuck in his back had he not reacted so expediently. But naturally, Hedyn Bawden wasn't done there as he came at Simon again and again, with even more spleen and aggression.

'Hell's teeth, Hedyn, enough! What is it that you want?' Simon said through gritted teeth.

'Your head on a silver trencher, Trebarr. But for now an apology would suffice.'

'Let me understand this. You wish me to apologise? Very well, then,' Simon muttered as he countered a defensive blow before stepping back and taking a deep bow that dripped with derision. 'Lady Elowen, I humbly ask that you accept my apology for saving your life.'

'You think this amusing?' the man barked as he lunged at him again.

'Somewhat, yes. But mostly I believe this to be ridiculous, as I stated before.'

'You damn cur, Trebarr,' the younger man roared as he lunged at him. 'You craven whoreson!'

He countered more of the younger man's strikes. 'I'm getting tired of this, Bawden. And you really do have some sort of destructive streak here.'

'Then fight me!' the man screamed as he pushed forward, striking again and again. 'Fight me as you would anyone.'

'But then again, mayhap you need to address that temper of yours first!'

'I said fight me!'

Elowen started forward. 'Please, Hedyn. Enough of this. Before anyone gets hurt.'

'That is actually the point, Elowen. To hurt someone, rather, to hurt Trebarr.'

'You should listen to your sister. At least she has some modicum of sense. Unlike you!'

And to prove his point, Hedyn Bawden roared and exhaled hot air before coming at Simon again and again, striking his sword as hard and fast as he could. And while the younger man had an abundance of aggression and anger, he lacked the power and skill needed to cause any real damage. Even so, his intention was to cause a blistering blow and he had used any excuse to attack Simon, and on Trebarr land. That was not acceptable.

Enough... Simon had enough of the younger man's stupidity and his unprovoked assault. If he wasn't going to stop this nonsense, then he would have to stop the man himself. He spun on his heel and thrust his sword, lunging at Hedyn with as much force as he could muster. He brought his sword down in a punishing strike, making his opponent fall and stumble, throwing his sword out of his hand. Simon ate up the short distance and picked up Bawden's sword.

'I think that's all the ridiculous display that I can stomach for one day, do you not think?' He nodded at him. 'If you would be kind enough to leave now, we can forget this whole sorry interlude ever happened.'

Hedyn stood, glaring at him, his nose flaring, his breathing laboured as his sister once again pulled at his hand, trying to shepherd him away. 'Very well, with the return of my sword, we shall leave you in peace, Trebarr.'

God, anything for this all to end. Simon sighed and held Bawden's sword vertically before pushing it down into the ground. It was then that he looked up and caught Elowen's eyes, giving her a small, understanding smile. And it was then Hedyn caught the exchange, flicking his gaze from his sister to Simon, his ire evidently mounting more and more as he came up with all sorts of mistaken assumptions about the two of them again.

It all happened so quickly then.

Bawden's snarl and roar; the force and pace at which he came at Simon, surprising and throwing him off balance; how they then rolled on the uneven ground, while Elowen pleaded an end to the fight; Hedyn attacking him and not realising how close to the edge of the cliff they'd got, as they fought to gain the upper hand; Simon managing to push him off and rolling away to get on his feet.

And then finally, what none of them had expected to happen, actually came to pass:

Hedyn Bawden losing his balance as he rose to stand and starting to flap his arms around in panic just as his sister had done only moments ago. This time, however, Simon was too late. This time he could not reach Bawden as he fell backwards, the shock and fear etched on the man's face as he plummeted all the way down to land on the craggy rocks below.

It was horrifying to watch as though time had slowed to that singular moment of sheer horror. And then the aftermath.

That scream. Oh, God, Elowen's piercing scream would haunt Simon until his dying days. He clamped his arms around the woman's waist, preventing her from looking over the edge at the terrible sight below, as she howled, cried and screamed hysterically.

No… Simon might have an end to the pointless altercation with Hedyn Bawden, but he had never wanted his death. He had never wanted this…

He had never wanted everything to change irrevocably. But it had…

It had.

Chapter One

Elowen glanced around the busy main hall in Bawden Manor and grimaced. God, but this was going to be yet another tiresome evening in honour of her father's young and spirited wife, Roesia, who was about to enter into her confinement. Again. And for her send-off, a celebration had been brought forth, asserting hope in the Bawden kin at the prospect of a new issue and a promise this time of a male heir.

There would be merriment, with plenty of mead and ale, an abundance of meat, poultry and fish cooked with spices and herbs, as well as fresh and dried fruits, warm baked breads on large silver trenchers, served on decorated trestle tables that stretched around the periphery of the hall. Musicians had been brought in to provide entertainment and a convivial atmosphere. Indeed, it was set to be a wonderful eventide, welcoming the promise of another child into the Bawden kin. And glancing at her father, who was so blissfully content with his new family, Elowen could not help but feel that she was now in the way. Indeed, she knew she was. Ever since becoming a widow, with her older husband, Philip of Hanford, passing away not more than a year after they'd wed, she had been forced to return back to Bawden Manor, especially as they had no children in their short marriage. And now more than ever before, Elowen felt like an outsider. At least the people and vassals of Bawden welcomed her with open arms, even though her father had not. To him she'd become an inconvenient reminder of a time that he'd rather forget. Meaning that his wife, Roesia, also treated her with barely disguised disdain.

God, but it was at times like this that Elowen felt sad and alone in the world. She knew that she no longer belonged here but with little choice for her future, there was nowhere else for her to go, unless she entered a Holy Order.

It was also at times like this that she missed her brother, Hedyn, who was the only person who had ever really cared about her. For all his faults and there had been many, she loved Hedyn. He might have been impulsive, hotheaded and far too quick to make assumptions, but he had nevertheless been her greatest ally. And he had been so fiercely loyal, her one and only person to defend her, even if he had been unnecessarily overprotective at times. These past few years Elowen had also missed that close bond that she had shared with her twin brother, a bond that tied them to one another even though they had been nothing alike. Indeed, she had never gotten over his loss. It still felt as though a part of her had perished as well that terrible day when he'd died. When it had all unfolded so disastrously.

What had started as a little bit of harmless banter, a

bit of teasing between Elowen and Simon Trebarr, had resulted in Hedyn misunderstanding the whole situation, overreacting before ultimately losing his life in the end. Even though she had thought at the time that Simon Trebarr had been intent on kissing her. And she had secretly wanted him to. How utterly ridiculous. Her chest clenched tightly in a painful ache. And now, looking around at the merriment in Bawden Hall, it was as though her brother had never existed at all. As though their world hadn't been ripped apart when he'd fallen to his death five years ago. Life had just continued, as Elowen supposed it should, but sometimes the reminder of it was like a knife in the heart. Her father, Breock, had wasted no time after Hedyn's untimely death to marry again and beget new heirs. However, their issue had been two beautiful little girls much to their parents' dismay, whom Elowen nevertheless treasured immensely, despite having little opportunity to spend time with them. She was rarely afforded much time with her two adorable infant half sisters, since their mother, who was only a year older than Elowen, believed that the little girls should be occupied in far better pursuits than the type of adventures that Elowen might suggest. In truth, Roesia just did not want Elowen anywhere near her daughters. The woman had never warmed to her, not that Elowen had warmed to her, either, but had initially wanted to make the effort for her father's sake. Yet, apart from her father's lack of interest, it had been the fealty and influence that Elowen yielded among both kin and the Bawden vassals that made Roesia also turn against her, although never openly. The woman would not stand to being challenged as mistress and chatelaine of Bawden Manor by the daughter of her husband, even if Elowen had never any intention of challenging her for that coveted role. Indeed, the woman had been frustrated and annoyed that Elowen had been forced to return to Bawden Manor after her first husband's death, but could do little about it apart from making Elowen feel unwelcome back home.

Had she provided her husband with an heir then mayhap Elowen's future would have been more secure and it would all have turned out differently. But life never did unfold as one wished it to.

Roesia caught her eye and summoned her to come to her, as her father rose to move among the guests and well-wishers.

'How may I be of service, Roesia?'

The woman patted the empty wooden bench. 'Sit beside me for a moment, Elowen. I would like to discuss something of great import to you, something that your father and I wish to tell you.'

Elowen raised a brow. 'Oh, what is it that you wished to say, my lady?'

'That you are a very fortunate woman.' Roesia smiled. 'To have such considerate and caring parents such as us.'

Elowen returned her smile even though it felt brittle on her lips. 'Indeed I am.'

'Yes, I hope always to be an attentive mother to all my children.'

Children?

God give her strength in moments such as this.

'Yes,' Elowen muttered lamely, uncertain of what to say to such a comment.

It was beyond preposterous that Roesia, who was

of the same age as her, wanted to assert herself as her mother. The truth was that she did not. The woman only wanted to assert herself over Elowen. 'So is that all you wanted to inform me, my lady?'

'No, of course not. Patience, my dear, is a virtue that you lack but no matter, since I do have exciting news to tell you. News that I hope you shall welcome.'

'Oh, and what might that be?' The woman's gaze darted around the hall until it rested at the entrance as a cluster of people were conferring close to the main wooden doors.

Roesia smiled excitedly without looking in her direction. 'I believe you shall soon find out.'

'What does that mean?' The woman merely nodded at the guards by the door, who then opened it after getting the signal to do so. 'Roesia, what is going on?'

'Wait, for goodness' sake! A little patience, as I said before, is what is required. Then all shall be revealed,' she muttered from the side of her mouth.

Naturally, Roesia seemed to be enjoying this—whatever this happened to be. More people gathered around the entrance, causing a stir at the opposite end of the hall. Elowen strained her neck trying to see what the commotion was about, when the crowd of people parted as if by magic and Simon Trebarr and his men swaggered into the hall, striding down towards the dais. The noisy din in the hall quietened down to a hush as every single person present stopped what they were doing and stared at the interloper who had come among them. God above, but a Trebarr had entered the Bawden domain. Nothing such as this had ever happened before. Elowen looked the man up and down and was shocked how much he had changed since the last time she had seen him five years ago. He had always been tall but now he had filled out, all sinewy, whipcord muscle and broad shoulders. His face had lost its boyish roundness and now was lean and slashed with sharp angles. His dark hair was far longer than it should be, and there was a small scar that ran through the corner of his mouth, adding a slight imperfection to an otherwise perfect face. But it was his eyes that almost had Elowen gasping in surprise. They might still be the same green eyes that the Trebarrs were famed for, but now they carried a glint of shrewdness that had never been there before; a certain coldness that made Elowen almost shudder with a certain apprehension. And yet, she could hardly deny that Simon Trebarr was the most beautiful man she had ever known and even more so now than before.

His gaze darted around the hall before it caught on to Elowen's. Something flickered into life inside her, a palpable, inexplicable heat that spread throughout her body. In that brief moment, everything stilled, everything seemed to melt away. It was almost as though there was nothing and no one else there apart from them. His eyes held hers for a moment longer as the corner of his mouth lifted faintly before he blinked and looked away.

God, how mortifying. Had she really looked at Simon Trebarr with unfettered longing? She had and he had known it. Indeed, her visceral reaction to him was just as annoying as his unwelcome arrival here in Bawden Manor. He was a reminder of everything that had happened and everything that he had inadvertently caused, even though she had in truth been as much to blame as he had. But Elowen did not want that. She did not need this added reminder of why her life was such a disaster, since she did that very well on her own. Indeed, she already carried the burden of unhappiness, guilt and blame.

'This? This was the exciting news that you spoke of? Simon Trebarr?'

'Of course not!' she hissed under her breath. 'I was speaking of your imminent betrothal.'

'What?' Elowen practically shot out of her seat. 'Betrothal to whom? To whom? Answer me… Roesia?'

Before Roesia could answer they watched transfixed as Simon stopped before her father, exuding the power and confidence that a man of his stature and influence could ever hope to, especially one who had recently succeeded to be Lord Trebarr after the deaths of his father and older brother.

'Good evening, my lord Bawden,' Simon drawled in a low tone, inclining his head in apparent deference to her father. 'I hope I have not intruded on your evening's revelry?'

Why was the man here? Had he forgotten the enmity between the Bawdens and the Trebarrs? That was not possible.

The sudden change and tension in the hall was palpable as all who were present were holding their breath, waiting to comprehend the reason for Simon Trebarr's visit to Bawden Manor and whether it would be well received or not.

'You are indeed intruding, Trebarr, or should I say *Lord Trebarr* now, of course?'

'Yes, I am.'

Her father rubbed his chin and his brows furrowed

in the middle as he watched Simon for a moment before he spoke again. 'What can I do for you, Trebarr?'

'It is a small matter, my lord. One that I know was of great import to my father right up until his death. And even though he may no longer be here, I believe it to be my duty to petition for this on behalf of all my kin.' Simon's gaze darted around the hall before returning back to her father. 'However, I can come at a more convenient time for a parley, my lord.'

Her father looked him up and down with barely disguised contempt before he finally answered. 'What manner of a petition?'

'If you would oblige me with your time in a more private setting then I can explain my reason for being here.'

The tension of the hall grew as all who were present waited to see what her father's response would be. But Breock Bawden only stared at the young man in front of him, stroking his beard before finally breaking the silence.

'Very well,' her father muttered. 'I would like it known that on this eventide, when Lady Bawden is set to enter her confinement and God willing deliver me an heir, we the Bawdens have agreed to parley with the Trebarrs. This, my friends, my family, my kin—this is a good omen.'

'Indeed it is.'

'But on my choosing, Trebarr, which will be directly after I finish my repast. And not to look inhospitable, you and your men may also sup here.'

'That is most generous of you, Lord Bawden.'

'I am in a generous mood,' he said coldly before standing and clicking his fingers to summon a serving girl to quickly sidle up to Simon and pour him a goblet of wine and hand it to him.

'Thank you, my lord Bawden,' Simon said, raising his goblet in the air.

'Come then, Trebarr, take a seat on the dais. You shall be allowed to take food here as your father never was.'

The noise dimmed once again to a sudden tense silence as everyone present waited to see whether Simon Trebarr would react to the slight slur directed at his late father or whether he was shrewd enough to let it go and not respond in the manner in which he was expected to.

Simon smiled and nodded. 'Very well. And I hope this eventide might bring forth a new peace between our two families.'

It seemed that the man was just as pragmatic as he looked, pandering to her father's ego. No doubt doing so in the hope that whatever his petition might be it would be met with success. Even so, it did not sit well with Elowen that the very man who was equally to blame for the death of her brother as she was—a Trebarr, no less, whom she had been taught to hate and distrust since she was a little girl—was now invited to sit at the head table in this great hall.

She cringed in embarrassment as she recalled their brief yet heated glance earlier. What was she thinking? How could she look upon him in that unguarded manner, surrounded by her Bawden kin? Yet, that was always the problem whenever she was in Simon Trebarr's presence. She always forgot herself as she did many years ago, when she caught him standing far off on the cliffs staring at her as she came out of the sea. And she certainly forgot herself when he had almost kissed her on that terrible day five years ago…

She shuffled along the wooden bench, moving far away, hoping that her presence was no longer needed.

'Ah, Elowen, serve Lord Trebarr from your untouched trencher.'

It seemed that she would not be so lucky to escape this. 'Of course, Father.'

'Come, girl, we haven't got all evening,' he said irritably, ushering Simon to sit beside her. 'Fetch Lord Trebarr a knife, a plate and some of the cuts of meat.'

Elowen did as her father bid, as he watched her every move in obvious dismay. 'Apologies for Elowen's slowness, my lord. I think it must be the excitement of learning of her betrothal that has her all aflutter and unable to concentrate on such little tasks.'

She passed Simon's plate to him in silence, wishing she was anywhere but here. God, but Elowen felt herself flush furiously in shame, watching her father turn his attention to his giggling wife after ridiculing her.

Elowen sat down and turned away, closing her eyes for a moment and taking in a deep breath. Not only had she felt utterly humiliated but in all the commotion of Simon Trebarr's arrival, she had forgotten that Roesia had also mentioned a damned betrothal, failing, however, to furnish her with necessary details of whom she was supposed to be betrothed to. If only Elowen could get away, just a moment to regain her composure.

'Could you possibly pass some of that fruit pickle there, mistress?' the annoying man from her side said.

God, at least she was not to be betrothed to Simon Trebarr. That she would never be able to accept. No, she could never be bound to a man who made her feel things that she had no right to feel. It was as shocking as it was unbearable. In truth, she should hate him. 'I believe you can reach for it yourself, my lord.'

How strange it was to call this man by his new lofty title but one that was now his.

'And I believe that your father said that you were to help serve, mistress.'

Elowen refused to take the bait by this man just as she refused to glance in his direction. 'My father says many things.'

'But you seldom follow his counsel?' he muttered and reached for the small bowl of apple and carrot pickle.

'I did not say that.'

'You did not have to, Elowen. Mmm… This pickle is delicious. May I offer you some?'

'I thank you but no.'

'Are you sure because it really is very good. Come, let me tend you as you failed to do for me.'

'I said no…thank you,' she hissed, trying to hold on to her temper.

'Very well, suit yourself.'

'Oh, I shall. Believe me, I shall.'

Elowen tried to ignore the man who sat beside her, even though it was exceedingly hard to do so. His size, his warmth, was proving far too potent and was even making breathing difficult. God, but it was as stifling as it was unacceptable. She looked away, wanting to expel these unwanted feelings about a man who certainly should not affect her in this manner after five long years. Instead, she trained her gaze sideways, noting her father, head bent talking with his wife. She could recall that she had once been her father's precious daughter but all that had changed the moment she had returned to Bawden Manor alone and without her brother five years ago. Indeed, her father had blamed Elowen for her brother's death and had resented her for being the one who had lived, the one who had had come back home. It was a truth that was reflected in his eyes even if it was not expressed in actual words. And if her father and his wife had arranged for another betrothal for her then so be it. He would rid himself of his unwanted daughter, even though the thought of being another man's wife, one whom she still did not know, made Elowen feel uneasy. She felt wary as though she were trapped with little choice in the matter. But she did. Elowen could decline the alliance if she so wanted, couldn't she? In truth, there was still so much to discuss before she accepted any such arrangement. Indeed, Elowen needed time to think, time to ponder, which was not altogether easy seated beside Simon Trebarr.

'So, you are once again betrothed, mistress?' It seemed that Simon Trebarr was not done tormenting her this evening. Something he had always seemed to enjoy.

'It would seem so, my lord,' she said, not wanting to divulge her misgivings to the man.

'Then felicitations. I hope that this marriage brings you a lasting happiness.'

Elowen turned her head, her eyes narrowed in suspicion, wondering whether she would find derision or mockery with those earnest words that he'd uttered, and was surprised to find none.

'I thank you,' she said, equally surprised at herself for meaning it.

'So, who is the lucky man?' he said, taking her off guard.

Elowen blinked several times, not knowing what to say. After all, what could she say? That she did not know whom her father intended to betroth her to, not that she had agreed to anything yet? She could hardly say that it was sprung on her this evening and that she still did not know any of the details.

'I very much doubt you would know him.'

He chuckled softly. 'There is no way of you knowing that, Elowen. Come, tell me, unless it is a secret?'

Why this need to know something so inconsequential? It was not as though anything about her mattered to Simon Trebarr. Yet, there were times despite being from families that despised one another, that they did. That they mattered to one another. Which of course, was absurd. How could it be so? When she was who she was. And he was a Trebarr.

'Of course, it is not. But the betrothal has yet to be announced so until then, it shall remain private.'

'Very well, keep your secrets.' He shrugged, taking a swig of wine from the goblet that he had been absently turning in his hand. 'It is not my concern.'

No, it was not. Yet, did he somehow feel that he was owed it—her secrets, her thoughts? As if they shared anything beyond what had always existed between their families despite her father's leniency on this night. Mayhap he did because of the handful of encounters they had had, from those secret heated looks to that almost-kiss that led to her brother's demise. Not that the harrowing tragedy of that day was something that Elowen wanted to dwell on. It would otherwise dig up those long-ago feelings of anger and resentfulness that she felt for Simon when in truth she should forget his very existence.

But this close, it was difficult to forget him, even if she wanted to. This close, his scent, clean and masculine, as well as the heat emanating from him, reminded Elowen of those elicit emotions moments before Hedyn happened upon them five years ago. When Simon had been holding her, staring intently into her eyes. When he had almost kissed her and she had wanted it desperately. Hedyn had not been wrong about them that day. He had taken one look at them and known the truth after encountering them in an embrace after Simon had caught her as she had nearly fallen down the cliff. And when he had challenged Simon, he had inadvertently challenged Elowen as well, reminding her of the bitter enmity that had existed between their families. They had both been shamed by Hedyn and he lost his life in the process, something that Elowen would never forgive herself for, nor the man who sat beside her.

'Why are you here, Simon?' she said quietly, trying to stop the bitterness from seeping into her words.

'Should I not be? After all, your father accepted my reasoning for this visit.' Simon must have noticed how she clenched her jaw tightly as he nodded, understanding. 'Ah, but you do not, do you?'

'No,' she muttered through gritted teeth, 'I do not.'

How Simon Trebarr had the gall to come here to Bawden Manor after everything that happened was beyond her comprehension.

'If you will excuse me, I shall retire now. I find that I have lost my appetite.'

And with that, Elowen rose and turned on her heel to leave as quickly as her feet could carry her. God, but she could not stay a moment longer.

Chapter Two

Simon paced the narrow antechamber outside Breock Bawden's small privy chamber, awaiting to being granted an audience with him as promised later that eventide. He had been left to wait for a long time in this airless room as he felt his frustration and annoyance grow more and more. He needed to get back to the vast wild Trebarr lands that overlooked the sea and the impressive castle that had become his ever since the death of his older brother Geoffrey, who had perished a few months ago after falling from his horse. His father had died a couple of years earlier, when Simon had been on a campaign in France. Not that his sire would have wanted to see him even on his deathbed. The man could not stand the sight of Simon despite all the glory and wealth he had accumulated for the Trebarrs. No, his father could never look beyond what Simon had done. Not that it mattered now. But what did, was the reason why he was here in Bawden Manor. For peace.

As the new lord of Trebarr, Simon wanted to gain some peace, which had always been so elusive to attain. Even now, there were many other problems that he'd needed to deal with since returning to Trebarr. One of which was what he would do with Anaís, his brother's young widow, whose welfare he'd inherited just as he'd inherited all of Trebarr, its castle and the demesne lands as well as its profitable mines. A young woman whom he was expected to wed. In truth, his brother's widow was the woman he *should* wed. After all, he felt nothing for the young woman and he could never marry anyone he was attached to, or God forbid, loved. No, the bitterness that coursed through his veins made his stomach sour as he once again vowed to himself that he would never be like his father.

And standing here in Bawden Manor, his mind was preoccupied on other pressing matters that had been troubling him for a very long time. It still revolved around the memories of what had happened in Trebarr five years ago. However much success he had had in his life since, it still ate away at him. It had mattered not that he had found himself in France and in the retinue of Edward the Black Prince of England, Duke of Cornwall and Prince of Wales. It had mattered not that Simon had been decorated by the young prince for saving his life as well as leading his men to victory in France and given even more lands and riches than he could ever have dreamt of. He still felt that same sense of guilt and remorse because of what had happened that day to Hedyn Bawden and the part he played in the young man's demise. All of which was the reason why he had swallowed his pride and come here. He'd even prostrated himself in front of all who had assembled in the hall, including Breock Bawden, who seemed to have enjoyed how he'd humbled himself in front of him, but he did it anyway. Simon had expected it and had put himself through the whole damn spectacle so that he could, in part, atone for his past misdemeanours. It was what he'd wanted to do for as long as he could remember and certainly once he'd become Lord Trebarr. But now being made to wait on Bawden for this long was more than he could accept.

'Do you believe the old goat might actually listen to anything that you are to put to him, Simon?' His oldest friend Ranulf Gibbons, who was known affectionately by all who knew him in Trebarr as *Gib*, was watching Simon pace the small area with a smile on his face. 'It is not as though he ever gave any concessions while your father was alive, so is it not doubtful that he would now?'

Trust Gib, his comrade who had always been by his side on all his campaigns, to be the voice of reason.

'Yes, but I must at least attempt to.'

Apart from Bawden was that matter of his daughter, Elowen, that had him feeling restless. Everything about the woman had perturbed him even though no doubt she neither wanted nor cared for his concern. Initially, when he'd entered the hall and caught her gaze, it felt as though they'd both been struck by a bolt of lightning. Yet, as always with Elowen, she quickly remembered who she was and whom it was she had been staring at so intently. When he sat next to her, the woman could barely meet his eyes. And when she did eventually, after much coaxing on his part, her brown eyes held such a depth of despair that it fairly took his breath away. Hell's teeth, but he had not expected that. Not from her. Not from the feisty and spirited Elowen Bawden, whom he had once known. She seemed hesitant and uncertain, as though she was no longer sure about her place in the world, when she had always been so confident before—mayhap a little too confident. Yet, it had been this very characteristic that Simon had always secretly liked about Elowen. Her assuredness, her spirit, her total belief in her family and their legacy. So what had brought about such a change to the woman? Was it what had happened to her brother, or becoming a widow, or possibly something to do with her father? Mayhap even a measure of all of it. Simon did not know, and he certainly did not comprehend why he was so fascinated by Elowen Bawden. Yet, he noticed everything about her as he always did; from the way she breathed, the rigid straightness of her back to the way she fidgeted with her knife, turning it around and around in her hand absently, as she glanced at her father from under her lashes when she believed no one was watching. The flash of hurt in her eyes when her father had been impatient and cuttingly called her *slow* in front of him made him cease teasing her altogether. It made him have the perverse notion of wanting to protect her of all stupid things— and from her own father. But he could not help feeling so. Just as he could not help notice her body close to his, reminding him of the last time he had been that close to her. When he'd held her five years ago, stunned with the knowledge and triumph that he had finally, finally touched her and far longer than necessary after she'd almost fallen down the cliff. But it had always been like that between them. That spark of attraction that was always difficult to accept and comprehend. Just as it had been five years ago when she had surprisingly curled her body into his, changing everything between them.

Indeed, the moment he had touched her he'd gone from want to guilt to remorse, the result of all that forbidden longing. God, but why her? Why did it have to be Elowen Bawden who affected him in such a manner? It was really quite pathetic, knowing that after all this time, his feelings had not been diminished, nor had the rush of awareness the moment he had seen her again. He'd even almost touched her again, when he sat beside her and God knew what happened last time when he had, even if it had been unintentional. He'd gone from wanting to kiss her to being challenged to a fight resulting in the subsequent death of Hedyn Bawden.

Yet, Elowen Bawden seemed different to the young woman she had once been. Oh, in appearance she looked much as she did five years ago and was just as beautiful, mayhap even more so, much to the disdain of the woman now married to Breock Bawden. But it was her eyes that had altered the most. Haunted, wary and watchful, she could not be more different than she was back then. It made Simon feel restless and annoyed as he always inevitably did when he thought of Elowen Bawden, knowing he should never notice anything about her. And this yet another reason why he was eager to leave this stifling place as soon as it was possible.

The doors of the privy chamber opened and a servant stepped out and bowed, ushering him inside.

'Ah, Trebarr, come, I shall see you now…alone.' Breock Bawden sat behind a wooden table with vellum and ledgers strewn about it, not even bothering to rise in courtesy as was the normal custom. 'I trust you have not been waiting long?'

'No, my lord, not long at all.'

They both knew that was a lie but kept up with the pretence.

'Now, what is this petition that you mentioned earlier?'

So the old man wanted to get right to the point now. The niceties were to be dispensed with altogether and at once it seemed.

'It pertains to old land border lines between our two great houses.'

'And where exactly are you alluding to as there are many land disputes between our *two great houses*.'

Naturally, Bawden was going to be difficult; this was, after all, what he had expected but not the condescending manner in which the old prig was speaking as though he was an unwanted speck of dust on his tunic.

'The main one, my lord.' Simon reached inside the saddlebag that he'd brought with him and got out an old vellum that had belonged to his father. 'It's regarding the northern border where it crosses the River Camel.'

A wry smile twisted around the older man's mouth as he scratched his short-trimmed beard. 'Ah, so we get to the heart of the matter.'

Simon frowned. 'My lord?'

The man pushed away from his chair and rose, meandering to the long wooden coffer against the wall, which had a couple of pewter goblets and matching pewter jugs on a serving tray on top. 'Would you like a goblet of wine, Trebarr, or some local ale?'

'I thank you, but no.'

'Suit yourself.' He shrugged. 'For my part I believe that I need some fortification before we commence with this…this petition of yours.'

Simon inclined his head. 'As you wish.'

Breock Bawden poured some wine into his goblet, returned to his chair and took a sip, watching Simon over the rim before speaking. 'The northern border where it crosses the river has always been contentious and a point that your father and I argued quite vociferously and vehemently about, when he was alive.'

'I know that.'

'Do you, Trebarr?' The man raised a brow. 'That is interesting. I had wondered when we would finally stop circling one another and get to the point of this visit.'

'Apart from paying homage to you, your lady and your kin, I have only come in peace and would like nothing better than for an end to these historic animosities between the Bawdens and the Trebarrs.'

'What is it that you want? The same as your father, who thought that I would just hand over a valuable piece of land over the River Camel that has been in my family for generations? And now you want to offer to end these historic animosities between the Bawdens and the Trebarrs, as you call it? How, exactly?'

'I thought to settle our differences in a fair, more equitable manner and yes, end the animosities that exist between us. With this we could begin to do just that.'

'Equitable, eh?' The man took another swig of wine and wiped his mouth with the back of his hand. 'Do you even know what that word means?'

God, but the man was insufferable. Simon ignored him even though it was becoming increasingly difficult to do so. 'I am willing to swap the land with the river running through it with one that you have coveted for a very long time, Lord Bawden.'

For the first time, Simon could register the sudden keen interest in the other man's eyes as he leant forward and tapped the wooden table. 'Oh, yes, where would that be, then?'

'The land border to the east, my lord. The large acreage that you have claimed has been yours can once again be under your control. But only if you relinquish the one over the river.'

The older man laughed a hollow, mirthless laugh. 'I must say that until now I had never seen anything in you that resembled your father, but with what you have just said, you remind me of old Trebarr and how ruthless he was.'

'Thank you,' Simon muttered through clenched teeth, wanting never to be likened to his cruel and hate-filled father.

Breock Bawden glared at him coldly. 'I do not mean it as a compliment.' He shook his head and exhaled through his teeth. 'Do you believe me to be simple and dim-witted to think this a good deal?'

'As I said, I believe it to be a fair and equitable proposal.'

'Fair?' he said, raising his voice. 'Equitable? Is that what you believe regarding this…this petition of yours?' He spat. 'Because there is no such thing here. Not when the land you offer up in this proposal already belongs to me.'

Simon had hoped that Breock Bawden would not take the same stance as he had always done when his own damn father had been alive, but it seemed he would be unmoveable regarding this issue unless he could somehow convince him. 'Not as far as the law is concerned, my lord.'

'The law? The law?' the older man repeated, getting louder and angrier with every word he uttered. 'You think that the laws that we had, our own Cornish laws, do not count for anything? But then again, why would you? You are a Trebarr, through and through. And what would you know of fair and equitable? What would a Trebarr know of what it means to serve our Cornish traditions? What would a Trebarr know of what it means to be from this great county of ours? All any of you care about is how to claw and grab what is not even yours. You are not even from the old esteemed families of Cornwall, but one that has been unfairly and inequitably risen by the English Kings for turning your back on your own—and Cornwall.'

'That is enough!' God, but Simon had to hold on to his temper. 'How quickly you descend to throwing insults and accusations, my lord Bawden, when all I have done is to come in good faith to end this dispute between our families.'

'So you believe you have come here in good faith, do you?' Bawden muttered, his lips curling into a sneer. 'When your only intention here was to insult and demean me.'

'I did no such thing.' Simon did not know why he was defending himself to this man but could not help but to do so.

'And this is the gratitude I get after inviting you in, letting you join in with our celebrations. This insult.'

'If this is your belief then why would you invite me to stay and sup with you?'

'I begin to wonder myself, Trebarr.'

Simon dragged a frustrated hand through his hair and

leant forward, wanting to try and salvage the situation one last time. 'Allow me to explain, my lord. This proposal that I have suggested is not meant as a slight or an insult but a way forward between our two families.'

'How can it *not* be a slight or an insult if your proposal rests on gains for the Trebarrs and losses for the Bawdens? A loss just like the one I experienced at your own hands, young Trebarr.' Breock Bawden stood and leant across the table, his clenched knuckles white and bony, gripping the edge far too hard. 'And do you think that I would do any dealings with the person who was responsible for the death of my heir?'

Simon shot up from the chair. 'That is a false accusation. What happened back then was nothing but an accident. A terrible accident. You yourself know this, Breock Bawden. Because again, I would ask why you would even invite me in, if you truly believed that?'

'To find out what you really want from me.' The man leant forward and spat the next words out slowly. 'And now I know. And while my son's death might have been an accident as you put it, that does not mean that I do not hold you and those who were also present at the time of his death responsible.'

Which meant that Breock Bawden also held his daughter responsible too. Christ, what a mess. Even so, it was futile to expect this man to understand what had happened at that time, or absolve Simon of any wrongdoing. The best he could hope for was to try and make Bawden see sense regarding his proposal.

'This petition that I have made to you has been made in good faith, my lord Bawden. You must see that.'

'On the contrary. Nothing that a Trebarr does is ever in good faith. I am not interested.'

'Enough! I shall not endure these insults any further!'

The discussion, which was quickly descending into more of an argument, was interrupted by a quick knock on the door.

'What is it?' Bawden tore off aggressively, not taking his eyes off Simon, who glared right back at him.

The door opened and Elowen hovered a moment before entering the small chamber. She inclined her head at both her father and at Simon before addressing the older man. 'My lord, I have been asked to come and remind you of Father Clément's blessing for your lady wife's confinement.'

'Blasted girl! Have you no sense to realise that I am not to be disturbed when I'm in discussion as I am here with Trebarr? You have once again bypassed my men and come marching in here.'

Elowen raised her chin a little, her back so regal and straight, her hands clasped together in front of her, and shook her head. 'I have been sent on this errand by Lady Roesia herself, who has asked for you to tend to her, my lord. At your convenience, of course, but I should add that the matter is of great import.'

'Lord have mercy on me, girl, I hope Lord Roger Prevnar, the man I intend to have you betrothed to, can shape you into something better than you are now—a pious and more obedient wife.'

The surprise and shock that crossed Elowen's face made Simon consider whether she had been aware of whom her father had intended her for. God above, but *Lord Roger Prevnar*? A man whom Simon was vaguely familiar with and whom he found to be taciturn and condescending. That was whom Breock Bawden would have his daughter betrothed to? Why would he foist his vibrant, beautiful daughter on yet another man old enough to be her sire?

'My lord?'

'What are you referring to, Elowen?'

'Your wife, my lord.'

The older man blew out an exasperated breath as Simon glanced with interest and concern between the two of them. 'What about my wife?'

Elowen dug her front teeth into her bottom lip and frowned. 'It is a little indelicate to discuss this in front of others.'

'Out with it, Elowen. I have no time for this!'

'Lady Roesia has started…she has started to birth your child, my lord.'

This was obviously not what Breock Bawden had expected to hear, judging from the startled look on his face. 'But it is too soon. She is not expected to birth *him* yet.'

The older man started for the wooden door and paused a moment without looking at Simon. 'This discourse is at an end, Trebarr. Your petition is met without success.'

With that, the man left the chamber and with him took Simon's hope of achieving what he set out when he had arrived at Bawden Manor. All the goodwill and expectation that he had held on to all dissolving into nothing. He had come with nothing and he would now leave with nothing but failure.

Damn…

Simon looked up and found Elowen staring at the space her father had just vacated, exhaling forcefully, her shoulders sagging. She rubbed her forehead with the back of her hand and as she turned to leave, her eyes met his, as if suddenly remembering that he was also in the chamber. He had a sudden compulsion to hold her as he once did and bury his head in that glorious flaxen silvery hair of hers that was plaited and pinned low on her neck.

Hell's teeth, he needed to be away.

Simon gave her a terse nod and made for the door. He had to get away from this place as quickly as possible. The very Bawden air that he breathed seemed so stifling and confined.

'I am sorry,' Elowen muttered softly as he moved towards the door.

He turned his head and frowned. 'Whatever are you apologising for?'

She shrugged. 'Not quite apologising but I am sorry that whatever you had wanted to achieve with my father has been met without success.'

'All I wanted was to end all of this enmity between our families once and for all. Yet, that can never be achieved with a Bawden.'

She stiffened but did not respond as she turned to leave the chamber. Simon stilled her by the elbow. 'Wait, Elowen, I am sorry too. My frustrations with your father have nothing to do with you.'

She raised a brow. 'Are you sure? I am still a Bawden, Simon.'

'Yes,' he said wryly. 'Although, it appears that is to change once more. Felicitations again on your forthcoming betrothal.'

'I thank you.'

'Lord Roger Prevnar, eh? I met him once in France on the battlefield. Like your father, he has many daughters from his previous marriages. I suppose he must be in need of an heir.'

And like her father, Prevnar was a man in his dotage rather than in his prime. Something tugged and clenched deep inside him, as he considered such a man being bound to Elowen Bawden.

'Yes, well, haven't you heard? There is very little use for daughters.' She gave a weak smile. 'However, if you must know, there is still much to consider and I have not given my consent.'

'Good, for you deserve far better, Elowen.' He knew the moment that the words had slipped from his mouth that he'd made a grave error. For it alluded that he wanted more for her; that he cared for her, when in truth, Simon had no right to. She should mean nothing to him bar this inconvenient attraction he had.

Elowen opened and closed her mouth a few times before speaking. 'If you'll excuse me, my lord, I am needed in the birthing chamber.'

Chapter Three

It had been almost a month since the birth of Elowen's small half brother, Grifiud, born small and slight, yet whose arrival had nevertheless been rejoiced throughout Bawden Manor. It had been a miraculous occasion with both mother and child doing far better than expected. And after staying on to help Roesia with her daughters and infant son after a difficult birth, Elowen was no longer needed. And well, she knew it.

Besides, Elowen had finally agreed to her father's plans for a marriage alliance between Roger Prevnar and herself. Her father had explained of the man's need for a wife and in particular to acquire a mother for his young daughters and had assured Elowen that he would be different from her first husband. He had convinced her that Roger Prevnar would instead be kind to her. So naturally, she had acquiesced to his wishes, especially since she was no longer wanted in Bawden Manor and was travelling to meet her betrothed in the nearby county of Devonshire, where the marriage ceremony could finally take place.

Lord Roger Prevnar could not take the time to travel to Bawden Manor to get married, so it was incumbent on Elowen to go to him. She would go alone apart from the small convoy of four men on horseback, and the wagon she was travelling on, along with all her worldly possessions.

Yet, despite all assurances, Elowen could not shake off her trepidation that this was an ominous start to her marriage with an absent and seemingly disinterested bridegroom. Or mayhap she was being unfair to him. The man might be preparing his new castle for her arrival and could not spare the time to escort her himself, hence the reason why she had to go to him. Even so, she wished she had had the opportunity to meet Roger Prevnar at Bawden Manor before she'd made her decision but it had not been possible, which made her more uneasy than she needed to be.

She exhaled through her teeth. Elowen would have to make the marriage work somehow; she would be the wife that Lord Prevnar needed her to be and be the mother to his daughters. Something she had always longed to be. She just hoped that it was enough. It had to be, even if the man was older than her father. All Elowen could hope for was that the man was kind. After years of taking scraps from her father, and absolutely nothing from her first husband, even a little kindness would have to suffice.

Yet, as the journey commenced it was clear that it was slowly becoming a disaster, and this before Elowen had even met Roger Prevnar. It started with the inclement weather that gradually turned into a raging, relentless storm hurtling through and ravaging the countryside. The men that her father had entrusted to escort her were, in truth, quite unsuitable to the task being far too old and lacking in the necessary strength. So it fell to her to trudge through the mud and try to manage the situation, screaming orders over the howling wind and rain that drenched them all through to the bone. God, but her father had sent far better men from Bawden Manor to escort the chest of silver that made up her dowry than he had for her.

Slowly and with great difficulty, Elowen herded them through the perilous conditions. And somehow, their miserable convoy eventually managed to reach the banks of the River Camel, which had risen and swollen so badly that it burst, overflowing and flooding the pastured land around it.

'It's useless!' her father's man Aleoic bellowed over the din. 'Do you hear me, my lady? We cannot proceed further. We need to turn back.'

'Turn back?' Elowen wiped her face, pushing away the strand of hair that had plastered itself across it, wet and dripping with rainwater. 'We cannot turn back.'

'We must, 'tis too dangerous. There is no way in which we can cross this river as it is. And the animals are getting fretful.'

'We can't do that! It will be just as treacherous if we turn back now. We must carry on forth.'

But it was becoming far more difficult to even move forward a little. The wheel of the rickety old wagon, which was conveying Elowen's older handmaid and all her belongings, got stuck in the deep sludge of muddy river water and became unable to move any further, however much they pushed it; it just would not budge. Elowen knew she would get no further help from Aleoic or any of the others, and had no one to rely on other than herself. Wading through the flooded water that had now risen to the same level as her knees, she reached the bottom of the wheel and felt about under the surface. She felt a barrier beneath the flooded bank, probably a largish rock that had stopped the wagon in its tracks.

She bent down and attempted to push it out of the way with her hands, her palms getting scratched as it scraped along the unforgiving jagged edge. Pushing her hair out of the way, she carried on, ignoring a sudden sharp pain, her hand being scratched and cut to bits. God, but had her life come to this? Relentless pain, continuous hardship, perpetual unhappiness? And no one but no one seemed to care.

No one…except one. One who had cared. One who had always looked out for just as much as she had done for him… And now he was gone. God only knew how much she missed her brother, Hedyn. They were two halves of the same beating heart and yet his was no longer there… It had stopped beating and she was forced to carry on alone. At least by acquiescing to this marriage alliance that her father sought, she was atoning for her brother's death in some way. In agreeing to it, she was somehow lessening the pain she had caused her father.

She heard voices muffled by the sound of the wind, voices calling or mayhap shouting nearby. But voices that she drowned out as she kept her focus on the task at hand. She had to loosen the large rock; she had to shift it so that the wagon could be free to move again. Otherwise, like everything in her life, it would continue to remain as it was, unyielding. Stuck forever in this cycle of misery and despair.

'Elowen, for God's sake, can you hear me?' A voice

getting nearer and nearer cried out over the incessant torrential rain that was plunging them into deeper waters. A hand gripped hers under the floodwater, large and assured. 'Let me be of some assistance. I insist, woman! Let it go.'

She blinked and looked up. *Simon Trebarr?* It couldn't be. But somehow it was. Lord Simon Trebarr was there, crouching over her.

'No, I can do this. I need help from no one,' she muttered as tears streamed down her face. She wiped them with the back of her hand, glad that the rain would hide them.

'Come, let it go, Elowen.'

'Let it go? You want me to let go of all the hurt and frustration and guilt that I carry with me? Or the fact that I'm standing in a raging storm with one who was equally responsible for my brother's death, and who I should hate with every fibre of my being? And yet I don't… I don't.'

That was just it. She could never hate Simon Trebarr as she was meant to. Oh, she would throw his teasing insults back at him whenever she encountered Simon before her brother's death, but it had all been an effort to show that she also shared the same enmity of the Trebarrs as her kin. But it had not been true. Not then and not now.

He watched her for a long moment and then swallowed uncomfortably.

'I am glad to hear that you do not hate me,' he said as he gently prised her fingers from the rock and pulled them out of the murky waters and held them in front of him.

God, how she wanted to be swallowed up by water for the shame of her outburst. What was the matter with her? It must be all the emotions of the day catching up with her.

'I am sorry,' she said, shaking her head. 'I do not know what came over me.'

'Think nothing of it, Elowen. Tiredness and frustration make us say and do many things we then regret.'

And Elowen had enough to regret in her life.

'But what are you doing here?' she said, pushing the thoughts away as the man stood right in front of her, inspecting her fingers. And strangely, it was this question that made him look up and give her a cold look, not her earlier outburst.

'I could very well ask you the same question, Elowen Bawden.' He dragged back the limp, wet lock of dark hair that had fallen over one eye. 'Have you finally gone mad, woman, to brave such terrible conditions? Although *brave* is really not the right word, rather ill-considered, misguided and above all foolish! Indeed, mad.'

Elowen tried to snatch her hands away from him but his grip was strong. 'If you think to scold me at a time like this, Simon Trebarr, then go. I neither want nor need your help.'

'I disagree, Elowen Bawden. You need me, and you need me more than you've needed anyone in your life.'

'*You?*' she muttered, shaking her head. 'Who is the one being foolish now? I do not need you.'

Yet, they both knew that was a lie. Elowen *did* need him and she was relieved that Simon Trebarr had come to her aid—again. And with that came the usual feelings of guilt and remorse for doing so from someone who was just as responsible for the death of her brother as she was. Elowen knew she wasn't supposed to trust or like Simon and yet could not help but do so, despite herself, despite his being a Trebarr. And what in God's name did that make her? Disloyal to her own. But Simon had saved her life before. He had helped her just as he was doing today.

'You know you do, sweetheart,' he murmured, the unexpected endearment coursing through her body, flooding her senses with warmth and something else that she did not want to acknowledge. Something that took her back and reminded her of that brief moment before her brother encountered them, when Simon was about to put his mouth on hers. He shook his head and frowned as he inspected her fingers. 'Why are you the one doing this anyway? Are there no strong men in Bawden Manor? You should not be the one to pull that damn boulder from underneath the wagon, Elowen. Just look at your hands, ragged and raw.'

Simon pulled her away from the wagon, taking her back to stand with Aeolic and the others. 'Stay here, my lady. My men and I shall attend to this. Come on, Gib, lend me a hand.'

She did as she was requested and watched in amazement as Simon and his three men, one of whom she recognised from when they'd come to Bawden Manor, helped her distressed handmaiden get down and single-handedly dislodged the large rock swiftly while his men pushed the wagon away. But Elowen's eyes were locked on to Simon Trebarr's tall, powerful body, which expended little effort in the exertion. He turned his head as he waded through the water and caught her staring…staring… Oh, God, she was staring, lost to the sight of him.

His shoulders and arms were encased in a tight leather gambeson, sculpting every muscle of his lean body. It was no denying that even in a situation such as this, the man was utterly mesmerising. Or mayhap it was because of a situation such as this. After all, he had once again come to her aid.

Elowen glanced away, mortified, feeling the telltale signs of heat creeping up her neck, spreading to her face, despite the cold in her bones and being wet throughout. Simon was right; she had gone mad but for rather different reasons. Mayhap in all the clamour and confusion, he had not noticed. Elowen turned her head back and let out a small breath. Oh, he had most certainly noticed. And he was staring back with such heat and intensity that Elowen thought she might go up in flames. What a time to notice, to stare, to be this breathless.

'Are you hurt?' Simon muttered as he approached her, the wind whipping through her body, making her shiver.

'No, I am fine.' She rubbed her forehead, trying to expunge the forbidden thoughts and feelings. 'And thank you, my lord. I would not like to think what would have happened to us, had you not found us here.'

'Oh, I have an idea, Elowen, and it is most certainly not good.' He pushed back his wet hair and frowned. 'I hate to think what would have happened had my men and I not been on patrol here, on Trebarr land, I might add.'

'Trebarr land?' She frowned. 'But that is impossible. I cannot believe that we have come off our planned route.'

'That is hardly important. What the hell possessed you to travel in such treacherous conditions?'

'It was not so treacherous when we started out.'

'You know how quickly the weather in this part of the kingdom can become so hazardous in a blink of an eye. You should have looked for shelter when the storms gathered, or rather, whomever was supposed to be leading this pitiful convoy should have.'

Elowen knew that Simon's words were true but could not allow for Aleoic or any of the other Bawden men to shoulder any of the blame.

'You know me, Simon. Not one to take orders from anyone, even my father's men.' She stood tall and lifted her head. 'I take full responsibility for this.'

'Of course, you do.' A ghost of a smile hovered around his lips. 'Where are you travelling to anyway, my lady?'

'I am travelling to Stromley Castle in Devonshire, to be wed to Roger Prevnar, my lord.'

Simon's smile vanished and his eyes looked at her in disbelief and incredulity. 'You must be jesting, Elowen. You cannot mean to say that the man did not come and escort you himself.'

'No.' All that had mattered to her was that she was leaving the stifling atmosphere in Bawden Manor. All that mattered was that her life was changing again. With a hope that it would all be for the better. After all, she would become chatelaine of Stromley Castle without being beholden to her father or his wife any longer. And more importantly, Elowen was about to become a mother to Roger Prevnar's young daughters. 'It matters not whether he came or not.'

'Hell's teeth, of course it does.' Simon exhaled in

frustration. 'It matters for it shows his character, which at this moment does not present the man in a good light, Elowen. I cannot believe that your father would allow it.'

Oh, he would allow it. If anything, her father had actually encouraged her to make the necessary arrangements and expediate the marriage as soon as possible. And with it, they would both then get what they wanted. To part and go their own way.

'Yes, he did allow it. And why should he not?'

Simon shook his head and muttered an oath under his breath. 'Without wanting to speak ill of your father, I believe he should have accompanied you himself, and if that was not possible, then he should have sent you to Roger Prevnar with an appropriate convoy. Not these old men, for God's sake.'

Elowen bristled. While she appreciated Simon's concern on her behalf, she could not allow him to disparage her father's decisions openly, not a Trebarr, even if she secretly agreed with him. 'My father might be many things but he, too, is unable to predict the weather, especially this savage storm that came about so quickly.'

Simon raised a brow, water droplets falling from the ends of his hair. 'We shall have to disagree on this point. But we cannot stand here all day and argue about it while getting further drenched. Hold out your hands, Elowen.'

She blinked in surprise but did as he bid and watched in rapt fascination as he tore off the bottom of his tunic worn beneath his gambeson and wrapped it around her one hand, tying the ends before moving to the other. His hands, big yet incredibly tender. He brushed his fingers against hers one last time before nodding at her. 'This will have to do until later. Come, Elowen.'

Come?

'What, where?'

But the man had turned on his heel and began barking instructions at her father's men providing escort, and his own men who helped her shivering handmaid onto the back of one of his men's horses. Before Elowen had time to think what he was about, Simon had commandeered the whole situation and at breathtaking speed. No wonder Edward of Woodstock, the Black Prince himself, commanded Simon Trebarr to the royal retinue when he ventured on a new campaign.

'What do you think you're doing?' she asked, frowning as she watched him finally turn his attention back to her.

'This.' He picked Elowen up, the weight of her sodden skirts heavy and cumbersome, and carried her across to his powerful-looking black destrier.

'Put me down, Simon!'

'Stop fussing, woman.' He helped her up and onto the saddle before he mounted the horse and sat behind her, putting his arms around and holding on to the reins. 'We leave now.'

'What do you mean by this? Where are you taking me?'

Simon's hands came to rest around her waist, anchoring her to him. 'Somewhere nearby and where you can take shelter for the night—Trebarr Castle.'

Elowen tried to put a little space between them so that she wasn't leaning back against the man. 'Trebarr Castle?'

'Does that worry you?' He leant forward, his hard body meeting the back of hers, sending a frisson through her, his low voice a caress against her ear. 'Or mayhap that angers you?'

'Anger me? No, of course not,' she sighed. 'I am indebted to you for coming to my aid, Simon. I would not be so churlish to mind that you are taking me to Trebarr Castle.'

He chuckled softly. 'The Elowen Bawden of old would certainly have minded breaching enemy lines.'

'Yes, but I am no longer that impulsive, rather foolish, maiden.'

'Shame, as I rather like her impertinent tongue. Whatever happened?'

'She grew up, Simon.'

She couldn't see, but rather felt, him frowning. 'We all have to do that, eventually.'

'And yet you wish to take me to Trebarr Castle—the one place that might not welcome the daughter of Breock Bawden. Even if it is closer than Bawden Manor.'

Elowen had had enough of being anywhere and anyplace that made her feel unwelcome. She had enough of being unwanted.

'You are not the only one who has changed. I am Lord of Trebarr now, Elowen. I demand my people's fealty. No one will dare show my guest, even a Bawden, discourtesy. I will not stand for it.'

Something that she hadn't even known she was carrying lifted from her tense shoulders, for the first time in a long, long time. 'Thank you.'

'My pleasure.'

His words, murmured soft and low, sent a ripple of heat from where Simon was holding her, seeping under her skin and rushing through her body, pooling in her stomach. It was as though the many layers of wet, sodden clothing clinging to their bodies were not there. As though his large, callused hands were touching her, skin to skin. A prickle of awareness went through her, knowing that such closeness to this man was a disaster. Still, a part of her wanted to lean back and be enveloped in his strong, protective arms. Elowen could not deny that she felt safe with Simon Trebarr, just as she could not deny her conflicted feelings towards the man. It was always there reminding her and not letting her forget, even in a situation such as this, when she was indebted to him for helping her, that she was not supposed to like him. That she should, in truth, hate him for his involvement in her brother's death. After all, Simon had also been there on that awful day. He had fought Hedyn, who had challenged him after he had seen them together as close as they were now.

Being in his arms, after helping her from a perilous situation, even in such different circumstances, made Elowen remember the last time she was this close to him. The same unwanted feelings, the same suppressed flare of desire. The same yearning for something she could never have. And with that came the memory of her brother's terrible death. The horror and total shock encapsulated in that moment as he looked into her eyes one last time before he fell.

Then in the aftermath, just as every day since, was the inevitable feeling of guilt when she thought of being in Simon Trebarr's arms as she was now and what it had led to. The perpetual cycle of that one singular moment that she had always secretly longed for, leading to that inescapable nightmare. It ran over and over again in her mind, as she tried in vain to find reasons why any of it had happened.

All of which meant that she should not feel anything about being in Simon Trebarr's arms. Nothing at all. Indeed, Elowen could almost hear the whispered thread of warning carried in the soar of wind rising with the words her brother had uttered on that fateful day:

Let him not be the one...

Chapter Four

Simon felt strangely at peace riding through the wilds of the Cornish countryside in the middle of a ferocious storm with Elowen Bawden nestled in his arms. He could not account for this feeling, and yet it was the only thing that brought about a measure of calm in his otherwise turbulent mind. And by God, he was damned furious about it.

He was furious with Breock Bawden, who had imposed this situation on his daughter, forcing her to venture out in this perilous condition. He was furious with Lord Roger Prevnar for not caring enough to come and fetch his betrothed himself. He was furious with the woman in his arms for blithely putting herself in such a dangerous position in the first place. And he was furious with himself for caring enough to come to Elowen Bawden's aid. He had no choice other than to bring her back to Trebarr Castle, after he had spotted the convoy getting into the difficulties it had. Above all that, for feeling the peace he did being so close to her and his body's reaction to the woman, even now when she was sat in his arms. As if she belonged here with him when she absolutely did not. After all, he had spent the best part of five years trying to forget his inconvenient attraction to Elowen Bawden.

God, but what on earth was he thinking? To help a distressed woman and on Trebarr land was naturally going to be his duty, and one that he was happy to carry out, but to bring Elowen, a Bawden, no less, back to the castle was nothing but courting trouble. She had been right about the welcome she might receive, not that he would allow it, just as he had told her. But Simon had only become the lord of Trebarr since his brother's un-expected death over two months ago. His recent triumph after the Battle of Crecy was one thing, but his rule was new and untried, especially in filling those revered boots as the new overlord. Simon might be well-known and well respected, but he had never been trained to be the lord of Trebarr, and he still had much to prove. So the idea of having Elowen Bawden under his roof might possibly be unwelcome, and it would certainly raise a few brows especially if his people knew how the woman stirred his blood. And there was also another difficulty, his brother's young widow, Anaís Trebarr née Le Brunde. A maid, who had never actually met his brother Geoffrey since she had been wed by proxy in her native Brittany. By the time she had arrived on their shores six weeks ago, Geoffrey was dead and Simon was left to pick up the pieces. All of which made the very idea of having Elowen Bawden stay in Trebarr all the more troublesome.

The best course of action would be if Simon ensured that he kept away from her while she sojourned at the castle, without making it too obvious that he was avoid-ing her. In any case, the woman would soon be gone and take with her the uneasiness that he felt by being so damn aware of her whenever he was in her presence. God, but he did not want any of it. He did not want to speculate on what Elowen's life had been like for the past five years. He did not want to know anything regarding her first marriage. And he certainly did not want to know what had changed so much in her life that had made her look so despondent when he'd seen her again last month for the first time in many years.

In truth, what did Simon know of Elowen Bawden apart from the handful of times that their paths crossed, before her brother's death when they, along with their Bawden kin, would deliberately trespass onto Trebarr land, and they would end up sparring and getting the better of one another? Nothing. He knew absolutely nothing about her. And it would be best if he kept it that way.

He felt her shiver as they rode as quickly as Gallosek could gallop across the landscape in treacherous conditions, the rain still lashing down on them.

'Never fear. We shall soon be at the castle, where you can warm yourself by the hearth,' he murmured against her ear, feeling her whole body shiver again.

'I await with much anticipation, my lord.'

Simon could feel her smile. Her words light, humorous yet just a little sardonic. Indeed, he could imagine her saying it with a roll of her eyes, as they glittered with amusement. And for some reason this filled him with a sense of relief with the knowledge that Elowen might still possess that resolute vivaciousness that he'd always liked about her, despite whatever she had evidently been through in recent years. Even if she had *grown up*, as she called it. Simon may not know her well or know what had happened to her, but this tenacious quality seemed to be still part of her, even if it was hidden deep inside.

'I am glad, my lady. I always aim to increase a woman's anticipation in such situations as this.'

Simon knew he was teasing her but his words seemed to suddenly stir an unknown emotion that he could hardly fathom. Good God, was he...nervous? A man of his stature and worldly experience nervous of bringing Elowen Bawden to his home, his abode? But then Trebarr Castle was personal; it held many memories and meant a great deal to him. But why should he care what the woman in his arms thought of it? No, it could not be something as absurd as that. And he did not care whether she would approve or not.

'Ah, so this is something of habit with you, then, is it?'

'Naturally. I always go into the country, especially during a raging storm, purposely in the hope that I might encounter a damsel in distress. And for this very reason.'

Elowen chuckled as she shook her head. 'I can quite believe your gallivanting at such a time would be because of these very reasons. But I have to say that I am glad of it.'

He could not help but smile despite the fact that he was bitterly cold and soaked through to his bones. But then he had always enjoyed this back-and-forth with Elowen Bawden and was relieved that they'd reverted back to it, finding comfort in his need to poke and ruffle her, while she bit back with her lacerating wit. It felt familiar. It felt safe. As though they both knew where they stood with one another rather than being out to sea with their untapped desire. Simon could recall their encounters when her brother Hedyn would goad him, after they'd purposely traipsed on Trebarr land, claiming that they could go where they want since the land was actually theirs, while Elowen would always try and temper her brother's volatile behaviour. And Simon and his friends? Well, they found the encounters with the younger Bawden siblings and their kin highly amusing. Yet, there had always been moments when there would be a spark between Simon and Elowen. Whispers and words in passing only between the two of them, when no one was noticing.

'Good, I aim to please.'

'I shall remember that. But you must know, my lord, that I have never stayed anywhere that neither my father nor my late husband were also guests.'

And he never had a Bawden stay at Trebarr Castle so this was a first for him too. 'And soon you shall be wedded again.'

'Yes.' She stiffened slightly. 'I shall.'

'To Lord Roger Prevnar, whom I'd wager you shall meet for the first time at the altar?'

'And if I am?'

'Nothing, my lady. Only I ponder why a beautiful eligible woman such as yourself would agree to such a scheme.'

'I thank you for bestowing such compliments but Roger Prevnar is actually the best option for me.'

At least she had not replied as she had the last time that he broached the subject of her forthcoming marriage. Simon had to admit he was intrigued by why a woman like Elowen Bawden would want to be bound to a man like Roger Prevnar, whom he found not only unpleasant but who was also older than her own father.

'The best option for you? How so?'

'Really? You wish for me to expound on the reasons why Roger Prevnar is a good choice as a husband at this time? When we are on this hazardous terrain riding fast while the wind and rain thrash against us?'

'I do.'

'Very well.' He felt her take a resigned breath into her lungs. It was as though she needed time to ponder and decide on what her answer might be. 'Because by marrying him, I gain the one thing that I want.'

'And what is that?' he muttered as he pushed Gallosek faster. 'Apologies, I did not mean to pry. I was just...'

'Security, safety. I want to feel safe, Simon, and... and above all I want to feel that I belong somewhere... and I also want to... I want to be a mother to his young daughters.'

This? This was all she wanted from life? He felt a sudden ache in his chest that a woman like Elowen Bawden would have such meagre needs, such paltry requirements. Nothing more other than security and a need to feel safe, which in truth were actually the same thing. And be a mother to another man's children.

It was humbling either way he looked at it. 'And you believe that Roger Prevnar would be able to do that. Do you believe he'll make you feel *safe and secure*?'

He felt her lift a shoulder and drop it in a shrug. 'I have no idea, my lord, since I have yet to meet my betrothed as I have already explained. However, it is my hope that he can.'

Her words served to convince herself seemingly more

than anything else. Even so, Simon had only met the arrogant man a few times and knew nothing of what he was like with his own people, his vassals and his kin. He might possess the kindness that Elowen sought, when he was among his own.

'As a powerful noble, I am sure he can. Indeed, I am certain he can.'

'Then our union shall be blessed.'

He flexed his hand, the one that was wrapped around her. 'I am sure it shall, my lady.'

With that, they fell into an awkward silence as they made their way along through the mud and rain, the elements slowing them down. Eventually, thank God, the turrets of Trebarr Castle came into view and before long he rode into the inner bailey of the new stone castle keep. He dismounted Gallosek and turned, holding out his hand to help Elowen down. She looked at his outstretched hand for a minute longer than necessary before deciding to take it, their touch punctuated by another wave of awareness. This seemingly happening at every turn. Every single time they touched, and even when they didn't.

Simon placed his hands on either side of her waist and lifted her into his arms.

Elowen instantly stiffened. 'You can put me down, you know.'

'I do know, Elowen,' he murmured, walking into the castle as he continued to carry her in his arms. 'But how do you think I usually help the stranded damsels that I stumble upon?'

'I'm certain that it's as gallantly as you can muster, Simon, but take note. Not all damsels need to be carried in such a manner. I am still able to walk quite well, actually.'

He looked down at her and smiled before letting her back on her feet. 'Very well, I shall endeavour to accommodate your wishes, my lady. I always aim to please the damsels that I help.'

'I can very well imagine it.'

'Good, and if you won't allow me to be the gallant hero carrying you inside, then at least let me escort you to the chamber that you shall stay in until it is once again safe to continue on your travails.'

'Thank you.' She paused and turned to touch his sleeve. His eyes fixed at the point that she touched him. She quickly removed her hand. 'Thank you for everything.'

He guided her through the castle by her elbow, stopping to greet some of his men, other vassals as well as servants, whom he requested to ready a chamber for Elowen's stay.

'I have to say that you are most attentive to a guest's needs. I wonder whether it is just me or all damsels whom you happen to stumble on.'

'Ah, but it is all part of the service.'

'And do you make it a regular occurrence, this stumbling on damsels?'

He shrugged as he escorted her up the wooden spiral staircase to the solar chambers. 'Only the special ones and only when I am needed, as I was on this day.'

'Yes, and for that you shall always have my eternal thanks.'

They had reached the top of the stairwell and walked to the end of the long hallway. Simon grabbed a torch from the metal sconce and opened a wooden door. 'You have already thanked me, Elowen. Come now, allow me to see to your roughened hand.'

'No, really, it is not necessary. You have already done enough.'

'I insist.'

He walked her over to the bench adjacent to the hearth and sat her down on it before turning to put the torch inside the decorative metal sconce. When he turned back towards her, he noted the concern and uncertainty etched on her face. 'This is all part of the service that we gallant knights are committed to do for fair damsels, Elowen, so there is really no need to fret.'

'Very well,' she muttered, looking around as servants moved about the chamber to attend to the hearth, changing the coverlet on the bed pallet and bringing in trays with a jug of ale and a couple of goblets, small pastries, cheeses and preserved dried fruits. When the last serving girl brought in a tray with all that he needed to bandage her hand and placed it on the table before shutting the door, Simon flicked his gaze to Elowen, who was watching him closely, now that they were all alone in the room.

He moved to the table and fetched the tray that contained strips of cloth, a small jar of salve and a bowl of water diffused with honey, then

knelt in front of her. He dipped his head and began to unravel the makeshift bandaging he'd made using his own tunic when he'd first encountered Elowen and her woebegotten convoy.

'Tell me, my lord, as I cannot help think that you have done this before.'

'Many times, Elowen. A good soldier always has to be prepared for a situation where he would know how to tend to cuts such as this. And preferably as fast as possible to prevent any bad humours from entering his body. I have seen far too many good men fall even from these types of small injuries.'

He slowly unravelled the dirtied binding around her hand and threw the long strip of wet cloth on the floor, before inspecting her hand, which had thankfully ceased bleeding.

'See. I told you that it is nothing other than a few cuts and grazes.' She tried to pull her hand away but he held it firmly yet gently in his.

'Yes, but even so, you would not want it to fester,' he murmured as he began to clean it with the soaked clean strips of honeyed water.

He rubbed his fingertips over the palm of her hand, noting the difference between his massive callused hands and her elegantly long, dainty fingers. Her hands were so damn soft, skin so unblemished and silky, that he wondered what they might feel like if they were against his skin, on his damn body. He pushed down the inevitable bolt of desire whenever he thought of her hands, her lips or any other part of the blasted woman on him, and instead focused on this task. To clean her hands, which he did most vigorously.

Once again, the surge of annoyance ran through him at why a woman like Elowen Bawden had put herself in such a dangerous situation. And why it had been he who had to come to her rescue. Not that Simon would have had any other be the one to do so. Still, he did not need to be here in a chamber alone with the woman or be cleaning her hand, for the love of God! He could have had any one of the many serving girls or even his brother's young widow, Anaís, to do the honour, not that the girl ventured out of her chamber often. Yet, Simon felt responsible for her as he did for everyone, and everything, within Trebarr. And it did not help that many of his people expected a marriage alliance between him and Anaís. But he just could not bring himself to entertain such a thing. Not yet and not so soon after Geoffrey's death. In time, however, once they both got used to one another, he would do his duty there as well. All of which made this insistence to attend to Elowen's few cuts and grazes now in her bedchamber, no less, highly unwise.

'I can do this myself, I assure you.' Elowen flinched a little as he drew away some of the grit and grime from the few deep scratches and cuts on her hand. Evidently, he had been rubbing it far too vigorously for her liking.

'I am sure you can but allow me this. Or do you find fault with my ministrations?'

'No, of course not.' She looked visibly bewildered. 'I would never dream of saying anything so disrespectful, especially with such gallantry on display.'

'Ah, so you believe I did this to display my many virtues of strength and valour?'

Damn, but he took some pleasure from watching her flush, a rosy tint diffusing her skin, even though he knew it was wrong to.

She snapped her head up and opened and closed her mouth several times before muttering something under her breath.

'I am teasing you, Elowen,' he said softly, a reassuring smile playing on his lips, and watched as she still looked a little uncertain and somewhat uncomfortable.

'Oh, I see.' Her brows furrowed in the middle. 'Yes, I knew you must be.'

'Good, because surely you know when I am just jesting with you after the many different encounters we have had over the years.'

Her frown deepened as they fell into a silence, the only sounds now the crackling of the fire in the hearth and the trickle of water as he dunked another strip of cloth in the water before resuming to clean her hand. He glanced up the length of her arm despite himself, took in her soft skin, the rise and fall of her chest, the slender swoop of her neck, her lips that parted slightly, those melting brown eyes and God, but that hair. Damn, but he wanted to unbind it and take it down so that he could see it spill down her body in all its gleaming glory. He wanted to sink his face in it and inhale her scent deeply.

And it was knowing how irresponsible and downright idiotic it was that he was here alone with the woman that Simon perversely had been drawn towards her. This knowledge of what had always been there between them, the pull and push of it all. And after everything that had occurred today, he had wanted to see to Elowen Bawden's needs himself so that he could prove to himself that he could do it and still remain unaffected by her. That he could touch her and remain unmoved. A necessary test that would show him that he was impervious to the woman. Indifferent to her very closeness.

'But do we? In truth, we know very little about one another, despite our many encounters as you put it.'

Well, Simon had not expected that. Not in the least,

but Elowen was right. They knew nothing about each other; nothing about their lives these past few years and nothing about who they truly were. In fact, what they did know came down to a handful of passing encounters and nothing more.

He shrugged. 'I suppose you must be right and yet I can hardly say we are strangers.'

'No, not that.' She shook her head slowly, carefully catching her lower lip between her teeth before adding, 'But I maintain that we know very little of real value regarding one another. After all, I am a Bawden and you…you are a…'

'A Trebarr. Yes, I know.'

And just like that, whatever comradery had existed between them dissipated at once. The reminder of their differences erected by invisible walls separating them and their two families. How disappointing that it always came down to this—the Bawdens and the Trebarrs and the enmity that had always existed between their families, and the terrible incident of five years ago when Hedyn Bawden lost his life. It seemed that no matter what Simon did, even by trying to breach the enemy line, or even coming to Elowen's aid and bringing her to Trebarr Castle, this would always remain between them. As would his own guilt regarding what had happened.

Mayhap because of all this, it would be best to observe their differences and keep his distance. After all, he had also failed in the test that he'd set himself. He did not remain unchanged and unaffected by her closeness or impervious to her touch. If anything, it was the damn opposite as it always was with her.

Simon once again cursed Elowen's father, Breock

Bawden, and her betrothed, Roger Prevnar, for their lack of care and for this unwanted predicament that he had inadvertently found himself in.

'I believe that my job here is done. Please do help yourself to the goblet of ale and the small repast here.' He rose to his feet and deposited the last wet strips onto the tray before bowing in front of her and turning on his heel. 'Now I shall leave you, until later, my lady.'

'Wait. Before you go, I wanted to say how grateful I am again for coming to my aid,' she muttered and then rose to her feet. But just as she was about to press her lips to his jaw, he turned his head, her lips landing on his instead. Awkwardly, the kiss lingered for a moment longer before she pulled away and lowered her feet. Her eyes widened in shock at what she'd inadvertently done.

Simon could not move and was just as stunned by what she had done, even accidently, as Elowen touched her lips with shaky fingers and then inclined her head.

Interesting that she had not meant to kiss him, even a fleeting one at that, and yet she had. It seemed the lady was still just as impulsive as he remembered.

Chapter Five

Elowen watched Simon leave the chamber and quietly close the wooden door behind him. She continued to stare at the door for a long moment with a sense of regret and confusion. She kissed his lips, even though she had only meant to kiss his cheek…but God, how mortifying. It had only been meant to be a kiss of gratitude yet, the moment her lips touched his, she wanted to linger for longer. And this after she had inadvertently insulted him. Although she had done so without entirely being certain how she had done so. Had he objected to her claim that they knew very little about one another? Mayhap, yet it was nevertheless the truth. They did know very little about one another and the lives they had lived. They had only ever encountered one another a few times and it had always been the usual spiky exchange between them. Nothing at all had suggested that there was more. Simon knew nothing about her life when she had married so quickly after Hedyn's death, and she knew nothing of his life as a soldier and a knight. But from the look he gave her, she was certain that her comment had not been taken well.

And after Simon had come to her aid and brought her

to safety in Trebarr Castle, the thought that she might have somehow insulted him, and perhaps not shown her appreciation and gratitude to him, was not something that sat well with Elowen. Well, that was one reason why she had then hastily kissed him.

God above, but the man had even tended to her grazed hands himself, which had also confused her. Why had he done it himself? Surely there had been no need to do so. None whatsoever. His fingers had brushed against her hand, sending a frisson that shot up her arm and travelled to every part of her body before it pooled in her stomach as she sat there, trying to feign indifference to his ministration. His large callused hands had mesmerised her and she could not stop staring at them. She had not stopped staring at him and, every emotion that flittered on his face, every movement he made, fascinated Elowen. Her whole body still hummed even now from the close contact as though it had been a plucked lute. And then to add more embarrassment to be found staring at the man was to kiss him before he had left the chamber. All of which had annoyed her. It annoyed her far too much. And just as always, when she felt irritated by being so affected by the man, she had uttered something true yet essentially impolite in her usual blunt fashion. No wonder her own family could not abide her presence, finding it something quite questionable.

But Simon never did find her questionable, despite his reservation, despite the fact that they were always supposed to despise one another. And neither could Elowen quite bring herself to despise him as she should, as was expected of her. She could not even hate him for defending himself against her beloved yet hotheaded brother on that terrible day. It had always been the same since the first time she had ever met Simon Trebarr.

She could recall even now that very moment as a young girl being in the same hall as the Cornish elders when they had gathered for a banquet to celebrate Edward the Black Prince being invested as the Duke of Cornwall over ten years ago. It was the first time she had ever seen Simon Trebarr. He had stood with his older brother Geoffrey and his father, back straight, head held up proudly as though he was supremely pleased to have been included, just as much as she had been, standing with her father and her brother Hedyn in all her finery. Even then, Elowen had had no doubt who he was or from which family he was. That Trebarr green gaze had swept around the hall and had paused when it reached her before continuing to take in his surroundings. And from that moment he had fascinated her in a way that no one had ever done since.

Elowen had always been aware of him whenever he was in her presence. Her brother had always wanted to confront the Trebarrs on their land. And Simon, to his credit, never rose to Hedyn's goading but instead found a way to dismiss him, as though he were an annoying pest more than anything else. Yet, he would somehow say something for her ears, tease her, annoy her, with his sharp wit and quick rejoinders. She would always feel a tingle run down her spine and that would be before she had even noticed him. And Elowen had always resented that. Resented the pull that he evidently held over her, so she had always masked it. She had always hidden that very secret part of her. Never wanting Simon to know any of it, hiding it with her cutting remarks and sharp tongue until that fateful day five years ago, when her life had suddenly been put in the balance. She had been stripped bare and she was at Simon Trebarr's mercy when he had pulled her to safety. But then just as quickly, her gratitude had turned slowly into dread that he could see right through to a place that always yearned for him, that wanted him desperately. After all, Hedyn had seen it in her; he had known the moment he had happened upon them together. And it had been that very reason why he had drawn his sword and challenged Simon Trebarr for even daring to look in that secret place deep within her.

Let him not be the one...

How those words that her brother had uttered haunted her, even after all these years. For it reminded her that after everything that had come to pass, she still secretly longed for Simon in a manner that could never be. It would always remain impossible. Since it also brought with it the sense of guilt. Elowen knew full well that if Hedyn had not seen the exposed longing on her face then mayhap he would not have challenged Simon. Mayhap he would still be alive today. So yes, the guilt was well placed, even if she had been equally to blame for her brother's demise as Simon. Mayhap even more so.

Yet, after all that had happened between them, after all these years, Simon had once again come to her aid in her hour of need, bringing with it not just her sense of relief and gratitude but also those feelings that always surfaced whenever he was close by. She just had to remind herself that it was futile as it had always been. Besides that, she would soon belong to another. Yes, that was what she had to remember. And by God, Elowen hoped that her stay here in Trebarr Castle would be of short duration.

She sighed and rubbed her forehead, trying to dispel the tension that had mounted in her head. Realising that it must be because after all the events that had occurred that day, she had not eaten for many hours. She rose and went to the coffer, helping herself to some ale and food, when she heard a faint knock on the door.

'Enter,' she muttered, but when no one did, Elowen strode to the door and opened it to find a maid stood outside, with her head bent low.

A delicate-looking maid with reddish copper hair that was braided and pinned tightly on either side of her head lifted eyes so pale, so blue, that they reminded Elowen of a midsummer sky.

'I have brought some clean, dry linen towelling for you, my lady.' The maid dipped her head and held out the stack of folded towelling.

Elowen took them from her and looked the maid up and down, realising that she was not a serving girl. Judging from her fine velvet dress and the decorative cream tunic and the pretty pearl necklace around her neck, the maid was a noblewoman.

Elowen dipped into a curtsey herself. 'How do you do, my lady? I'm afraid that I have not had the pleasure of your acquaintance.'

'I am Lady Anaís Trebarr née Le Brunde, and I am happy to make yours, Lady Elowen.'

'And I yours.' She was a *Trebarr*? Elowen pushed away her surprise at who this young woman might be and what her connection was to the family. 'Please, would you come in?'

'Thank you.' The young maid dipped her head and tentatively walked over the threshold, coming to stand inside the chamber.

There was something awkward and unassuming about Lady Anaís Trebarr. 'Would you not sit, my lady? May I fetch you a goblet of ale?'

The young woman sat down on the bench that Elowen had vacated and stared down at her hands clasped tightly in her lap. Surely Anaís Trebarr could not be nervous of her, could she?

'Yes, I thank you.' She muttered this so quietly that Elowen strained to hear her. She turned back to the coffer table and poured ale into another goblet before returning to the bench and lowering herself to sit, pressing the ale into her guest's hands.

'So, my lady, you are part of the Trebarr family? I must say your English is exceedingly good.'

'Thank you and yes, I am or rather I was. I was married to Geoffrey… Geoffrey Trebarr, and since his death a few months ago, I am… I am now his widow.'

Of course, Elowen had heard some time ago of Geoffrey Trebarr's imminent marriage but with her own changed circumstances and then his death recently, she had forgotten. There was much she had forgotten.

But, oh, God, the poor young woman. 'I am so sorry for your loss, my lady. It cannot be easy for you to have lost your husband after such short a marriage.'

'No, it has not,' Anaís Trebarr muttered and seemed to want to say more but then decided against it. Instead, she sipped the ale and fidgeted in her seat.

Oh, the unfortunate maid. She was the same age as Elowen had been when she had married her first husband, only mayhap a little younger. 'It cannot be easy being here alone.'

'No, it has not,' Anaís repeated, absently biting down on her lip before turning towards her. 'Although I am here with a few of my ladies from my home, from Brittany, and they do, in truth, give me comfort while I wait to find out what will become of me.'

Elowen knew too well the difficulties and uncertainties a widow faced, especially one so young and so newly wed, after the loss of her husband. It was a situation that she could definitely relate to. In her case she had been married a year to her first husband, who, like her betrothed, was older than her father, with grown adult children. His daughter had gone to her husband's house after her marriage but the heirs lived with them. And in that time, Elowen slowly lost her value to him and also lost sight of herself, as she failed again and again to get with child. Her husband eventually looked on at her with total disdain, treating her with contempt and scorn, which made his whole household do the same, relegating her to the sideline as he returned to his favourite mistress. And then after his death, there seemed no reason to stay. So Elowen had gone home and received the welcome she had not believed she could ever receive. She hadn't expected warmth and the open arms of her father, but neither had she thought to receive his indifference and derision.

'Yes, our situation in life is never easy,' Elowen said absently.

'Though I very much doubt that any lady's situation to be quite as peculiar as mine, Lady Elowen.'

'I do not understand.'

A small sad smile played around the maid's lips. 'I straddle between being a married woman—or rather a widow now—and never having actually been one, my lady. Not really.' She shook her head and sighed. 'You see, I married Geoffrey Trebarr in Brittany, yet without him actually being present and only by proxy through a Trebarr representative. And by the time our ship arrived here after being waylaid due to poor weather, rough seas and winds, Geoffrey Trebarr was already dead. So you see, I am a widow in name without ever actually being wed. Without actually ever meeting my husband.'

Elowen was so amazed and bewildered, her jaw dropped a little as she tried to comprehend Anaís Trebarr's words.

'I am astonished, my lady.' She leant forward. 'Let me understand this. You are saying that you had never actually met Geoffrey Trebarr—your husband?'

'No, never,' the young maid muttered, staring down at her hands in her lap. 'And now I wait to find out my fate, which is now more uncertain than ever, after such an unexpected arrival.'

'Yes, that is a most extraordinary situation.' Elowen reached out and covered the maid's hand. 'I am sure that whatever happens, you shall be treated with the respect and honour that is your due, my lady.'

Anaís Trebarr removed her hand away slowly and lifted her head. 'I really do not know how you can make such a claim. You do not know me or my situation.'

Elowen frowned and was unable to hide her surprise. 'Have you experienced unkindness? Or disrespect?'

'No, not at all. That was not my meaning, Lady Elowen.'

'Good. I am glad to hear it.' Elowen could never have imagined such a thing to be true of Simon. He would do all in his power to protect and safeguard his brother's wife. But that did not mean that the maid would not feel alone or uncertain. In which Elowen was well versed. 'And no, I do not know you, Lady Anaís, but I should very much like to during my short stay here.'

The girl's shoulders seemed to visibly sag. 'Thank you. I should like that too.'

Elowen smiled. 'We young widows must band together. Although in my case I shall soon be wed again.'

'Yes. And so shall I,' the younger woman said, grimacing as though she were swallowing something unpleasant. 'I believe, although I am not certain.'

All at once Elowen understood her meaning. That it was Simon whom she was referring to. After all, Lady Anaís Trebarr née Le Brunde might have wed Geoffrey Trebarr, but she had never actually consummated the marriage. She still carried the family name, so who better to wed now that the husband she had never met had died, than his own brother. It all made sense and it all made Elowen feel a pain so sharp in her chest, she could hardly breathe. She rubbed her forehead, sensing the first signs of a head malady. God, but she had no right to feel any of this feeling of loss. It was not as though she had a claim on Simon Trebarr.

'In that case, I wish you happy, Lady Anaís,' Elowen muttered finally, conveying that she understood her meaning well. But something else occurred to her. Anaís Trebarr's words a little earlier made a little more sense, on reflection.

Now I wait to find out my fate, which is now more uncertain than ever, after such an unexpected arrival.

Lord, but had Elowen's arrival here in Trebarr pose as some sort of threat to her? Did Anaís Trebarr see Elowen as a rival for Simon's affections? Surely not!

Indeed, she could see how this would be the best situation for both of them, even if it did make her chest ache. Elowen hoped that the young woman sat beside her would make him a good and kind wife. Their arrangement had nothing to do with her but she wished it all the same, did she not? Yes…yes, it was for the best. After all, Elowen was destined for Roger Prevnar and Simon was meant for Anaís Trebarr. She took in a shaky breath as she reminded herself of this.

There was another knock at the door that broke the silence that had descended over the two women reflecting on their own unfortunate circumstance. Elowen opened the door as a few serving maids came in carrying a wooden tub and a few others carried buckets of water.

'Lord Trebarr… He asked for a bath to be readied for you, my lady,' Anaís muttered.

'I am very much obliged to you. Both of you.' She hoped that the young woman understood that she was not here to come between her and Simon. That she would soon be leaving.

'Yes, I daresay Lord Trebarr is all kindness. Mayhap a little too kind.'

Elowen ignored the last comment and said instead, 'He is. Indeed, I really do not know what would have become of me or my convoy had he not come to our rescue.'

Anaís Trebarr got up and awkwardly dipped into another curtsey before turning away. 'I shall leave you now, my lady. But I would like to say that I am pleased to have another lady here. I should like to say that very much, Lady Elowen.'

'Thank you but I am only here until the storm clears and the roads are safe to continue with my travails.'

'Even so, we shall have the pleasure of your company until then, and for that I am very glad of it.'

A faint smile curled around her lips. 'As am I, Lady Anaís. As am I.'

For the second time, Elowen stared at the door as another guest left the chamber that she had been assigned to, closing it quietly behind her as she left.

Good Lord, but that whole encounter was not at all one she had expected. Not one bit. Elowen had been stunned by everything that she had unravelled after her short discourse with Anaís Trebarr née Le Brunde. First, the revelation that the young woman's marriage to Geoffrey Trebarr had never been a real one and because of that, Simon would be expected to do his duty and marry the maid, and thus not have the need to return the young woman nor her dowry back to her family. In every manner this whole arrangement made sense, and Elowen had no doubt that Simon would do what was required of him. Whatever his feelings on the matter, he would do right by Anaís. On that, the young maid will have no concern. Simon Trebarr was nothing if not the honourable man she had always known him to be. But oh, God, did the knowledge of all this have to hurt as much as it did?

Chapter Six

The storms raged on relentlessly for another three days and nights. And in that time Simon kept himself busy, making certain that he distanced himself from Elowen as much as possible. He rode out in the torrential rain, visiting tenants and farmers, lending his expertise and his men in shepherding valuable livestock and cattle from the sodden pasture and into the safe enclave of their stables. He then spent the past two days down the copper mines that brought Trebarr its main source of income. It felt good; indeed, it had been satisfying, wielding a mallet hammer and double-speared chisel down the mines, breaking into the craggy rocks and cutting strips of rock away. It was what Simon would do, ensuring that his people were safe in such precarious conditions in terrible weather, yet for Simon it was also a good distraction, keeping him away from the castle far longer than necessary and especially from one particular guest. One who had his head spin into a whirl ever since he had seen her again—Elowen Bawden…

Damn, but she had kissed him! Inadvertently. But Elowen Bawden had still kissed him and he would never forget the shock of that. That she had placed her mouth on his even for a moment had surprised the hell out of him. It was a fleeting impulse, a momentary lapse of judgement and Lord knew he'd had all manner of kisses in his time but no, it was more the woman who had kissed him that surprised him the most.

Simon had not seen Elowen since he had brought her to Trebarr Castle that day when he had encountered her with her ill-begotten convoy. And as soon as he had left Elowen in the chamber given for her use, and after the kiss, he had kept away. It was better this way and soon, once the storm passed, the woman would leave Trebarr and be on her way again, leaving him in peace. She would bind herself in marriage to a man who seemingly thought little of her, judging from how he had seen to arranging her journey from her father's house to his. It had been badly done and did not speak well of Roger Prevnar or what he thought of his betrothed's welfare. Not that it was any of Simon's concern. It was nothing to do with him and yet he found that he did care. He did mind how little Elowen Bawden's safety had been thought of. How little she had been cared for. All this went around and around his head while he purposely kept away. And then there had been the anger and despair that she had vented in his direction when he had come to help her. All the years of pent-up anger that she had held inside came out in that short but blistering outburst, and yet Simon knew that her guilt for what had happened had been directed at the one person who had shared it; so yes, he'd taken, not challenged, her accusations.

It had been in part his fault, part Hedyn Bawden's own folly on that day. But in the end the whole incident had been a terrible accident. A damn tragic accident. Still, if it had helped Elowen to overcome her guilt by lashing out on him, then he would take it. Indeed, he perversely welcomed it as a way for him to atone for that time. For his misdirected pride and overinflated arrogance.

This and more were what he had needed to process since the start of the storms that seemed strangely to mirror the conflicted feelings he had in his head. But he knew it could not last. He knew he could not hide and stay away for good, otherwise it would be noted and whatever else Simon felt, he would not want to make Elowen feel uncomfortable or unwelcome.

He strode back inside the castle and after changing into more appropriately dry clothing, he walked inside the bower chamber, the same one that had once been his mother's domain, where Elowen sat with Anaís and a handful of her maids who had travailed with her from Brittany. The women all had stitch work on their laps to occupy them, a table laden with sweetmeats and jugs with mugs set aside and a fire blazing in the hearth. The whole room was awash with a warm glow from the flickering flames.

The two young women lifted their heads as he walked towards them and stood to curtsey.

'What a lovely surprise, my lord,' Anaís muttered with her barely audible voice. 'It has been a while since we have seen you.' He noted that she was the only one of the women who was not occupied with her stitch work but had instead a piece of parchment in her hand along with a frown etched on her forehead.

Simon ate up the distance between himself and the two women who sat back on the bench and took Anaís's hand in his and bent over it before turning and taking Elowen's hand and doing the same. He tried hard not to meet her eyes or even worse, have them drop to her lips. The very lips he'd had pressed against his, albeit briefly.

'You do me a great honour, my Lord Trebarr, by coming all this way into the bower.'

'I had been meaning to see to both of you.' He smiled. 'I hoped to find you well, Lady Anaís? And you as well, my Lady Elowen? Indeed, all you ladies?'

'I thank you,' Anaís murmured softly as she stared at the parchment on her lap. 'We are passing the time together as I make our guest here feel welcome while this terrible weather passes.'

'Good…very good.'

Well, that chastised Simon, if nothing else. And *our guest* was certainly a comment that raised an eyebrow. Since it alluded to a certain presumption that made him feel a little stifled, a little uncomfortable. Simon knew very well what was expected of him in relation to Anaís, and he knew what he owed his family name, but he would not be pushed into marriage with the young maid. He would not be made to feel as though he had no choice in the matter, even if it was somewhat true. After all, he did need to marry and what better way to forge an alliance with the same family in Brittany that his father had sought for Geoffrey. A marriage between himself and Anaís Le Brunde, or rather Trebarr, was a sound choice and it would mean that he would keep her substantial dower lands and money that came with her to the marriage. He watched the young maid, who seemed uncomfortable with what she had said. In truth, for having said anything at all. Still, it was certainly a step forward that Anaís was now leaving her chamber and keeping Elowen company; something she would not have done even until recently. But then there was something odd about her this evening, something that made her seem distracted, her attention elsewhere, somewhere outside this chamber and possibly to do with whatever the contents were of the parchment she held tightly to her chest.

Simon tilted his head and wondered as he did many times how a woman like Anaís, meek, mild and unobtrusive, would have fared with his brother Geoffrey, had he not fallen from his horse and broken his neck. How would she have been married to a man like him—stern, brusque and unyielding? He might well have ended up breaking her spirit and crushing her dignified nature.

After all, Simon only had to look to the woman sat beside Anaís to remind him of how one such marriage affected a woman of Elowen's fiery and tempestuous spirit. He hoped to God that Roger Prevnar would be worthy of Elowen Bawden and be the husband that she deserved, giving her the security and safety she longed for.

It was a reminder that he was responsible of Anaís, a young woman whom he felt obligated to. He would not allow anything to happen to her when he had the power to do right by her. Yet, the notion of being bound to her made him give pause. God, but when he imagined it, his heart rejected the notion. Still, many marriages were arranged on less.

'May I offer you some ale or wine, my lord?' Elowen shot up from her seat and moved towards the wooden coffer set against the side wall.

He caught her eye and inclined his head. 'I thank you, my lady.'

This was yet another thing that he had in common with Elowen Bawden, the weight of expectation from his family name and the little choice he had in whom he would have to wed. Just as she had in her first marriage and seemingly in the one she was about to commit to. He kept his eyes locked on to her, watching her every movement. She returned back from the coffer and pressed the mug into his hand. Their fingers touching, lingering a little too long. She lifted her eyes slowly to his, a slew of messages flashing in her beautiful brown eyes, but none that he could not fathom. She clearly wanted to wordlessly convey something to him and all he could do was smile faintly instead. Elowen gave him the smallest shake of her head and returned to her seat beside Anaís, bending her head and continuing with her stitch work. The woman was clearly preoccupied with something.

'And what has taken so much of your time, my lord?'

Simon blinked and flicked his gaze away from Elowen to Anaís, who had asked the question. 'Many things, my lady. I have tended to my affairs here in Trebarr as I always do. For one, I have visited the mines with Gib, I mean Sir Ranulf Gibbons, and my men, and for another, seen to the welfare of my tenants and the livestock.'

'Such dedication.'

He inclined his head, a little taken aback with Anaís's shy observation. Despite that, this had been the most he had ever actually conversed with her. Or indeed had seen her since her arrival to Trebarr. 'Yes, my lady. I take my duties very seriously.'

'But in such treacherous weather as this, Lord Trebarr, you must take care. I should not like for anything untoward to happen.'

'You are all kindness, Lady Anaís.'

Anaís smiled so faintly he wondered whether he was imagining it. 'But I wonder whether you should see to such important matters in such terrible conditions, my lord.' Her voice was like a light wisp. 'Would it be too presumptuous for me to say that we have missed your esteemed company? Is that not so, Elowen?'

Simon let his gaze drop to Elowen, who continued to work on her stitch work, refusing to look in his direction. But Simon could see that his presence was somehow making Elowen feel uncomfortable. Indeed, both women seemed a little uneasy yet he could hardly account for it. It seemed that he had walked into a chamber where he could barely comprehend the subtle messages, the nuances to what was being said and even all that remained unsaid. Again, he wondered whether it had anything to do with the parchment that Anaís held on to.

'Is something amiss here? Lady Anaís? Elowen?'

Anaís shook her head, while Elowen merely looked away for a moment before answering. 'I was just mentioning to Anaís on how long it was since either one of us had seen you and now here you are.'

'Indeed, here I am,' he said, his eyes flicking from one woman to the other.

'And what of the conditions outside, my lord? Are they still as bad as they seem?'

'Unfortunately, they are much worse, my lady. The rain has not only been relentless but now many of the roads and main pathways are flooded. In some cases, very badly. The many riverbanks, too, have broken and flooded the nearby land and pastures.'

'Oh, God, I am sorry to hear that.'

'Indeed, many crops will be destroyed.' He sighed through his teeth with grave resignation. 'And I'm afraid that even after the storm passes and when the rain subsides it will take time before any of the roads and pathways are open again.'

Elowen frowned and stared at her lap. 'Oh, I see.'

'And yet in all of these conditions, I have been fortunate to receive a scribed parchment through a messenger who arrived here from Brittany.'

Simon was suddenly alert, frowning with concern. 'I hope all is well, Lady Anaís.'

'Of course it is,' she said softly, staring at the wall ahead. 'Why should it not be?'

Simon had come all this way to attend to both ladies who were under his care even temporarily. And instead of being welcomed he'd been given a far more frosty reception. He'd been more or less ignored by Elowen Bawden, even though he had also kept away. While the other lady had a haunted look and clutched at her parchment tightly. What in God's name was wrong?

He turned his attention to Anaís instead. 'Truly, Lady Anaís, is everything well?'

'Why should it not be?' she sighed in exasperation. 'I am here in a country that is not my own, missing everything and everyone I hold dear. I have no idea what shall become of me. I am tired, I am lonely, I am… I am sorry, I have said too much and I have said words that are unworthy of the kindness you have shown me. Forgive me.'

'There really is nothing to forgive, my lady. I understand your sentiment perfectly. It must have been difficult to leave your family, your kin, and travail to an unknown place. And then to discover that everything that you had envisaged about the future had changed irrevocably so.'

'Yes, exactly so,' Anaís whispered, nodding absently, her gaze falling back again onto the parchment she clutched between her fingers. 'I seem to be poor company this evening, my Lord Trebarr. Lady Elowen. If I may, I believe I shall withdraw now, and bid you both a good evening.'

Elowen also rose. 'I shall come with you, Anaís. I, too, should retire for the evening.'

'No, no, stay.' She motioned with her hand. 'Stay and keep Lord Trebarr company. I should like my privacy in any case.'

'If that is what you wish.'

'It is, I thank you.'

'Then I bid you a good night.'

Anaís curtsied again and moved towards the door with her maids following behind. Simon watched her leave and felt both relieved and somewhat perplexed. It seemed that Anais Trebarr née Le Brunde had much on her mind and all of it related back somehow to Brittany.

He flicked his attention to Elowen, who sat on the bench but had moved and shuffled along a little, her back slightly turned towards him.

Ah, so it seemed that she had been avoiding him, just as he had been avoiding her for the past few days. He sighed again and dragged his fingers through his hair. This all somewhat irrationally irritated him as it mirrored his own feelings. He, too, had kept away in the hope of whatever attraction had been there between them would have now lessened. After all, they had now seen one other again after many years, and spent time in each other's company, so the fascination that once held him captivated about Elowen Bawden should have evaporated. It should have…

'You seem quiet this evening, Elowen.'

'I am still considering the information you have imparted regarding the weather. Notwithstanding the devastation it has caused, which I am very sorry for. The impact it will have on my journey is something I am pondering on.'

'Keen to get to your betrothed?' he mused.

'Yes, and I am certain you should be glad to see the back of me.'

In truth, he should be, but found that he was not. Despite keeping away from Elowen these past few days, he was in some way relieved to know that she was safe. Here in Trebarr. And that in itself was a feeling he was reluctant to admit, even to himself. He found that it was an uncomfortable feeling knowing that he cared for her.

'No, I would not want that. I am glad that you are here in Trebarr and hope that your stay here has thus far been comfortable.'

'It has. I thank you. Anaís is a sweet maiden and has been very attentive to me.'

'I am glad, although she seemed very distracted tonight.'

'Mayhap you should take time to know her, my lord, and find out what is troubling her.'

That was just it. Anaís had very little interest in him at all. She had not once sought his company and neither had he pushed her for it. Since her arrival to Cornwall and learning of Geoffrey's death, the young maid had retired to her chamber and rarely come out. Simon had initially thought it was the loss of the life she had been promised that she had been grieving for, and that had made him feel the burden on his shoulders in securing her position in marriage to him. Yet, the more he observed Anaís, and the more he conversed with her, the more he realised that he might be wrong regarding that. He was now no longer convinced that it had been for a loss of being Lady Trebarr in Cornwall she had been mourning for at all. Nor for a husband she had never met. It was something else entirely, something that was rooted in whatever and whomever she had left behind in Brittany.

'At this moment I would rather know what is troubling you, Elowen.'

'Nothing… Well, actually, yes, there is something since you mention it.' She raised her gaze to meet his and sighed. 'It has been on my mind for the last few days, Simon, and it is something that you must allow me to apologise for again.'

'Oh, and what is that?' he muttered, knowing full well what she was about to say.

The kiss…

'You must know how mortified I am that I… I behaved inappropriately that night when you brought me to Trebarr Castle. What must you think of me?'

'Quite well and please do not fret, Elowen.'

'How can I not when I shall soon be wed to another, myself? It was unbecoming, unpardonable and after the gallant way that you came to my rescue…' She shook her head and exhaled through her teeth. 'All I can say is that I was overwrought and overcome with everything that had happened that night.'

And thank God for it.

'And had I known about your arrangement with Anaís, then I would never have presumed to behave so…so…'

'Wantonly?' he said, unhelpfully biting back a smile.

Elowen swallowed uncomfortably and seemed so flustered that she dropped the cloth that she had been stitching. 'I am sorry, I… I.'

Simon dropped to his knee in front of her and retrieved the long scarf that she had been adding some green and red embroidery to. He ran the soft cloth through his hands absently, rubbing his fingers along the fine stitch work back and forth, back and forth. 'No need, it's my fault. I was just teasing.'

'You have always enjoyed doing that?' she said on a whisper. 'Why is that, I wonder?'

Why, indeed… If only he knew the answer to that.

He shrugged, unable to say more. 'And there isn't an understanding between myself and Anaís, Elowen. She is my brother's widow, despite their short-lived marriage, and she is also still in mourning.' And he still did not know what he was supposed to do with the young maid.

'I see.' She held out her hand. 'May I have my scarf back?'

'Certainly. Your stitching is…beautiful,' he murmured as their fingers touched again in the giving and taking of the long linen cloth.

This time, however, he did not pull away and instead allowed his fingers to explore hers, softly brushing against them, palm to palm. The scarf fell away from their entwined hands once again, landing in a puddle of soft folds on the wooden floor between them. Yet, all he could think about was tracing the elegant lines up and down her fingers, while linked together, feeling the heat pulsating between them.

God above, but had he actually believed that he might somehow manage to dispel this fascination that always held him captivated with Elowen Bawden? What a fool he was. It was like an awakening of the feelings he had always had for her, which had lain dormant while he had tried to valiantly rid himself of them time and again, was flickering back to life. But now more potent than before. He turned her hand around and brought her palm to his mouth, kissing the centre reverently.

Elowen gasped and closed her eyes. But just as Simon leant in closer, her eyes flew open and she yanked her hand away, breaking whatever spell had been weaving around them.

'I believe I should also retire for bed as well, my lord.' She shot up to her feet and dipped into a quick curtsey before turning on her heel and leaving the chamber as he watched her, stunned and still kneeling on the floor.

Simon dropped his head and exhaled a shaky breath. He noticed that Elowen had left her scarf on the floor in her haste to leave. He reached down and picked it up, running his fingers over the delicate stitch work of flowers and thistles and wondering if he could ever rid himself of this torrent of feelings he had towards this woman. A woman who was not only wrong for him in every manner possible but always made him forget himself as well. And God only knew how dangerous that was for a man in his position. Hell's teeth, he hoped he would conquer it. He had to…

Chapter Seven

The treacherous storms continued for the following few days, subsiding momentarily, giving the impression that they had died before whipping up again for another bout of torrential rain, wind and gales battering across the Cornish coastline.

It was so relentless that Elowen wondered whether it would ever pass. The clattering of noise against the wooden shutters, the devastation it was seemingly leaving in its wake, made it impossible to plan ahead and think of anything beyond the safety within the walls of Trebarr Castle.

She hoped that her father, his new family and all at Bawden Manor were also protected from these perilous conditions. Yet, Elowen wondered whether they had spared a thought for her? Had they worried about what had come of her, after she had left Bawden Manor for Devonshire, without actually arriving there? Did Roger Prevnar wait within his estate prostrated with concern, or had he forgotten her existence in all the mayhem of these uncommon and unexpected storms? Mayhap… but then, knowing her family, mayhap not.

Still, all these thoughts were far better than to allow

herself to reflect on the master of Trebarr Castle. Elowen absently brushed the tips of her fingers down the centre of her palm where Simon had placed his mouth, hot and wet in that stirring kiss, that unexpected moment when he had marked her on her hand, of all things, with his mouth, lips and tongue a few nights ago. God, but his breathing had become ragged and it was then when she'd looked at him and seen that unfettered desire swirling in his eyes, that she had known—oh, she had known—that she had wanted him more than she had ever wanted anything in her life. So much so, that Elowen had needed to get away. She needed to distance herself from it in case she got burned by its intensity. Simon had even used the word *wanton* and in jest but oh, she had felt so very wanton. She had run to her chamber if only just to breathe.

Since then, thankfully, she had seen Simon when he had visited the bower chamber and had managed to pretend as though that intense short interlude between them was a figment of her imagination—as though it had never happened. There was civility and conversation about nothing in particular between Simon and Elowen, yet at least it lacked the heated glances from their last few encounters. At least there were no more repetitions of the time when Simon had first brought her to the castle and she had kissed him after he had tended to her hands. At least she had avoided a repeat of that mortification, thank God!

'Where shall I put these linen cloths, Elowen?' Anaís looked up from over the top of the folded stacks of cloths that she was carrying.

'The wooden livery cupboard in the corner would

do very well to keep all the essential household goods.'
Elowen brushed her hands on the apron she had tied
around her waist and pointed in the direction that she'd
had all the storage cupboards moved to. 'All the dried
goods can be stored there along with household linens,
string, dried beeswax for the candles and kindling. The
larger coffers can store all the spare yet clean and dried
bed linen and coverlets in that corner too, Anaís.'

They had been rearranging the dry goods in the stone
vaulted undercroft in the castle, which was surprisingly
watertight and dry despite the incessant rain during the
ongoing storms. The undercroft had been in dire need
of rearranging and cleaning as it had all been left in a
mess, mayhap because it had been without a mistress
of Trebarr for many years. But now that Anaís was here
the situation might change, even though it made Elow-
en's chest clench tightly when she thought of Anaís as
Simon's wife. Not that she should and not that she had a
right to. Yet, Elowen noted no attachment in that regard
between them. They laughed and chatted well enough
but more as siblings or friends. But then mayhap that
was a good basis to form an attachment—as friends and
easy companions first, before later getting wed to one
another. Again, Elowen felt the stab of pain in her chest
just thinking about such a union. God, she felt wretched,
which was another reason why she had thrown herself
headlong into being busy while she remained a guest
at Trebarr Castle. It gave her much to do and little time
to think of her own betrothal to man she did not know.

She pushed that thought away and pondered on Anaís,
who had never been given instruction on how to run a
castle as large as Trebarr. Strange, as all maidens from

families such as theirs would need to know and cultivate these skills. In this, Elowen, however, was in her element, supervising the many serving hands to carry the goods into storage and the barrels of ale and wine that had to be put into different sections under the arches. As well as showing Anaís how to be a chatelaine of a castle as vast as this.

'And what of the various salves and unguents used for ailments?'

'I would keep them separate from all the herbs and spices used for the kitchens. In the far cupboard in the corner.'

'Oh, yes, that is a good notion.'

With the kitchens flooding, many more items had been brought into the undercroft by the kitchenhands to prevent perishing, while many other hands drained the kitchen floor.

'But I must say, Anaís, that it should be you telling me where you would like everything to be organised here. After all, it is you who might soon be mistress of Trebarr.'

Anaís stopped stacking the linen cloth in the cupboard and turned her head. 'I do not know about such a thing, Elowen.'

'But why? After all, you were to be the next Lady Trebarr, were you not?'

'I might have been had Geoffrey lived but he did not,' she muttered softly.

Elowen blinked in surprise. 'Yes, but…would you not want Simon to honour the marriage settlements that were made before his brother's passing?' Elowen didn't know why she was asking Anaís this. It was not her place to, yet she could not help herself. 'Would you not want him to step into his brother's shoes in more ways than one?'

'No. It is not what I would have Lord Trebarr do.'

Elowen let out a breath she had not realised she'd been holding on to before moving towards her young friend. 'I do not understand. Surely you would wish for the security of being chatelaine of this castle? Its mistress?'

'Oh, Elowen, I do not know.' Anaís sighed as she rubbed her brow. 'Presently, I cannot think of such a thing. After all, marriage may not be what fate has in store for me.'

'But mayhap it could.'

Anais smiled tentatively, with a smile that did not quite reach her eyes and continued with her task. 'We shall see.'

They continued with their tasks in silence as Elowen reflected once again on everything that Anaís had said. Could there also be the added indifference that Simon showed the young maid inadvertently? Beyond that of a solicitous friend or brother? Could Anaís be holding back because she was uncertain of Simon's intentions? After all, on Elowen's arrival here the younger woman had behaved with more assuredness in regard to both her future place in Trebarr and Simon's resolute protectiveness of her situation and mayhap even more. So what had brought about the change in Anaís? Had it been whatever had been in the missive she had received, or Elowen's sudden arrival? Or mayhap a combination of both?

In which case, Elowen must do something to help Anaís, with both the instruction she needed to become the chatelaine of Trebarr Castle and also securing its master. God, but Elowen wished that she could avoid it. Indeed, she wished that it might have been different for her but what was the point of wishing for things she could never have? Elowen was pragmatic enough to know it was for naught. Her fate lay with getting to Devonshire and her betrothed as soon as the weather cleared and the roads were safe enough to travel again.

It was the one thing she could do to help the young maid as in only a short time, Elowen had come to like and admire Anaís Trebarr née Le Brunde very much. The maid might be quiet and reserved but she was also fierce and proud and dare she think it, but she also reminded her of her own situation when she had been younger. At least, however, Anaís had a handsome prospect in Simon Trebarr who was protective, loyal and honourable and would in time come to love and admire Anaís. Even if a union between them did make Elowen's heart ache, she could see that it would be for the best. For all of them. She would just have to get over it and never think of Simon Trebarr again. Indeed, she had to forget the forbidden feelings she had always felt for him.

That eventide in the bower chamber, Elowen ensured that Simon and Anaís sat together, while she remained conversing with Anaís's maids, knowing that the more time they spent together, the more opportunity they might have to start that initial stirring of attachment in earnest. And however difficult that might be for Elowen to navigate, it would be the best outcome for all of them. Mayhap then once Simon's affections were fixed onto Anaís as they clearly should be, the feelings Elowen had for him would begin to fade away. Yes, mayhap in time they would. God, but she hoped so.

Elowen put down the scarf that she had been embroidering, the very same scarf that Simon had sheepishly returned to her after that time they were left in the chamber alone, and rose. She moved to the coffer to pour ale into her mug as she surreptitiously watched Simon and Anaís sat together on the furthest corner of the room. It was a very good thing that they seemed to be getting better acquainted than even a few days ago. For Anaís had even informed her that until Elowen's arrival, she had mainly kept to her own chamber. She took a sip before Anaís appeared at her side, taking the jug and pouring a measure into two mugs.

'It seems that you two are quickly forming an attachment, Anaís,' she whispered from behind her mug.

Anaís raised a brow and shook her head. 'I would not say so.'

'Then what would you say?'

'That as much as I like him, I could never wed Simon. We would not suit and there is no reason for it in any case.'

'How can you say such a thing? Only moments ago, you were conversing and laughing freely with one another.'

'But as one might with a kindly friend or brother, which in truth is what Simon has ever been to me ever since I set foot on Cornish soil.'

Elowen frowned. 'Are you certain?'

Anaís sighed and nodded. 'My marriage to Geoffrey might not have been real in the truest sense, Elowen, but now it seems that the wheel of fate has given me the freedom to choose, if I so wish it, which I was not at liberty to do before. I am not bound to agree should Lord Trebarr even ask me, which he has not.'

'And if he does?'

'This conversation is far too soon to be had, especially in view of the fact that I am newly widowed. But I can say with certainty that I shall not accept Simon Trebarr, much as I admire him.' Anaís smiled as Elowen exhaled slowly.

'I see.' But no, she did not. Mayhap it was because of her. Mayhap if Elowen was not present in Trebarr or even in this chamber, matters might progress more naturally. While Simon could never be destined for her, he could nevertheless be bound for someone as lovely as Anaís, even if such a thought did hurt her deeply.

She walked alongside Anaís towards where Simon sat and covered her mouth to stifle a pretend yawn. 'I believe that I shall retire now and bid you good-night.'

'Are you well, Elowen?'

'Yes, perfectly, just a little tired after organising the undercroft earlier, which I might add was a task I could not have done without Anaís.'

Simon inclined his head. 'I thank you. I am very much obliged. Your efforts have not gone unnoticed.'

'It was my pleasure, my lord. Especially after everything you have done.' She felt herself flush as she noted his inscrutable gaze. 'It was mainly Anaís in any case.'

'It certainly was not.' Anaís smiled, shaking her head. 'I do not know where any of us would have been without Elowen organising it all.'

'It was the least I could do for you allowing me to stay here while the storm rages on. You have both been such wonderful hosts.' She curtsied. 'Now, if you'll excuse me, I shall take my leave. Until the morrow.'

Simon watched Elowen gracefully vacate the chamber, leaving behind the stitching that she had been working on once again, judging by the crumpled-up folds of cloth left where she had sat.

Now, what had all that been about? The past few evenings they had enjoyed a cordial albeit polite time convened together in the bower, which Simon had to admit reminded him of those long-ago moments when his mother had been alive. It had been a far more restive, companiable and contented time and especially after long and difficult days. The only thing that had perturbed Simon a little was how wary and a little distant Elowen had seemed. And yet, after the last time he had overstepped with her, and in this very room, Simon had also kept his.

'Is everything truly well with Elowen?'

'I believe so, my lord,' Anaís said on a shrug. 'Although she is someone that likes to keep busy, I believe, since it prevents her from having to ponder on matters that might otherwise be uncomfortable to.'

Simon nodded, once again marvelling how astute the young maid was. 'You might be right.'

'Indeed, her situation and her future particularly cause Elowen much worry and consternation.'

'I wish it wasn't so,' he said on a sigh as he absently moved to retrieve the scarf that she had left behind.

'Yes, as do I,' Anaís agreed. 'Why do you not attend to Lady Elowen and escort her back to her chamber, my lord? I am sure that she has not gone far.'

Simon rose slowly, keeping his eyes on the young woman whom he was becoming rather fond of. Indeed, these past few days, the more he had come to know Anaís the more he realised that despite expectations from all around them, she was also reluctant to enter into the married state with him. And this knowledge built a comradery between them that he had never known before with a woman. One whom he only saw as a friend or, in Anaís's case, a sister.

And another discovery regarding his brother's widow was that Anaís might be mild and meek but she was far shrewder than he had ever given her credit for. Her quietness hid many facets of her character such as observing everything around her and comprehending much at the same time.

'Very well, my lady.' He rose and bowed over her hand. 'If you are certain that you have no need of me this eventide then I shall bid you a good night.'

'Make haste, my lord.'

Simon did as Anaís bid and quickened his pace and grabbed a lit torch from the metal sconce and rushed towards the stairwell that led to the solar chambers two floors above. He took two steps at a time that wound up the spiral staircase, noting the sound of the rain thrashing against the stone keep.

He saw the flicker of light above him and could just about make out Elowen's back. She must have heard his footfalls as she turned around and waved her torch about to find out who had followed her.

'Simon?'

'I thought to come and escort you to your chamber, Elowen.'

She frowned. 'That is hardly necessary when I am practically there.'

'True, but I had forgotten my manners and was reminded of it belatedly.' He took a step up towards her; his head was level with hers as he turned them both around slowly so they faced one another. 'So here I am.'

He noted a flash of something akin to desire blaze in her eyes before she lowered them. 'Your manners remain intact, sir, and I thank you. However, I believe I can manage a handful of stairs on my own and the short walk along the hallway before I reach the bedchamber.'

'And if I insist?' he murmured, manoeuvring them so that Elowen now had her back against the stone wall.

She wet her lips, her voice a little raspy. 'There is little I can say since I am a guest here and this is your castle.'

That surprised him. 'Are you annoyed with me, Elowen?'

'Not in the least.' He watched in fascination as her top teeth sank into her lower lip. 'After all, where would I be without you?'

He took another step towards her, his face mere inches away from hers. 'Where indeed?'

'Either way, you should not be here. Not like this.' She dropped her arm holding the torch, shaking her head slowly. 'You should be by the side of your intended. You should be by Anaís's side, Simon.'

He placed his hands on either side of her against the stone wall, with one holding on to the torch, effectively caging her in case she decided to bolt. 'Interesting. Anaís thought I should be by yours, Elowen, escorting you to your chamber of all places.'

'Is it?' She wet her lips again before she answered huskily, 'Interesting?'

'I believe so.' He removed his hand from the wall and with one finger lifted her chin and watched her throat work as she swallowed, her eyes finally meeting his. 'For someone who is my intended, as you put it, despite the fact I have never actually declared my intentions, Anaís is only interested to remain a faithful sisterly friend. And apart from that she is rather diffident and uninterested in me, if you must know.'

'An excellent start to a marriage, I'd wager.' A ghost of a smile played around her lips.

'You would, eh?' He trailed a finger down the length of her long neck, feeling the soft, satiny skin and watching her response as she shuddered. 'Is that your general estimation of the marital state?'

'Yes,' she whispered. 'Anaís is young and she is confused with the situation she finds herself in. She might still wistfully long for Brittany. Mayhap her heart beats for all that she left behind there but I am certain that she is willing to do her duty now.'

'You take an eager interest in her,' he muttered, wanting to cease this discourse about anyone else other than the two of them here alone in the stairwell. Nothing at the moment mattered to him other than being this close to Elowen Bawden.

'How can I not, when I was once in very similar shoes? She, too, has a father who has recently married and who has been nothing but unkind to the poor maid. And she, too, finds herself at the mercy of her husband's family awaiting her fate. But in Anaís's case there is a gallant knight waiting to come to the damsel's rescue, as he is oft to do.'

He dragged his finger along her jawline around the shell of her ear, wanting to know every part of her. 'And what if she doesn't want to be rescued? What if that heart of hers beats still for whomever it belonged to back to in Brittany?'

Elowen pulled back a little. 'I never said that!'

'No. I did because I would wager that it is the root of all her woes.'

'And what if it is? We women can rarely follow what we hold in our hearts. Indeed, we can never reveal what it is that we want, nor what we long for.'

'And what is it that you long for, Elowen?' Simon spread his fingers around the curve of her neck, feeling the pulse from the long purple vein running down her neck beneath his hand, beating wildly. 'What is it that you want?'

'I… I cannot say.' Her eyes were soft and heavy lidded. 'But I know that you should stop this, Simon.'

'Should I?'

'Yes,' she hissed. 'I am bound for another, while you…you should…'

'I should do what?'

'I do not know.' She swallowed. 'But surely you must care about Anaís beyond just mere essentials?'

God, but he did not want to discuss Anaís. Not when he was this close to Elowen and when everything and everyone else melted away when she was with him here.

He cupped her jaw. 'And surely you must understand that Anaís was never meant for me.'

Elowen frowned, her brows meeting in the middle. 'Then who is?'

'You...' he muttered softly before catching her lips with his.

Chapter Eight

Elowen melted against him and groaned the moment Simon kissed her, his lips surprisingly soft yet firm. He slanted his mouth, covering hers, coaxing her lips open and deepening the kiss. He cupped her jaw with his large hand, his thumb brushing back and forth, back and forth along her skin, before his hand skittered down and settled around the column of her neck. Those long, sturdy fingers that always fascinated, stroked and caressed her, holding her still as he plundered her mouth, sending her blood rushing to her stomach. He tasted of so much want, need and the promise of sin that it almost made her knees buckle. God, but she felt so light-headed with this onslaught that she could almost swoon at his feet. But she would not; she could not.

It was all wrong; nay, it should not be happening, yet Elowen could never end this kiss. Even if she wanted to, which God help her, she did not. Not yet, not while she tasted his hot, wicked mouth on hers. And Lord knew it was wicked. It was all that she had secretly yearned for since she could remember. For so long, wondering what it might be like to be touched, stroked and kissed by him. She oft thought back to the time when his breath had caressed hers in passing as he whispered a quip in her ear, or when he had stared at her so intently as she had walked out of the sea and then of course the time when he was about to kiss her five years ago.

And now she knew. His mouth, his tongue, his teeth and those hands of his on her skin, on her body. God, but it made her wild just thinking about it; it made her wanton and at that very moment, Elowen did not seem to care. Her whole being was present in this potent moment. All her senses awakened to the myriad feelings that Simon was drawing out in her body and only by using his mouth. Against hers. God, but what a mouth. And yet, she should care. She should most certainly care.

'We should stop, Simon,' Elowen whispered as she writhed against him, his fingers trailing down her neck again followed swiftly by that mouth.

'Should we, now?'

'Yes! This is all wrong.'

He lifted his head and gave her a smouldering look. 'The little noises that you are making suggest otherwise, my lady.'

God, but the impertinent arrogance of the man. How he had neatly cornered her, knowing that she was incapable of resisting him, his touches, his kisses. Even if one were to even call his mouth on hers a mere inconsequential commonplace thing as a kiss. God above, but there was nothing inconsequential about it, since it felt more like he was devouring her.

Simon's fingers grazed along her exposed skin and down to the edge of the neckline of her dress, with his mouth, his tongue and teeth following the trail.

She gasped. 'You must know that we should not.'

'Aye, there are many things we should not do, Elowen,' he murmured, kissing her neck. 'We should not be drawn to each other. He sucked on the beating pulse against her neck and nipped it lightly, making her moan. 'We should not touch one another like this. We definitely should not kiss each other like our lives depended on it. And we most assuredly should not be constantly wanting each other.' He kissed her on the sensitive skin just above her neckline. 'But alas, we do. No matter how much we try not to.'

Simon had in this time loosened the lacings with his nimble fingers, so that it gaped open a little at the front. And before she knew what he was about, he had gently pushed it, tugging down the neckline of her tunic, exposing more of her skin, lower and lower until he had bared one of her breasts.

Simon groaned as he cupped her breast in his large hand, his thumb brushing against the sensitive tip of her nipple, again and again before he bent down and pulled it into his mouth. He used his tongue to lick around the sensitive bud and then sucked it into his mouth, over and over again, making her writhe uncontrollably in his arms. He was relentless, holding her still as he worshipped her.

Dear God above!

Her whole body was now alive, sensitive to every touch, and burning, burning in need for him. Wanting and needing more just to assuage this fire that had been lit in her veins. God, but with just a few kisses and touches, what had Simon reduced her to? This wanton need. This unrestrained yearning. She was losing herself more and more to this pleasure, even though her head was warning her that she was hurtling towards a perilous path. But she was in no mood to listen. She did not, in truth, care. Not at this moment.

All she wanted was to give in to the sensations that he was igniting in her. Even though it was wrong. Even though her aim this eventide had been bringing Simon together with Anaís. How spectacularly she had failed in that regard. How indifferent Simon had seemed when she had spoken about Anaís. And God help her but how at this moment, nothing else seemed to matter except her and him, together. At long last giving in to the pleasure that had always been denied.

Elowen had been a married woman and was now a widow. Yet, her late husband had never been able to make her feel as Simon did. He had never kissed nor touched, nor caressed nor made her feel like she was about to lose all control and shatter into a thousand pieces as this man did.

Simon's lips were once again on hers, licking into her mouth so deeply. He trailed to the side of her mouth, sucking on her lower lip before kissing and sucking on the sensitive skin beneath her ear. 'Tell me what you want.'

You, she wanted to cry. *Endlessly. This. Now. Always.*

But she said not one of those words. Instead, she muttered, 'I do not know.'

'Come now, do not be coy, Elowen.'

'But...*this*...this is...'

'What, Elowen? What is *this*?

He pressed his hard body against hers and claimed her mouth again, his hand caressing her breast, the other hiking up her skirt and grazing the inside of her legs. Slowly, slowly, his fingers caressed her in circular brushes and gradually moved higher along her thighs, giving her time to stop him if she so chose to. But heaven help her, she did not. Elowen would rather die than stop anything now. His hand moved higher until his fingers found the damp heat of her, between her legs. They both moaned when he gently pushed away the fabric of her chemise and slid the tip of his finger inside her and then excruciatingly slowly pulled it out again. He pressed against her as she felt the hard contours of him against her, despite being fully clothed.

'Tell me,' he whispered against her ear. 'What is *this* between us, then?'

'Surely you should know.' Her voice was so ragged, so unlike her own. 'Because at this moment, I cannot… Oh, I cannot…think.'

She could feel his hot breath against her ear before he licked the outer shell and moved to the spot beneath her ear. 'Oh, I do know.'

His finger slipped in and out of the centre of her heat, again and again and again while he kissed her. And she matched him in everything that he did. Kissing him, tangling her tongue with his, touching him. Her hands roaming all over his chest, shoulders and neck through the layers of clothing he was wearing. She wanted, nay, needed, to feel every sinewy muscle, every sharp plane, every corded strength of him.

'I have never known this… I haven't known it to be like this.'

And Elowen had not. Her late husband had only ever sought to find purchase in his own pleasure. Hers was never a consideration. Never.

She had never even believed that her body could ever react in this manner. But mayhap it was because of the man who was rousing her in this way. Mayhap it was all because of Simon Trebarr.

'I know,' Simon murmured hoarsely against her damp hair as her breathing became more and more laboured.

She curled her arms around his neck and sucked on that pulse along that vein throbbing and beating so fast, and heard a startled hiss from his lips as she nipped him with her teeth, wanting to mark him, as he had done to her.

His slick finger continued to penetrate her heat, unrelenting, ruthlessly moving inside her deftly and creating sensations she had never known existed. He dragged his other hand down the length of her body, stopping to knead her breast before moving to cup her backside and giving it a squeeze. He thrust her forward to meet the hardness of his body through all the layers of clothing they were both still wearing. They both moaned as his mouth found hers again and again.

She pulled away and arched her back, her head thrashing from side to side. 'I... I... Oh, God, I feel like I am about to break.'

'I shall catch you.' He kissed and sucked down her neck and along her collarbone. 'Let go, sweetheart. Let go.'

'This... This is too much.'

'No, Elowen, *this*... This is...everything.'

She felt his hardness rub against her heat, his hand cupping and caressing her backside and that one finger rolling against that sensitive spot deep inside. He pressed lightly again and again, his heavy breathing against her neck. And with an inexplicable feeling that made her soar higher and higher, she did. She broke.... Elowen came apart in his arms as he caught her mouth with his, muffling her scream. She shuddered, sagging against him, her hair mussed and her forehead damp, while he had indeed caught her, holding her up against him, his own breath coming in frantic bursts.

She could feel him panting against her skin.

Elowen gradually came back to herself, as her breathing returned to a semblance of normality. But no, nothing could ever describe what had just happened between them as normal. She took in her surroundings, pinned against the stone wall in this damp spiral staircase, with her breasts bare and her skirts hitched up to her hips and her fingers tangled in Simon Trebarr's hair, and wanted then for the ground to open up and swallow her whole. What had she done? Not only had she allowed this but also had encouraged him, giving herself to the carnal pleasures that Simon had awakened in her body, wanting more and more and more.

Dear God, but she felt wave after wave of mortification engulf her senses.

Elowen gently pushed against Simon's chest, making him take a startled step back away from her, and looked up into his eyes, wanting to see something, anything other than the confusion that she felt reflected back. But all she saw was the same visceral shock of how quickly everything had caught aflame between them. How they had both given in to *this*, whatever this was, and let go of all reason, restraint, as well as their good sense.

Please say something, she willed. *Please say some-*

*thing to make this not as sordid and shameful as it feels
right now.*

Yet, Simon had stilled and was staring at her and then
at his hands, and then back at her as though he were
considering how those clever, expert hands of his had
managed to achieve what they had.

God, how lowering.

Elowen felt a sudden wave of anger replace all else.
She was angry with him, with herself and all the emotions that came crashing through her at that moment.
Emotions that she had been holding a tight rein on from
the moment she had first seen Simon Trebarr again in
the hall at Bawden Manor. Ever since she had found out
that she had been betrothed to yet another man she'd
never met, even if she had later agreed to it willingly.
Ever since she had fallen into that muddy water and attempted to lodge the wheel of the wagon away and having Simon come to her rescue. Ever since she had come
to Trebarr Castle and meeting the young maid whom
Simon Trebarr should marry. And ever since she had
lost her brother in the manner she had. God, how everything always seemed to come back to Hedyn and
her guilt. The burden of guilt that she carried everywhere no matter what she did. Why did she feel such
guilt? Because of this damnable attraction to the man.
This terrible, all-consuming desire that she could never
quite rid herself of.

And now Simon Trebarr had unleashed it all with a
little help that she had willingly given.

'Well, now I know what *this* is,' she said coldly, meeting his gaze.

He frowned. 'What does that mean?'

But Elowen had already pushed past him after smoothing down her skirts, letting them fall down to the floor and pulling her bodice up and over her shoulders, righting herself as much as she could. 'That whatever you might believe, my lord, I was never meant for *you*.'

Simon stared at the disappearing silhouette of Elowen Bawden as she rushed up the stairwell, in anger, disappointment and incredulity. All of which was his fault, and because of what he had just done.

Damn but he had behaved as though she was some tavern doxy, staying her on the steps of a stinking damp stairwell of all places and kissing and touching all over her glorious body in a manner he had no right to, and when anyone might have come upon them. He had behaved unpardonably towards her even though her body had all but sung when he had touched, and caressed her. God, but he had felt her. And her response to him was sweeter than he could ever have imagined possible. Indeed, he had never known such passion, want and need come together so perfectly in a single potent moment that encapsulated all he had craved for so long. And damn, but the heat of Elowen Bawden's body, slick and wet with desire, was still making his head spin. He was astounded and staggered by her reaction, and when she had come undone in his arms with the low light of the flickering torch skimming her smooth exposed skin with a warm glow...

He glanced down and noted the scarf that she had left behind...again. He reached out and retrieved it, sliding it through his fingers, and exhaled irritably. He had to dispel these thoughts and put it all out of his mind.

How had it come about to all that fevered heat and frenzied passion so quickly, though? It was the one thing that he could not fathom, in his dazed, confused state. Indeed, this loss of absolute control to a woman he'd no right wanting, was something he could not abide. Apart from which, Elowen Bawden was his damn guest for the love of God, and look how well he'd managed to extend that welcome on this night. Yes, he had behaved inexcusably, while he had always been careful to foster the opposite in every situation, especially with a woman who was under his care, even if it was for a short duration. And yet, he had lost all restraint and given in to his desire, effectively taking advantage of her.

Hell's teeth!

There was nothing for it. Simon had to apologise and he had to do it as soon as possible. But with Elowen rushing off to her chamber he would have to do it on the morrow.

Yet, Simon did not see Elowen the following morn. Nor was she present in the hall when one of the outriders rushed into the hall to inform him that most of the local rivers had breached their banks, flooding nearby land.

And when he walked into the bower chamber that evening, to find Anaís sat there with all her maids, and Elowen elusively missing once more. Simon knew that it had not been an accident. She had been evading him all day.

'Ah, Lady Anaís, but where is Elowen this eventide? I don't believe I have seen the lady all day.'

'And have you been looking for her all day, my lord?' the young maid muttered with a raised brow as she continued with her stitch work.

'No, only an observation, my lady.'

She smiled and lifted her head, as she continued to stitch with remarkable deftness. 'Ah, well, then it would be my observation that there is something amiss with Elowen this evening. But I assure you that there is nothing to concern yourself with. However, since you seek the lady, then you might want to see to her comfort yourself and take her a goblet of this fortifying wine from my homeland. It is rich, red and full of restorative properties. Well, it was always given to me as a child in any case.'

'I thank you. It is most considerate of you, my lady,' he muttered as he sat for a moment across from the maid. 'And it brings to mind the scarf she forgot yesterday as well.'

'Ah, so you did not manage to give it to her, then?' she asked innocently.

'No, my lady. I did not.'

'I see,' she said, tilting her head and giving him a penetrating look. 'It seems that you did not see Elowen last night, then and did not escort her to her chamber?'

'No,' he muttered, shifting a little uncomfortably.

'And yet I cannot help think that Elowen mentioned to me that you did, precisely, those things.'

Simon did not say anything but felt a little irritable by this astute young maid's interrogation. 'Well, it must have slipped my mind. In any case, it's of no consequence.'

'I know, it was merely an observation,' she murmured, giving him a wry smile.

'Are you jesting with me, my lady?'

'I must admit that I am a little.' Anaís sighed and put

down her stitch work. 'May I be so bold as to offer another observation, or rather my meagre counsel, such as it is, my lord?'

'By all means.'

'I would say that life can be so uncertain, so unpredictable, with much hardship and strife that we have no choice but to endure all that is thrown at us in the end.' She shook her head, her blue eyes taking on a wistful gleam. 'But when we find something so precious, something pure and good, we should... Indeed, we must follow it.'

He frowned. 'I confess, I am at a loss. We must follow what, my lady?'

She leant forward and lowered her voice to a conspiratorial whisper. 'Follow our heart.'

He drew back suddenly. This was the maid's counsel to him? And yet, something else puzzled him. 'And did you? Did you follow your own heart?'

She nodded slowly. 'Yes, but sadly in my case that path led me to loneliness and heartbreak.'

'Then I am sorry for it.'

Her brows shot up. 'Even knowing that the person whom I lost my heart to was not... That it could not be your brother...my husband?'

Simon could see that it had taken a measure of courage for Anaís Le Brunde to confess what she had. Courage that his brother Geoffrey would have crushed as surely as he would have crushed Anaís herself, wanting only a dutiful, pious wife who would bear him heirs and nothing more.

'Even then, Anaís.' He smiled softly, wanting her to

know the truth of it. 'But tell me who was this scoundrel who broke your heart?'

She frowned and sat back on the bench. 'But I am your brother's widow, my lord. It was unseemly for me to have said anything at all about my own situation.'

'Anaís?' he said softly. 'You were married in name only to Geoffrey, so there is no disloyalty here, I assure you.'

She exhaled and said the name that must have been tormenting the poor woman, evidently for far too long. 'Gregor Bartele.' She breathed out and shook her head. 'His name is Gregor Bartele. And he never broke my heart, not intentionally anyway.'

'Then what?'

'Our families…they would not consent,' she muttered on a shrug without needing to say much more. 'I am certain that you must understand.'

He nodded absently, knowing the truth of it. Indeed, he understood too well. Far too well the nature of families, their feuds and how destructive it all could be. But then he had hoped to end it all with Breock Bawden, this long and oft painful animosity with the Bawdens that brought nothing but strife. Yet, the distrustful old fool put pride before pragmatism and refused to see reason.

Simon thought of Breock's daughter alone in a chamber within the walls of his castle and pondered on her reluctance, a different one certainly but a reluctance all the same, as she refused to see him today. Well, she would not refuse him or his apology now.

He rose and bowed, suddenly needing to see the blasted woman. 'I shall take leave of you, my lady, and deliver this fortifying wine to Lady Elowen now along with her stitch work.'

Anaís smiled and inclined her head. 'You may wish to take another goblet of wine as I believe you might need some fortification yourself, my lord.'

He smiled faintly and inclined his head before leaving and turning in to the small hallway that led to the spiral staircase, taking two steps at a time as he climbed to the solar. He walked through the antechamber and reached the chamber at the far corner that had been assigned to Elowen Bawden and knocked on the wooden door.

Elowen opened the door and took a step back, surprise etched on her face. 'My lord?' she gasped, remembering quickly, it seemed, to give a perfunctory curtsey. 'What are you doing here?'

He returned her courtesy with an elegant bow of his own. 'I have come to offer you my apology, Elowen. Something I have been meaning to do, had I the opportunity to encounter you today.'

She frowned in confusion. 'Have you been looking for me?'

'I have,' he said, raking his hair back with his fingers. 'I believe that you might have been avoiding me?'

She stood with her back straight and lifted her head, her eyes slowly meeting his gaze. 'I have.'

'May I enquire to the reason, Elowen?'

She sighed and opened the door wider. 'Please, would you come inside? I cannot have this discourse by the door.'

He took a tentative step inside her chamber, his eyes flicking all around the warm and comfortable space. 'Well?'

'Do you really believe that I could see you, face you, so soon after what transpired between us yesterday evening on the stairwell?'

'That is also the very reason why I wanted to see you, Elowen. To offer my apology.'

She spun on her heel and turned to face him. 'You want to apologise? Why?' She tilted her head to one side in that way she did when she was considering something.

'You need to ask that?' He folded his arms across his chest. 'Very well. I need to apologise because I treated you…nay, I took… I made you…' *I made you burn with desire…* 'God, this is much harder than I anticipated. Please just allow me to apologise, Elowen, so that we can at least forget the interlude even happened and return to how matters were between us.'

Even as the words left Simon's lips he knew how impossible that would be. God, but he could never forget the feel of her mouth, her skin, her scent, her body.

'Forget that it even happened? And how exactly do we do that? Because I know I cannot just erase what happened, even if I wanted to. And you wish to return to *how matters were between us*?' She stepped in front of him and smiled softly. 'And what is that exactly, my lord?'

He raised a brow at how adamant she was. 'Come now, Elowen, you know what I am saying.'

'Do I? For it is all I have been pondering on all day.'

'And what is your summation, for I thought that you were both ashamed and embarrassed by what transpired between us, and why you left in haste.'

'Yes, I was… I was both ashamed and embarrassed,

Simon,' she sighed deeply. 'However, after some reflection today I realised that I am not quite as ashamed by what occurred as I should be.'

'Why?' He frowned, wanting to hear her answer.

'Because…because it would be a lie.'

He exhaled a shaky breath as relief flooded his senses.

'I am glad to hear it, as I feel the same. I could never regret what happened between us, even though I believed I must have behaved badly for you to have had that look of horror on your face once you…once you came back to yourself before you rushed off. And that, my lady, is why I felt the need to apologise.'

'If you apologise then surely I should as well. For I behaved just as badly as you.'

He smiled softly. 'Whether we behaved badly at all, then, in that case.'

'Indeed, for far too long I have not been honest with myself…regarding you.'

He caught her hand in his and pulled her a little closer. 'And now you are?'

She smiled and raised an impish brow. 'Honest and true? Of course.'

He chuckled. 'Never have two words been so further from certainty when spoken in relation to a Bawden.'

She gasped in evident mock outrage. 'Are you disparaging my good name?'

'And if I am?'

'Well, then I shall have to retaliate and say how typical it is that when we have finally reached some semblance of understanding between us and our two houses, it is a Trebarr who would resort to casting aspersions on our good name.'

'And don't forget that your good name is supposedly one of the oldest and most revered names in all of Cornwall.'

'For shame, my lord, for now it appears that you are now mocking our family name, which makes me think that you should offer yet another apology.' She grinned, her face filled with mirth. 'And when I recall that most of what is now part of the Trebarr land and mines once belonged to the Bawdens—that very old and revered family.'

A flash of annoyance flashed across his eyes until he realised that Elowen was still jesting with him. 'It might have once but Edward the Black Prince, and Duke of Cornwall, has seen fit to bestow the land and mines to the Trebarrs, for our allegiance to him in the past few years.'

'Hardly fair.'

'Nothing in life ever is,' he murmured, knowing it to be so damn true, especially regarding the woman who stood in front of him.

She watched him for a long moment and sighed. 'It seems that you'll always be a Trebarr at heart.'

'Yes.' It was an honest statement of truth. 'As you are always a Bawden at heart.'

'And never the two can come together?'

'Apparently not.'

But they had, unequivocally.

'And it is for that reason, and for as long as I can remember, that we have evaded one another, looked the other way, just to avoid *this*, which has, in truth, always existed between us.'

'Ah, so you have realised what *this* is, finally?' he

murmured, watching as a warm flush spread on her cheeks and neck.

Elowen held up their entwined fingers as though she were studying a rare sight that she'd never beheld before. 'I tried to plead ignorance. I pushed it away and dismissed it, not wanting any of it to be true. But it is. It always has been and I am tired of constantly fighting it—this very inconvenient attraction that I felt from the moment that I first met you.'

Simon stood there stunned by all that she had revealed, knowing that he, too, felt the same. Yet, he could not move for shock. Words, too, seemed to have been stuck in his throat, unable to get out. But they needed to be said.

'I, too, have struggled, Elowen,' he croaked, swallowing uncomfortably. 'I, too, have always felt the same.'

She nodded and dropped his hand, turning away from him, as though this confession was of little consequence, when in truth, it was not. Not to him. 'So you see, after all is said and done, an apology is quite superfluous, do you not think? When for once, we gave in to what we have both wanted for so long.'

Their desire...

Simon did not know why Elowen's sudden pensiveness was both alarming and endearing, in equal measure. And why, after everything they had said, they were now both being coy about saying *this* out loud.

Or mayhap they had both said all they needed to say. Mayhap they had both been *honest* and *true*...and there was nothing left to say.

'I should leave you now, my lady, and bid you a good night.' Simon bowed and spun on his heel to move to the door.

'Simon?' her voice caught and was barely audible from behind him as his hand reached for the latch on the door. 'Stay?'

He turned around slowly to face her, his heart thumping in his chest. Had she just invited him to stay with her? Or was it possible that he had misheard her…misunderstood her meaning.

'What did you say, Elowen?'

He could see her take a shaky breath before she spoke again. 'I asked… I asked if you would stay.'

His lips curled slowly into a smile as he sauntered towards her, taking his time to reach her. 'And what if I stay?'

Elowen returned his smile, her eyes dropping to the tray that he'd forgotten he was carrying. 'Then I shall be forced to invite you for a drink of wine from the tray you brought with you and have seemingly forgotten about.'

He nodded slowly, never taking his eyes off her, before he prowled towards Elowen Bawden.

Chapter Nine

Elowen had known the moment that she'd been escorted to Trebarr Castle that it would be difficult to hide her *true* and *honest* feelings, the ones that she had guarded so closely, for such a long time. It was either that or continually going through the perpetual cycle of remorse and shame that she always had for her feeling towards a man whom her Bawden kin hated. Yet, after what had happened between them the night before, that was no longer possible. Not to her. And it was also not fair to the man who had helped her, taken her in and given her shelter during these raging storms.

So she had told him. God above, but she had invited him to stay with her…in her chamber because she could no longer fight it. She could no longer deny this want of desire for Simon Trebarr, even if she was bound for another. She would have this, she would have this one night that was just for her, before she settled and became the dutiful wife of Roger Prevnar. A man she had never met.

Simon set the tray that he had been carrying down on the wooden coffer and poured a measure of red wine into the two goblets and handed one to her.

'Restorative wine sent by Lady Anaís with her compliments.' He raised his goblet before clinking it against hers. 'To your health.'

'And to yours, my lord.' She took a sip, letting the rich, soothing wine slip down her throat. 'Mmm, indeed it's very…restorative.'

'And before I forget your scarf.' Simon untied the material that she had been working on from around his sword belt and presented it to her. 'You left it in the bower last night and then…in your haste you left it again.'

'So I did,' she said, gulping down more of the wine before taking the fine linen from him.

'And may I enquire what it is that you're stitching, my lady?'

'I am using the Bawden colours of blue, brown and gold to embroider our motto of *Karensa a Vynsa, Covatys ny Vynsa.* And including our emblem of round gold bezants and an eagle in the corners of the scarf.'

'Ah, so that is an eagle, is it? I had wondered,' he said wryly, earning him a light dig from her elbow to his side, making him chuckle. 'No…no, of course, now that you mention it, I can see that it must be one.'

'Very amusing. I am gratified that you find my stitching so lacking. But I do try, my lord, even if I might not be as proficient as Anaís.'

'I would never dream of using such inflammatory language, especially in terms of a lady's accomplishments and artistry. I only mentioned it since it is I who is lacking.'

'Lacking?'

'Why, yes, in imagination.' He slipped the soft fabric between his fingers before passing it to her. 'After all, your family's motto of *Karensa a Vynsa, Covatys ny Vynsa*—Love Would, Greed Wouldn't—resonates far more in a…dare I say it…romanticised view of Cornwall than the Trebarr one, which is short, to the point and direct: *Franc ha Leal, Atho ve.*'

'Ah, but some might think it far more honest and true, rather like a rallying call, showing your allegiance to the traditions of Cornwall and the kingdom to declare, "free and loyal am I," with your Trebarr motto.'

He took another long sip and nodded. 'And yet, I maintain that I along with our honest and true motto are still somewhat lacking in spirit and imagination.'

'Well, now that you are Lord Trebarr you might change it to one that inspires and epitomises the new spirit and ethos of House Trebarr. If you so wish.' She lifted her head and smiled at him. 'But I must admit I still admire your forthright one, even if you believe it to be lacking. Since being free and loyal are far more noble aspirations than anything that might be construed as *romantic.*'

Elowen knew the moment those words had slipped from her lips that it was a mistake. For such views were not only unusual for a woman to have but offered a window into her mind, nay, her very soul, and she did not want anyone to be privy to that. Not even Simon Trebarr.

How had Simon moved so close, so effortlessly, to her? He lifted her chin with his finger and stared into her eyes, trying seemingly to comprehend more meaning from them. 'So you believe that anything that might be construed as romantic to be…unworthy?'

'And if I did?'

'I would say that that such a notion is not only sad but to be beneath you, Elowen.'

She pushed away from him and strolled to the coffer. 'And I would say that I have been married, while you have not, Simon.'

'Ah, so that is the basis of your beliefs, an unhappy marriage?'

'My unhappy marriage as you call it, did at least teach me the folly of believing in such idle nonsense as following one's heart and anything that might be construed as *romantic*, as I said before.' She held up the jug. 'May I offer you some more wine?'

'Yes, I thank you,' he muttered as he placed his goblet on the coffer. 'I recall that you would have comfort, security and protection as your main requirements for a successful marriage.'

She sighed, wanting an end to this particular discourse. 'They are more prudent than any romanticised notions of marriage and I am no longer that maid who believes in such things, Simon. So, yes, I would rather have that along with the Trebarr maxim of freedom and loyalty, as those, too, are highly commendable.'

'Well, then, I'd drink to that,' Simon murmured, raising his goblet up in salutation before knocking back the wine. 'Although, my lady, I am not certain that a woman can, in truth, be free once she has wed.'

'I do know that.' She ambled back towards him. 'But until then a woman might enjoy it, can she not? The illusion of such a thing?'

He inclined his head. 'Of course, but may I ask what she might do in possession of such freedom?'

'What would she do?' Elowen sank her teeth into her

bottom lip before she uttered the most brazen words she'd ever said in her life. 'She would invite the man she most desired in the whole kingdom to stay with her in her chamber…all night.'

'How very scandalous.' Simon's green eyes blazed with so much potent heat, that she found she could scarcely draw breath.

Elowen knew from the moment that she had uttered those words, which were indeed very scandalous, what she was saying to Simon. And ever since the scalding kiss and intimacies from the night before, she had known there was nothing for it. Not anymore. Elowen could no longer deny that she wanted him still and with an intensity that shook the very foundations of her soul. And mayhap, just mayhap, by giving in to this visceral, all-encompassing desire that she felt for the man and for one night only, it might possibly be remedied for good. Mayhap she would no longer feel the way she did for Simon, after they spent the night together. And he might not desire her in the same way, either. Not after they both got what they had craved for so long.

Besides, this would change nothing in Elowen's plans to follow through with her marriage to Roger Prevnar. Why should it? He was, as her father had reminded her, the most sensible choice for a woman in her situation, from a highly respected venerable family, with young daughters who needed her. And she was still young enough to give him heirs. But more importantly to Elowen, Roger Prevnar was also a man whom she would never have the deep regret nor guilt as she did about Simon Trebarr, as she would never have the same depth of feeling for him. No, there would never be another quite like Simon Trebarr, who made her heart quicken and made her long for things she could never have. But mayhap she could on this one night.

After all, the older man, whom she had yet to meet, was hardly *her* choice for a husband. Not that Simon could ever be that, or anything more than what they'd share tonight.

It had been her desire for him that had been the reason for her brother's ire, which then caused his untimely death, after all. So no, despite it all, despite finally giving in to her desire to this man, it changed nothing about how it had all been her fault, nor made her forget its cause. And because of that, her plans for marriage to Roger Prevnar would remain unchanged.

There might have been a time once when she wanted more from her life, but that no longer held true. Elowen had grown up from those long-ago ideals of marriage. It was not true and certainly not for someone like her, whose only purpose was to make a strategic alliance for her Bawden kin. At least then this marriage agreement would assuage her feelings of guilt and would be a restitution of sorts for her father for the loss of his heir, a matter which he had always rightly blamed Elowen.

So this, tonight, was for her, for Simon, just the two of them, before she entered the marriage that she had been pledged to; one that held no ridiculous romantic notions of courtly love. And because of that, it was one she was fully intending on honouring.

She flicked her eyes to find that Simon was staring at her. He took the goblet from Elowen's hand, placed it on the coffer before turning around and taking her in his arms, covering her mouth with his in an intoxicating kiss that sent a lick of flame coursing through her whole body. She moaned as he deepened the kiss, his mouth and tongue exploring hers, sending darts of pleasure through her.

It was a kiss, only a kiss, just as it was last night. But now, just as then, it felt like so much more. From the moment that Simon's lips touched hers, she was lost to the sensations of his mouth on hers, exploring, lingering, devouring. And yet, she could not help but feel that he was still trying to grapple with his desire, holding himself in check, as though he feared that he might not have the power this time to settle for anything other than to have her beneath him. And this time she would acquiesce, since this time she wanted the same.

She trembled in his arms as her hands skimmed up his broad chest and curled around his neck, pulling him down to her. She wanted, nay, needed, to be closer to him. Have her skin pressed to his. Indeed, Elowen had just as difficult a task holding on to her control as much as he seemingly did.

Simon's fingers fumbled a little at the lacing at the back of her dress, as he kept his gaze locked on to hers before bending down to take her mouth again and again. His hands tugged the dress over both her shoulders and allowed it to skim down her body, pooling at her feet. He reached for her tunic and she took a step back, shaking her head.

'I think, my lord, that it is now my turn to divest you of your clothing as you did of mine, last night.

'You forget that I only got thus far as I have tonight.'

She shrugged. 'I, on the other hand, believe that I shall get on much further.'

He chuckled and raised a brow. 'How very bold of you, my lady.'

'If only you knew how my heart has quickened so, you would realise that it was all bravado. However, I have been flattered and encouraged enough now to show that I, too, can possess the imagination and artistry needed at such a time as this.'

'I have every faith in both your imagination and your prodigious artistry. But may I ask how you intend to… exhibit it?'

'Ah, but you shall have to wait and see, my lord.'

'Of course.' He gave her a slow, wicked grin. 'Then by all means go ahead, my lady. I am but your humble servant.'

She returned his smile but was also feeling a little nervous. 'I am very glad to hear it.'

Elowen proceeded to help him to take off his leather belt and then the matching gambeson, shrugging it off his shoulder and then placing it on top of the wooden bench. Next, she untied the ties to his moss green tunic that brought out the vibrant green of his eyes. She kept her eyes fixed on his as she pulled the tunic up and over his head, throwing that on the bench as well.

Simon now stood in front of her with his chest bare and his hose tied low around his narrow hips, covering his well-defined legs.

'May I touch you?' Elowen could not believe that the question had actually been uttered. She flicked her eyes to his to find them almost black with unspent longing.

'Nothing would give me more pleasure, Elowen,' he muttered hoarsely.

'Very good, but only if you keep absolutely still. And

only if you refrain from touching me. That is, until I say so.' She did not know where she'd acquired her newly found confidence but revelled in the power she yielded over this magnificent man, even if it was fleetingly so. No one but no one made her feel the way Simon Trebarr made her feel.

'Very well, do as you please.'

Her heart was hammering in her chest as she reached out and touched his skin, her fingers skimming the contours of the muscles of his chest, up along his shoulders and then his powerful arms.

His breathing became ragged as he kept still while Elowen explored every part of his upper body, as if she were putting to memory every scar, every muscle, sinew and even the smattering of hair that ran from his chest down a long line until it disappeared under his hose. She leant forward and pressed her lips to his chest and felt him tremble a little, enjoying the control that she exerted, or rather, Simon allowed, for the moment at least, while her hands skimmed all over his body. She continued to use her hands, lips and tongue to explore Simon as he hissed in pleasure. His chest rose and fell beneath her fingers; his brooding eyes darkened with pent-up desire while his hands were clenched tightly on either side as she moved closer to him, dutifully keeping to what she had asked. But it could not last for long. God, but his body was now so taut, so hard, that if Elowen continued as she was, he might likely snap.

Elowen's fingers moved down his body until they reached the ties of his hose. She heard him exhale through gritted teeth as she continued to torment him as she slowly, slowly untied them. Elowen flicked her eyes to meet his and smiled as she had finally parted the two ties, holding them for a long moment in each hand. She then pushed them down his hips, making him shudder, revealing all of him in all his naked glory. And then it was Elowen's turn to stand there, unable to move, unable to breathe, as her eyes skimmed Simon from top to glorious bottom.

Dear God...

There was something quite exhilarating about being dressed while in the presence of a gorgeous yet powerfully rugged man who had nary a stitch of clothing covering his body and almost pulsating with need and desire.

Her breath shuddered and her hand shook as she reached out and wrapped her fingers around his erect manhood and felt him groan as if she'd caused him pain.

'Oh, I am sorry, I did not mean to hurt you.'

'God, no. You...are...not...hurting...me...' he muttered, his voice low and strained.

'Yet, I cannot think I am implementing matters correctly.'

'Allow me... Allow me to show you the correct application to...to implement, then.'

Simon covered her hands with his and guided her how to slowly caress him intimately. He threw his head back and growled, muttering an oath under his breath before he pushed her hands away.

'Enough, enough... My God, enough, woman!'

And before Elowen knew what was happening, he frantically divested her of her clothing, pushing, tugging and actually tearing at her dress, her tunic, her chemise, before she stood bare to him from head to toe. Elowen's mind was a whirl. She had not noticed that he had walked her backwards until her legs had hit the edge of the bed and all the while, Simon's fingers tangled in her hair, his mouth was on hers, kissing her deeply.

She gasped in surprise when he suddenly lifted her in his arms and laid her down in the middle of her bed, untied the bed curtains and crawled in beside her.

'I have dreamed of this moment for such a long time and now it is here,' he murmured as he rose on top of her, his arms bent on either side of her head, taking his weight in his arms.

'And now it is here…' Elowen repeated as she wrapped her arms around him, pulling him closer so that she could feel his skin against hers.

'Yes,' he rasped and pushed her legs apart with his knees, settling himself in the middle before he thrust inside her as she welcomed him, wrapping her legs around him.

Elowen matched him as Simon drove inside her, gathering more and more pace. He bent his head and licked and sucked her breasts until she was moaning and writhing beneath him. Heavens above, but the pleasure that he was eliciting from her body was unlike anything that she had ever experienced before. She leant up and latched her mouth along the column of his neck, sucking on the throbbing pulse beating rapidly.

All thought had dissipated from her head and all that remained was her and him together on this bed and how they had come together as one. She arched her back, taking him deeper inside her body, wanting the sensations that he was igniting in her body to last forever. Simon quickened his pace, his hands all over her, his clever mouth and wicked tongue put to use in every curve and crevice of her body. She felt boneless. She felt consumed. She felt that she wanted to sink inside his skin. And melt into him.

Dear God…

The pleasure was building more and more and more until she felt tremors begin to cascade through her. Until the exquisite pleasure suddenly gave way to a release rippling through her whole body unlike anything she had ever felt before. She screamed out his name again and again before Simon leant down and caught her mouth with his, kissing her with a fierce intensity. His thrusts became ruthless, relentless and wild as he then stopped, tipped his head back, and with a roar pulled out of her body just in time as he, too, found his release.

Simon watched her intently before he pressed his forehead to hers, breathing heavily, as Elowen slowly came round to herself. And in that moment, she wondered after all the true and honest consideration she had duly given regarding the matter, whether she had misjudged, after all. She hoped to God she had not as she could not afford for it to be anything more than what this was. Just one night.

Chapter Ten

Simon nestled Elowen in the crook of his arm and turned to give her a swift peck on the forehead. Their breathing began to gradually come back to its normal cadence, as he held her in his arms. He could not quite believe what had transpired between them and nor could he have imagined as he climbed the stairwell that this, here, with Elowen Bawden in his arms, would be the outcome after coming in search of her this evening. And yet, it was and nothing could have been sweeter…

God, but Simon had oft wondered what it might actually be like to bed Elowen Bawden but nothing, nothing, could have prepared him for how incredible the whole experience would be.

From her shy yet confident manner in which she divested his clothing, to taking hold of him by her hand, uncertain of what to do, to the little noises she made as he filled and stretched her, to the manner in which she came undone in his arms.

'What are you thinking, Simon?' she said softly, her fingers running up and down his chest.

'That while this was wholly unexpected, it was quite simply glorious, Elowen.'

'For me too.' She reached up and cupped his jaw.

'I'm glad to hear it, sweetheart.' He turned his face around to kiss the palm of her hand. 'I feel sated and replete.'

'As do I.'

'So what happens now, Elowen?'

'Now? Well, I had hoped that we might fall asleep.' He felt her smiling.

Simon turned his body so that he was now on his side, resting his head against his hand, his arm bent. 'In time, I would like nothing better, but I was actually referring to us.'

'Us?'

Her brows furrowed in confusion as though she did not quite comprehend what he was referring to. 'You cannot deny that matters between us have now changed after what has just happened.'

'I am fully aware of what just happened, Simon.' She sighed deeply before speaking again. 'But I cannot think why that would then need to change anything between us.'

'Can you not?' He trailed a finger along her jawline.

'No, my lord, I cannot.'

'Are you certain?' he murmured as his finger moved down the column of her neck before sweeping around the curve of her breast, making her shiver.

'No…yes…'

'So is it a yes or a no?'

'How can I answer that when you are touching me like this?'

He continued to let his fingers graze all over her body. 'Ah, so you enjoy these caresses?'

'You know full well that I am enchanted by your touches and caresses.'

'Enchanted, eh?' He ducked his head down and licked her skin, tasting her. 'I am gratified you think so, my lady. Now, what is your answer?'

'I cannot remember what you just asked of me.'

'Can you not?' he drawled as he cupped her breast, his thumb grazing around her nipple again and again.

'This is hardly fair, my lord,' she whispered before a groan escaped her lips.

He smiled. 'I cannot recall saying that I would do anything fairly, Elowen.'

'But even so, you must understand that…that whatever happens between us in bed will have no consequence outside of it.' She gasped.

'Understood.' His other hand ran down the length of her body before settling between her legs. 'For now.'

He curled one finger and then another inside her, and started to explore her intimately, watching her eyes widen in surprise yet welcoming him inside her slick heat. She closed her eyes and arched her back as he put his hands on her.

God, but she seemed to want him again as he wanted her, and so soon after their first time together. He rose over her and slowly, languidly entered her body again, feeling so damn content, as though they belonged to each other.

'I believe you said that you were sated and replete, my lord,' she gasped aloud.

'I believe I thought so too.' He began to move inside her. 'But it seems that when it comes to you, my lady, I can never be sated and once is never enough.'

And it wasn't. Simon made love to Elowen until they both came apart again in each other's arms. Until their bodies sang sweetly as one. Until they fell together in slumber, boneless, finally replete in tangled limbs only to wake up to reach for one another a few more times in the night.

It was dawn before Simon's eyes fluttered open and found that Elowen was awake and watching him intently. He turned his head and pressed a kiss to her naked shoulder. 'Good morrow.'

'Good morrow to you.'

He glanced at her and shook his head. 'Are you making a study of me?'

'And if I am?'

'I would say that you must know my likeness by now,' he muttered, yawning before closing his eyes again.

'I do.' She chuckled softly. 'But it is not merely your likeness that I am putting to memory but everything about you, Simon. From the way you raise just one brow when you're intrigued by something, to that small little scar on the corner of your mouth. Or mayhap the way in which you pull your top lip into your mouth when you are uncertain of a particular matter.'

'It seems you that have made a very detailed study.'

'I have but not just this morn. Indeed, it has been quite a long time, Simon.' He did not know why but the truth in what she'd said made his chest suffuse with a sudden warmth that spread throughout his body.

'Have you, now?' He said this in jest but she must have realised she'd revealed too much as her eyes shuttered and she rolled over to her side.

'Well, I might have.' She raised one shoulder in a

shrug. 'Incidentally, you shuffle around in bed incessantly and even talk in your sleep.'

'What?' He smiled, taken aback. 'I do not believe such falsities. You slander me, my lady.'

'I do nothing of the sort, my lord. It is an observation I have made.'

'An observation, eh? He pulled her back towards him. 'And what of my observations of you, Elowen?'

'I would gladly know it.'

'Well, you sink your teeth into that plump bottom lip of yours when you're nervous,' he said, brushing the pad of his thumb over it. 'And you always tilt your head to the side like so, and frown when you're pondering on something of great import.' He leant down and smoothed away the frown that was beginning to form on there. 'And you make these mewl-like sounds when you take your pleasure from me.'

'I do no such thing!' she said in mock outrage.

'Ah, but you do, and you flush a pretty shade of pink that always starts along the column of your neck and spreads—' he held up the coverlet and looked down the length of her covered body '—everywhere.'

'For shame, my lord.' She chuckled and tried to move away but he pinned her to his side. 'You are nothing but a scoundrel.'

'That I am, Elowen.' He winked at her. 'Never forget it.'

Elowen lifted her head and kissed his lips quickly. 'Yes, but you were my scoundrel last night.'

'Aye, Elowen, I am. And today?'

The smile seemed to freeze on her lips. And with that, Simon seemed to have his answer. After all, this was what Elowen had said about their night together—that it would only be one night. That was all she could promise.

'And the last observation that I have made, Elowen, is that with everything that has come to pass between us, you're pondering whether this really should be just one night of this incredibly fiery intimacy between us.'

Simon had made no such observation, as this was more of what he was trying to discern and unravel than anything else. He would dearly like to know whether it was true for her as it was for him—to have more time together and not restrict the passionate and unbridled pleasure they had found in each another to just one night.

Elowen shook her head slightly. 'You know that can never be.'

'Do I?'

'Yes, or at least you should.'

'May I enquire why?'

'Because surely you can see that for us, one night was all this could ever be.' Elowen pushed herself up so that she was now sitting up, pulling the coverlet up to cover herself. 'Besides which, you must see that if this continues between us then more and more of your people will become aware that their lord is...involved with a Bawden, something which they would never approve of. It was bad enough that you allowed me to stay at Trebarr Castle during these storms.'

Simon scowled. 'Have you encountered unkindness or discourtesy while you have been here?'

'No, but I think their expectation for you to forge an alliance with Anaís might have allayed their uneasiness about having me stay here.'

'There will be no alliance between myself and Anaís. We are both in agreement on that, Elowen.'

'I realise that now but remember that the people of Trebarr do not know this.' She sighed and grazed her fingers along his jawline. 'Quite apart from that, Simon, I think it would be a reckless thing to pursue.'

'I see that no matter how much you were enchanted by my touches and caresses, you would still impose such limitations on…our time together.'

'If you shall not then I must. And our time together was only for one night. It was all I could give. Surely you can understand that?'

Simon pushed up to sit beside her. 'What I understand, Elowen, is that despite admiring our motto of loyalty and freedom, and despite coveting this in order to have the freedom to choose the life you seek, you shackle yourself to whatever you believe is expected of you as a Bawden, so that in some way you can gain your father's approval by giving him what he wants.'

'And how exactly can you know this?'

'Because this is yet another marked observation that I have made of you over the many years I have known you.' He noticed that she had stiffened as he took a shaky breath. 'And because this is something I did myself so that I could finally win my own father's approval and respect.'

'And did you earn it?'

'No, I never did, no matter how hard I tried to please him.'

Simon had never told this to another soul and did not know why he was doing so now. And yet, after their closeness, after what they had just shared last night, he found that he wanted to share this part of himself with Elowen too. Something that he had always held close to himself.

'I cannot believe that he would treat you in such a manner, Simon.'

'Yet, nevertheless he did.'

'Are you telling me that your father, Lord Trebarr, never acknowledged all your incredible achievements, especially those that you accomplished on the battle-fields in France, in Crecy by the side of the Prince?'

'Oh, my father would certainly take any favours, honours and stipends of land and any valuable mines given in lieu of any acknowledgments, but he seemed to see that more of an extension of himself, an extension of the Trebarr name was his due, than anything I was doing. In truth, it was what he'd expected of me, so no, he never once welcomed me back from those gruelling campaigns with open arms and a slap on the back, praising my achievements, not that I wanted his acclaim but some sort of acknowledgement would have been welcomed, Elowen.'

'I am sorry for it, Simon,' she murmured, brushing her hand up and down his chest. 'I cannot imagine why your father was unable to see your worth. To know what he had in you.'

'Thank you.' He lifted her fingers and pressed his lips to them. 'But I do know the reason for my father's antipathy and why he could never bring himself to ac-knowledge and praise anything I had ever done.'

Elowen frowned. 'Why? Why would he show antipa-thy towards his younger son? It makes no sense at all.'

'Because I took away from him the one thing that

he cherished and loved the most in the whole kingdom, Elowen, even more than the Trebarr name—my mother.' He took a breath before continuing. 'You see, she had a difficult time birthing me and died only a few days afterwards, changing my father's relationship with me forever. From that moment onwards he held a deep-seated anger and bitterness towards me that remained unchanged until the day he died.

'I am so sorry.'

'As am I,' he sighed. 'She meant everything to him and after my mother's death, he could never look at me without resenting me for being the one who survived.'

Elowen lifted her head and nodded. Her eyes filled with sadness and regret. 'I do know what that rejection might feel like, Simon. My father, too, has resented me all these years for being the one who survived while it was my brother, Hedyn, who had fallen down those cliffs to his death. He, too, could never look at me again without scorn or displeasure at everything that I did and still do. Indeed, he always finds fault in me. I can never seemingly do anything that might please him.'

'Is that why you have agreed to enter into a marriage with Roger Prevnar, without ever meeting him beforehand?'

'Yes, in part.'

'And the other?'

Elowen fell silent for a moment as though she were considering whether she wanted to disclose this to him or not. 'Because I would gain the home and security that I seek and would be chatelaine of Stromley Castle. I would also become a mother to his young daughters, Simon, something that I have oft longed for. And with this marriage, to a man of my father's choosing, I would also settle what I owe him. I would settle it for good.'

'I see.' But no, he did not, not completely. 'I comprehend why you would want to be mistress of your own domain and be mother to the man's children, as you do love to look after everyone and everything, sweetheart. But what, may I ask, is it that you believe you owe your father?'

Simon thought for a moment that mayhap Elowen might not respond. But eventually she broke the silence. 'Reparation.'

He watched her carefully for a moment. 'Reparation? I'm afraid that I do not comprehend you.'

'I can well believe that. But in truth, I need to make amends for my brother's death.'

'Even though it was not your fault?'

'But it was.'

'How can that be when Hedyn's death was nothing but a tragic accident, Elowen? Your father knows this now as he did back then. But it is easier for him to blame you or even me, than to accept that. In truth, if there was anyone who was more responsible for Hedyn's death, then it would have to be me.'

'No, Simon, that will not do. You were never responsible. You were only protecting yourself after Hedyn challenged you.'

'Yet, there was a time that you believed differently.'

'There was and I was sorry for it, as you were never to blame. I, unlike my father, eventually realised the truth of that day.' Elowen took a deep breath before continuing. 'But my father had the right of it in blaming me for Hedyn's death, even though he never knew the real reason.'

'How can that be so?' Simon frowned, shaking his head. 'After all, we were both there that day. We both know what happened and that it was an accident.'

Elowen sighed and moved to the edge of the bed, with her back to him. 'Yes, but it's not just about that day, Simon. It is what led to Hedyn challenging you in the first place that is the heart of the matter. And for that, I am wholly the one who's responsible.'

Chapter Eleven

Elowen was uncertain why she had blurted out such deeply held secrets that had always been kept so close to herself. And yet, she had. Mayhap it was being in this bed, with this man, that had lulled her into confessing to so many things that she should not have. Yet, with this realisation came a feeling of uneasiness, making her want to put a little distance between Simon and herself. Indeed, she needed to get away. Elowen pulled back the bed curtain and rose, just as Simon's hand shot out and stilled her from behind.

'Where are you going, my lady?'

'To get washed and attired.'

'Now? After what you have just disclosed?'

She looked over her shoulder at him. 'Mayhap I should not have said anything.'

'Hell's teeth, Elowen, it's too late for that now,' he said from behind before shuffling to the edge of the bed to sit beside her, and taking her hand in his. 'Tell me what this is about. What do you mean that you were responsible for your brother's death?'

'I say it because it is true, Simon. I was responsible for his untimely death.'

'But how, for heaven's sake? How can you possibly think that when I was also there? And what precisely do you mean that it was not just about that terrible day?'

Elowen did not know how she had got into revealing so much about the past, nor did she know how to put an end to this uncomfortable discourse. Still, she had already said more than she had intended and revealed far more than she should, so disclosing more now could hardly come as a shock.

'Because on that day Hedyn finally must have realised and understood the depth of my attraction…to you, Simon, which had always been something that I had kept hidden and locked away inside, as I knew it to be so very forbidden to have such feelings for a Trebarr.' She looked across at him as he squeezed her hand, urging her to go on. 'The truth was that my brother Hedyn and I could always read one another, mayhap more than other siblings might since we were twins. And you must remember that he was the only friend I ever had, when I was a young maid. But at the time he rightly guessed, on the very day that I became betrothed to my first husband, that I had…well, that I admired another. I really do not know what had given me away. Possibly the delightful pink flush that you referred to earlier, which does indeed spread from my neck, but in any case, Hedyn realised that day that there had been truth in what he'd said in jest. From then on, he would pester me every day and every night into revealing the identity of the one I secretly admired, yet I kept my lips sealed. Then on that fateful day, when he encountered me in your arms after you'd saved me from falling down the cliff, he saw…well, he saw you, Simon, with me.

More than just finding me alone and in your arms, he must have seen something that made him believe that it was you whom I had always liked and admired. And so that was the reason why Hedyn reacted in the way he had. That was the reason why he then challenged you to a fight, Simon.'

'I see.'

'Now do you comprehend the reason why I was responsible for my brother's death? Because, in truth, I am.'

Simon shook his head. 'I do comprehend your reasoning, Elowen. However, I do not take the same stance as you. Let us suppose for one moment that everything you have so eloquently explained is true. Don't you see that even with your brother believing he knew what you felt for me—and by the by, I am honoured beyond measure that I was the forbidden knight you secretly admired for all these years—there could still be no way of knowing that he would have had the erratic reaction that he did. Don't you see that Hedyn's subsequent impulsive reaction would have resulted with the same tragic consequence, whichever way you look at it? And what then happened was actually nothing more than a terrible accident, which was wholly out of your control. You must believe that, sweetheart.'

Elowen wanted, she desperately wanted, to believe that her brother's death was as he described—a tragic accident—but could not see how that was so. 'Alas, I still know that if he had not stumbled upon us that day, and if he had not found out my secret then he would not have challenged you and would be alive today.'

'You have no way of knowing that, I am afraid.' He lifted her hand to his lips and kissed the back of it.

'But as someone who has seen the futile loss of life that occurs on battlefields when one small mistake can be fatal, I know firsthand that there is no sense to be made of these things, despite how much we try. It sometimes comes down to bad luck. And I believe in Hedyn Bawden's case that was precisely what it was.'

She dropped her head and shook it slowly. 'I do not know that.'

'Yet I do, Elowen. Believe me, I do.' He sighed deeply before continuing. 'I understand the need to make sense of what happened that day but this will not do—taking responsibility for your brother's death when it was nothing but an accident. You cannot interpret what happened and twist it to be a narrative that conveniently suits your father's aims of having you under his thumb. And then for you to add credence to that and believe it as the truth, Elowen. Because all you are doing is punishing yourself for something that you had no control over. And what would be the purpose of that? What would that achieve apart from misery and hardship with this continued burden of guilt? I, for one, cannot imagine that your brother would have wanted that for you, sweetheart.'

Elowen had not realised that her eyes had filled with tears. She looked up as a single drop fell on her cheek. And before she could brush it away, Simon caught it between his thumb and finger. She coughed, trying to dislodge the lump that had caught there. 'I'm sorry, I do not know what has come over me. In truth, I have a little something in my eye, that is all.'

'Of course, how can it be anything else?' he muttered as he put his arm around her, sliding her close to his side.

'Thank you for all that you have said. It means a great

deal that you would try to make me feel better about what happened back then.'

'My pleasure. However, what I said is also from what experience has taught me, Elowen. I have lost far too many good men, whose lives were lost needlessly and without warning; their demise never easily be explained. And neither can the burden of responsibility of such tragedies be placed on one person solely because they happened to have been present at the time.' He dropped a kiss to the top of her head as she nestled into his arms, feeling safe, feeling protected and at peace for the first time in such a long time. 'I cannot believe that for all this time, you have believed such a thing regarding your brother's death, aided by your father, who was wrapped in his own grief for losing his son. It is a cruel situation, Elowen.'

She pulled away and caught his gaze. 'Just as in the situation with your own father, Simon.'

'Yes, there was little I could do about a man who believed his infant son to be responsible for the death of his wife. Who then treated him with such scorn. There is no logic or reason in that.' He exhaled deeply and shrugged. 'But it took a long time for me to realise all of this, Elowen. Indeed, it took until after my father's death to release myself from the shackles of blame and contempt that I had willingly bound myself to. Once I realised that no matter what I did, my father would always despise my very existence, which came as I said after the old man had died, I broke the endless need for repentance and self-flagellation. It had been enough.'

Elowen could not bear that Simon had thought of himself so lowly and had done for so long. It amazed her that a man could treat his own son in such a deplorable manner. 'I am so sorry, Simon.'

'It is all in the past now. And I will not allow it to affect my future. For one thing, if I was so fortunate as to sire children, I would never blame them for a situation that was out of their control. No, I will never be like my late father. Not in any way. Not in the way he wed, not in the way he loved and not in the way he fathered his children.'

Up until this moment, Elowen had never realised how alike their respective fathers had been by treating them so poorly. And for the first time in a long time, something lifted from Elowen's shoulders, something that had inexplicably weighed down on her for so long. And all because of this incredible man who was sat beside her, who had welcomed her into his castle in her hour of need and had given her refuge and safety. And today, despite all that had happened before, he had taken the time to explain that she needed to let go of the past. To let go of all the twisted, pernicious beliefs that she had been harbouring for so long. She cupped his jaw as he turned his face to kiss the centre of her palm.

'Simon?' she murmured softly.

'Yes?'

'Take me back to bed.'

He blinked in surprise before a slow, wicked smile spread along his lips. 'With pleasure, my lady.'

Simon gently pushed her back onto the bed and smiled at her, his fingers grazing her face. 'So beautiful, Elowen.'

'As are you.'

'I thank you,' he murmured. 'And look, look…there

is that infamous pink flush that I know well, coming forth.'

She giggled as they both took a long time to explore each other, with fingers, mouths and tongues, slowly, languidly and with a reverence that had not been there before. And when she came apart, shattered in his arms again, she felt as though nothing would ever be the same.

Elowen was beginning to realise that quite apart from her attraction to Simon, which she had always acknowledged even secretly to herself, now other emotions were beginning to stir, ones she had never thought she could possibly possess. Indeed, her heart, which had always remained impassive and disaffected, was becoming more and more engaged. It made her ache; it made her restless. And it made her feel vulnerable and raw. Was this normal?

No, I will never be like my late father. Not in any way. Not in the way he wed, not in the way he loved and not in the way he fathered his children.

Simon had said those words earlier and it was only now in the glow of the aftermath of their intimacies that the full shock of their meaning resonated with Elowen. Good Lord, but Simon meant that he would never want to love his wife with the same intensity that his father did because it broke him when he lost her after she had birthed her child. And the startling realisation of that made Elowen feel sad for Simon and somewhat unsettled by it. Not that she harboured any thoughts of capturing Simon Trebarr's heart for herself. Still, she did not know why her stomach had knotted into such a tight coil. After all, despite what Simon had made her start to think regarding Hedyn's death, she was still promised to another. She would still wed another.

Simon could not comprehend why both of them had revealed much about their pasts and in his case, disclosed the truth about his father's antipathy towards him. It made him feel uncomfortable and uneasy confessing all the sordid information of why his father held little interest in his achievements and how the old bastard had continued to blame Simon for the death of his mother, even as he lay on his death bed and refused to absolve Simon and make peace with him before his rites were read out.

Reparation...

That was what Elowen had said was the reason she had agreed to wed Roger Prevnar, a man of her father's choosing, believing in doing so, she would finally absolve herself from the blame she held for the death of her brother. Which was ridiculous, of course. It was for this very reason that Simon then made the decision to share his own sorry tale regarding his father. To make Elowen comprehend how futile it was to continually condemn herself because it was not true, and it would change nothing in her father's regard and acceptance of her. And he should know, as he experienced quite a similar censure from his own sire. In this, they shared the same disdainful judgement from their fathers. And Simon wanted to spare Elowen the continued pain and hurt that it would cause, should she want to carry forth with such a belief.

He held Elowen tightly and kissed the top of her head. 'We should get up, my lady.'

'Yes,' she murmured without making a single move to get out of the bed.

'We should at least attempt to rise.'

'Yes,' she said again sleepily. 'But why must the day intrude on the little time we have left together?'

'Ah, so we're back to that, are we?' he said as he wrapped a few strands of her hair around his fingers. 'We are back to negotiating the few meagre hours that I endeavour to spend with you.'

Simon did not say it but inferred that their time together would be until they had to part. Which of course they would, eventually. After all, nothing in life lasted forever.

'I believe we agreed that it would be unseemly, especially if your servants and your people were to discover our involvement.'

'Naturally, I forgot that our involvement would be so frowned upon,' he said sardonically. 'After all, the Bawdens and the Trebarrs can never be involved, now, can they?'

'No, my lord.'

Simon chuckled, shaking his head. 'It really must be time for us to rise from this pleasure bed if you are back to *lording* me.'

He gave her a wink before pushing off the bed and allowing the bed curtain to fall back.

He could just make out through the soft, sheer bed curtain that Elowen had sat up, covering her nakedness with the coverlet. 'Where are you going, Simon?'

He pulled up his hose and tied the laces loosely around his hips before pulling his tunic over his head. 'Back to my own chamber to wash and change my attire. There is much I need to attend to this morrow and if I am not mistaken, from what I can hear or the lack thereof, it seems that the storm might finally have broken. But I shall need to confirm that and see what devastation has been left in its wake.'

'Of course.'

Simon picked up the remainder of his clothing and strode towards the woman who had sent his mind into a whirl. He lifted up the bed curtain and leant in to kiss Elowen full on the lips. 'Until later, my lady.'

She did not say anything but touched her lips and nodded. Taking a step back, he then inclined his head before turning on his heel and leaving the chamber and closing the door behind him.

Simon dragged a deep, long breath into his chest and dragged his fingers through his hair as he pondered on everything that had been said and done with Elowen Bawden since the previous night.

Hell's teeth, but what a night of pleasure and revelations it had been. It had been extraordinary; it had been exhilarating. And it had been heartbreaking in a very unexpected way. Simon had felt an ache he never knew existed somewhere in the depth of his soul when Elowen admitted that she had secretly admired him from the first moment she had seen him. God, but that had been like a punch in the gut. And then for her to carry that secret with her for so long as well as the belief that it was that unwanted and forbidden attraction that led to her brother's death was inexplicable. That had certainly taken him aback, and while he had been shocked with all that she had disclosed, he wasn't surprised that her father had used her not only to take the blame for Hedyn's death, but also to force her to do his bidding, whenever he so much as clicked his fingers.

Reparation...

God, but what an ugly sentiment that was, and in Elowen's case, totally unnecessary as she did not owe her father anything. Simon certainly did not believe so, even if the lady did herself. And in the midst of all of that was his own sorry confession regarding his father, which Simon had not meant to reveal. But in doing so, he had uttered out loud what he'd always known about himself—that he would never be like his own father. And he would never allow love, the kind that destroyed his father's relationship with Simon, to ever enter his life, despite what he'd said in jest to Elowen regarding romantic endeavours. No, he would never be fool enough to love anyone and certainly not in the all-encompassing manner in which his father had.

That would be foolish indeed.

Chapter Twelve

Simon had been right; the storms had finally broken. It brought with it a tangible relief after the endless days and nights of uncertainties and difficulties that the terrible weather had inflicted upon them. And in the days that followed, Simon, along with many of his men, patrolled the Trebarr land, inspecting the damage reaped by the storm on buildings, dwellings, the Cornish countryside and its environs.

During that time Elowen, with Anaís by her side, helped in every way she could to supervise, direct and organise people to clear the debris and give aid in all the areas that had flooded. It was a huge undertaking but with many hands to the task, it was accomplished in a matter of days. And in those days, Elowen had seen Simon all but fleetingly; however, at night he'd come to her, after sitting with Anaís in the bower before scurrying to Elowen's chamber, where they would lose themselves in each other's bodies again and again.

That one incredible night of promised pleasure had turned to many, but it could not last. And they both knew it. Indeed, the time for Elowen to continue with her travail to her betrothed in Devonshire had come.

Even though she would now do it reluctantly and with a heavy heart. Since, in truth, she knew that it would be difficult to say goodbye…to Anaís who had become a good friend to her. And then there was Simon. Elowen could not contemplate parting from him but knew that she had to. It would be better to go sooner so that she could spare her heart the grief staying longer would bring.

Since that first night, when they had confessed their feelings and so much more as they lay in each other's arms, Elowen had pondered on everything Simon had said to her, especially his view on Hedyn's demise. She still did not know if she could ever share his stance on it, and she was uncertain whether her beliefs regarding her brother's death would ever change, but at least Simon had offered her a different perspective. A different way to view that fateful day from the past and not through the prism of guilt and remorse.

Yet, despite everything that Simon had said, Elowen knew in her heart that her decision to be bound to her betrothed, Roger Prevnar, would have to remain unchanged. Indeed, it would still go ahead. After all, this is what had been arranged with the betrothal documents signed and verified. But that was not the only reason that Elowen would honour it. She would do it for her kin, for House Bawden, and she would do it because she was needed by Lord Prevnar's maiden daughters.

Elowen had mentioned to Simon one night in bed, that the time had come for her to continue with her journey, and he had looked stunned but had remained silent, his demeanour suddenly shuttered. Indeed, he might seemingly have been despondent but as he later explained, it was because most of the roads and paths were now flooded so badly that it was impossible for Elowen to take a normal route to Devonshire. Her choices were to wait a little longer until the roads were safe enough to pass through, or to travail to the coast, where she could board a vessel, a Trebarr vessel, and sail on the sea along the Cornish coastline until she reached Devonshire, and from there resume her journey to Roger Prevnar's castle.

With those two choices before her, Elowen had not known whether to choose with her heart and stay a while longer and continue with her furtive liaisons with Simon, or with her head and carry forth to her betrothed. After all, she was already waylaid because of the storms, and she could not afford to stay in Trebarr Castle much longer, even though she would have liked it above all else. It was not prudent to do so, especially since it was not certain how much longer she would then have to wait until the roads were safe.

With her mind made up, she had given Simon her preference and noted the look of disappointment in his eyes before it had been masked over. He had nodded and told her that he was happy to oblige and would escort her himself along with his best friend, Sir Ranulf Gibbons, and half a dozen of his men to one of the many Trebarr vessels moored at the nearby dock.

A new convoy had been set to depart from Trebarr, and this time without any of her father's decrepit old men, who'd originally accompanied her, as Simon had the foresight to send them back at the earliest convenience.

When the hour finally approached for them to leave

Trebarr, Elowen realised with an ache in her chest how much she was loath to leave the castle and its people, who had started to respond to her with a little more respect than when she had first arrived, and seemed to have appreciated her efforts in Trebarr. Strange as it might have seemed, Trebarr had become a home to her in such a short space of time but in part because of the people who inhabited it, namely Trebarr's lord.

On the crisp, bright morn that she departed Trebarr, Elowen clung on to Anaís as she bid her goodbye, hoping that they would be reunited one day again in the future. Not that Elowen knew when that might be or what would become of the maid since both she and Simon had vehemently decided against marriage between them. Mayhap Anaís might get her wish and return back to Brittany, although Elowen wondered about the reception her family might give her as a young widow, but hoped that it was better than the one Elowen received when she had gone home after her first husband had died. Indeed, she hoped Anaís would be welcomed back with kindness.

It was just after dawn when Elowen had left Trebarr, riding alongside Simon, his men and the rest of the convoy. Their party rode on much slower than they would have liked, but the wagon behind them carrying Elowen's trunks and other possessions dragged them back, as did the conditions, which were still treacherous, despite the blue skies that had greeted them that morning. And quite apart from the monotony of a slow journey was the fact that the man beside her had barely said a word to her since the night when she had told him that she had to leave and hasten her progress to reach her betrothed.

'Do you believe that we might reach the coastline by dusk?' she asked, peering at him as he rode his magnificent destrier beside her.

'I should think that if the conditions would allow it, we should arrive a little sooner than that.'

'Ah, so mayhap before vespers?'

He turned his head and raised a sardonic eyebrow. 'Are you that much in a hurry to get to your betrothed, my lady?'

'I did not say that, *my lord*.'

She could not comprehend why Simon was now being so very rigid, so very caustic, so very formal. Initially, she had wondered whether the reason why she had barely seen or spoken with Simon was because there had been much to do to ready this convoy so expediently, but now Elowen was not so certain. Mayhap this formality as well as the silence that greeted her after she had disclosed her plans to him was more of an expression of how frustrated and despondent he had been with her decision. Indeed, she had wondered if the crestfallen and disappointed look she had detected in his eyes after she told him that her destiny still lay in marriage to Lord Roger Prevnar had been real or not. Elowen did not know whether what she had seen was true or a figment of her imagination. Not that she would change her plans now.

She could not believe in a marriage founded on love as she had once done; that notion had been drummed out of her by her first husband, who'd left a lasting legacy with his unkindness and neglect, making her know how ridiculous she had been for believing in such a thing. And Simon himself had inadvertently declared that he would not wed for that sentiment either, wanting never to be like his father. So there was nothing left to say on the matter, even though there was. There was still so much to say before they parted.

In truth, she did not know how she was going to give him up, even though she knew she would have to. She had to bid him farewell once they reached Roger Prevnar's castle, not that Elowen knew how she was supposed to do that. The intensity of the feelings she had for Simon Trebarr had never abated, even though she believed they might after their intimacies. If anything, the pleasures that they had shared as well as all the many things they had discussed late into the evening strengthened the depth of feeling and regard that she had for Simon. But it mattered not. There could never be a future between them and this wonderful interlude that they'd shared would one day be just a passing memory. One that Elowen would never forget, not until she breathed her very last breath.

'Either way, my lady, we shall be at your desired destination before long,' Simon muttered in a low, strained voice, keeping his eyes ahead. God, but he seemed so distant now as though with each step closer to the vessel that would take her away from these shores, he was becoming more and more remote. The gulf between them becoming even more insurmountable.

'Well, I am glad to hear it, my lord.' She smiled, a smile that felt so brittle on her lips. 'I would not wish to importune you any further.'

He snapped his head around and shook his head slowly. 'Is that what you truly believe?'

'What I meant was...'

'That I have been *importuned* by you?'

Elowen expelled a breath. 'I only meant that I have been an imposition from the moment you came to my rescue and brought me to Trebarr Castle.'

'How can you even believe such a thing? How can you believe that you were…that you were somehow an imposition?'

Elowen's gaze flicked to his clenched fists gripped tightly around the reins to the shuttered look in his eyes, his spine straight and rigid, and realised that she had angered him. 'I'm sorry, Simon, I meant no insult.'

'I'm sure you never meant for it, my lady, despite it still remaining one.' He kept his gaze in front, not even looking in her direction. 'You believe that I have somehow been importuned by you? That you were an imposition? Dear me, Elowen, whatever happened to being *honest* and *true*?'

Indeed, it seemed that she had angered him a great deal. But even so, Elowen could not be either honest or true, not in regard to Simon Bawden. Not in regard to the way she felt about him. God, but this would not do. She was a woman who would soon marry another.

'You are right. I attempted to express my heartfelt gratitude to you, Simon, and instead used words that were taken in the wrong way. I apologise.'

They continued to canter along the lush, green, undulating landscape, with the convoy following up behind them for a long moment before Simon responded. He turned his head to face her. 'I have no need of your apology, Elowen. And I especially have no need of your damn gratitude.'

'Then what?' She frowned, pulling her palfrey away from his horse a little. 'What is it that you want from me?'

* * *

Simon let out a slow breath through his teeth, trying to hold on to the last vestiges of his composure. God, but the past few days had been a trial. Ever since the storms had broken and the weather had improved, Simon had known that their time together would be limited to a scant few nights that they had left together. He'd always known this, that their time together would be brief, would be fleeting. They had only ever promised one night to each other and then that had turned to another and then another until there had been no more left. But he still wanted more, so much more of Elowen Bawden.

He had always known that despite all their conversations, her course was still set for Devonshire, and set for her new marriage to a man she had not even met, not that Simon actually tried to dissuade her. He never said anything that might entice her to stay. And yet, now that the time had come for her to leave his life for good, he wanted to bundle her back to Trebarr Castle and keep her there forever. Lord knew she deserved better than Roger Prevnar. Indeed, she deserved a far better man, far better than Simon as well. And yet, the thought of another kissing her, touching her, taking her to bed, made him want to punch his fist through something sharp and painful. He also knew that he had absolutely no claims on the woman. Elowen belonged with another; she always had. And besides, he had nothing to offer her, least of all a marriage. After all, he would never want a marriage that in any way resembled the one his father and mother had had. God's breath, but theirs had driven his father to despair after he had lost the woman he loved and fostered an enmity with Simon from the moment he had been born. No, it was not a future that Simon envisaged or wanted for himself. The only reason he would wed would be for an alliance that would serve Trebarr interests. And he would marry a maid who would never have his heart. He realised then, with a sudden bolt of clarity, that that would be the very reason why he could never wed Elowen Bawden as the depth of feeling he held for her would make Elowen an unsuitable wife. Not that she would ever agree to him anyway.

Anaís Le Brunde Trebarr would have been a perfect choice in that regard but neither the lady nor Simon had wanted to take any steps towards marriage. Indeed, Anaís had advised Simon to follow his heart. Not that he believed in something as asinine as that.

What is it that you want from me? Elowen had asked him only moments ago.

Dear God, but the question had nearly knocked him off his seat.

You, he had wanted to say, but kept his mouth firmly shut.

No, that would never do. Elowen Bawden would never be the woman whom he could keep, even if he had wanted, which he never could.

'Nothing, my lady,' he muttered as he nudged his destrier forward. 'There is nothing that I want.'

From you...

He could not say the last two words that he should have, since they were caught at the back of his throat.

'I want to say something, as I may not have the opportunity again, Simon. I want you to know that...'

'Come now, Elowen, surely there can be nothing left to say between us, can there?' He exhaled through his teeth. 'Surely we have now exhausted every topic of discourse.'

'If you say so.' Elowen seemed to bristle atop her horse, looking perfectly regal, perfectly majestic, in her finery. By God, she was beautiful. Elowen wore a long navy cloak, and her silvery pale flaxen hair that he'd had the pleasure of burying his face in was plaited and knotted at the back of her head, with a thin cream-coloured veil pinned to keep it in place. His heart lurched just looking at her.

'I do, sweetheart,' he said, closing his eyes momentarily. 'I feel that it is futile to say anything more to one another when you shall shortly sail away from me.'

And wed another...

'I comprehend your sentiment, Simon. I shall miss you too.'

He turned his head sharply 'Is that what I said?'

'I believe that it was inferred.'

He raised a brow. 'How well you must know me now, Elowen.'

Simon knew that he was being petty and did not know why he was responding to Elowen in the manner he was, but only that the closer they were getting towards the coast, the more and more frustrated he was getting with the situation they were in.

'That is not what I said.'

He let out an irritated breath, knowing that his frustration was directed more at himself than Elowen. 'Apologies, my lady, I am being surly and prickly, something which I had no intention of being.'

Elowen pulled the reins of her horse, forcing him to

do the same as she sidled up alongside him. 'I shall miss you, Simon. I shall miss you greatly.'

He swallowed uncomfortably. 'As I will miss you, Elowen.'

'And I wish you to know that the time that I have shared with you at Trebarr Castle has been the happiest I have ever known.'

'Then stay,' he whispered, hating that he was pleading with her.

'Please do not ask me, since you know that I cannot.'

'Why not?' Simon took the reins from her horse, forcing her to stay as he addressed her. 'Or are you that adamant that you should become Lady Prevnar?'

'As opposed to what, becoming Lady Trebarr?' Elowen was studying him carefully. But whatever she seemed to glean was evidently taken as some sort of confirmation as she then said, 'No, I did not think so, Simon. Not that I would have agreed even if you had asked me. So, now we both have what we want.'

'Is that what you think?' He clenched his jaw in total and utter irritation. 'That I have what I want? Because I can tell you, Elowen, that cannot be further from the truth.'

'Then mayhap it is just as it should be,' she said softly, with solemn resignation. 'Mayhap you and I are destined never to have what we want. And we shall somehow have to be content with that.' She nudged her horse forward, leaving him behind with her words to untangle.

Simon pushed his horse forward to catch up with her. 'And what if that is not enough?'

'It will have to be, Simon.'

'Why must that be?'

'Because we have no other choice.' Elowen sighed deeply and her face was etched in despair and regret. 'I am sorry.'

'As I am, too, my lady.' He gave her a curt nod. 'It seems there is little left to say.'

'Yes, it seems so.'

He took a deep breath before saying more. 'Then let us continue on, Elowen.'

They rode on through marshy terrain and flooded land, avoiding areas that had been particularly affected by the rise of the floodwater. Their journey, however, as they rode in silence beside one another, was stifling, uncomfortable and damn awkward. Simon wished now that he could have avoided escorting the woman in person, as this journey was becoming more and more unbearable. But bear it, he would. And in any case, he could hardly stand by as Elowen readied herself for this journey and offer no assistance while she travailed through hazardous conditions as her father had done. And as always, when Simon thought of Breock Bawden, he became infuriated with the total lack of care and protection he'd given his eldest daughter, as she made her way through the country. It was unforgivable to allow Elowen to travail in that sorry state, when he'd found her as the storms first started to rage. But then Breock Bawden was a man who thought of nothing other than his own comforts, and all his relationships centred around what he might gain.

They made their way through a small, dense coppice of woodland, with a thicket of bushels and tall trees, their long branches acting as canopies overhead. They meandered through in single file along the uneven muddy pathway until they could see through to a clearing opening out to the edge of the coastline. It was as they were coming through to the other side of the woodland that Simon suddenly felt uneasy as the hairs on the backs of his arms rose. No, something was wrong, he could feel it in his bones, not that he could put his finger on it. And this was something that had always fared him well when he had gone on long campaigns—his intuition. Yet, as he looked about the area, he detected nothing that was out of the ordinary. Nothing that he could detect and yet still, his senses were alert, heightened as their convoy exited the woodland. It was then that he saw what he'd feared, even though he had hoped that in this case he might have been wrong. But he was not.

There in the distance beyond the gently sloping cragged landscape, was the mighty sea, peaceful and calm. But there was also something else, something that was not as peaceful nor as calm but waiting, seemingly for their convoy and on Trebarr land. It was a large company of men on horseback waiting menacingly, wearing chain mail shirts over their leather gambeson, as though they were about to go into battle.

Simon pulled his rein and raised his arm, making the rest of the convoy also come to a stop in their progress.

'Who are those men, Gib?' Simon turned back and cried to his second in command, Sir Ranulf Gibbons, who rode up from the rear to Simon's side.

'I do not know, my lord, but I can ride out with a few men to ask what their purpose is and to demand they leave Trebarr immediately.'

'Very well, Gib.'

'That may not be necessary,' Elowen muttered from Simon's side, making both men turn and look at her, waiting for her to explain. 'Judging from the standard bearer, I would say those men are from Bawden and the man in the middle of the group is my father.'

Simon continued to stare at Elowen for a moment longer before he blinked. 'And what pray is your father doing here, Lady Elowen?'

'I know as little as you do, my lord.'

'Then in that case I suggest we find out.'

Their convoy continued towards Breock Bawden and his men, moving with more pace. The tension grew more and more the closer they got to the damn Bawden men, who had seen fit to trespass on Simon's land. It would not do.

As their convoy reached within thirty yards of the Bawden men, Simon raised his hand again, bringing their convoy to a halt. 'Good morrow, Lord Bawden, it seems you have lost your way, seeing that you and your men have found yourselves on my land.'

'And a good morrow to you, my young lord. I am just as lost as my daughter, who has somehow, it seems, found herself to you. By misadventure, I daresay.'

Simon was not amused by the man's implication. 'If by misadventure you are alluding to the storms that have been raging and battering Cornwall of late, which I am certain that you cannot have missed, then yes, Lady Elowen was caught in the middle of it before I came to her rescue.'

'How very gallant of you.'

'I like to think so,' Simon growled. 'It is a shame that you did not think of such things, my lord, and sent her with a handful of useless retainers who stood back while your daughter waded through murky water so that she could shift the wheel of her rickety old wagon.'

'Such impertinence!' Breock Bawden barked. 'How dare you?'

'I speak only of the truth.'

What are you doing here, my lord?' Elowen asked her father.

He snapped his head to glare at his eldest daughter. 'What does it look like, Elowen? I am here to demand that Trebarr releases you.'

'Releases me? What in heavens are you referring to, my lord?' she said. 'Simon is escorting me to the coast where I can then continue my travail to Devonshire and Lord Prevnar by sea.'

'*Simon* is it, daughter?' The man sneered at Elowen, sitting atop his grey destrier. 'I see that I had the right of it. Trebarr has made you his whore and before you say you are going to your betrothed. You bring dishonour to me.'

'What is it that you want, my lord?' Elowen said, no longer cowering to her father as she once did. Instead, her spine was straight, her head held high and she glared at her sire directly.

'I believe I have said so.'

'I think not. I think you have only thrown insults at me and at Lord Trebarr, who came to my aid during the storms.'

'And to think a daughter of mine, a Bawden lady, has stayed under the same roof as a Trebarr and for as many nights as you have,' Breock Bawden bellowed, trying it seemed to get his men on his side.

Simon could not comprehend the reason for this nor

for why the man was here in the first place. Their whole stance seemed to be an outright attempt to intimidate or threaten, neither of which he would allow to pass.

'I want you to turn back around and leave my lands, Lord Bawden, and I want you to do that now.'

Breock Bawden's nostrils flared. 'You believe you can order me...*boy*?'

A muscle leapt into the corner of Simon's eye as he remembered the same derogatory manner in which his own father had used that word...

Damn you, boy! Come here when I say so! And to think I endured the loss of my beloved wife for a creature as worthless as you... Devil take you, boy!

'I hate to inform you, Bawden, but it's been many a year since I was a mere boy. But if you wish to put that to the test, we can do so.'

'No, stop this madness. Why are you here, Father?'

Elowen's pleading voice made Simon halt for a moment and consider what he had said to the older man, her father. And what had happened the last time he faced another Bawden man, who was at the time far more a boy, in truth. Simon could not do it. He would not rise to this man's baiting. He would not fight another Bawden.

'You ask me what I am doing, daughter?' The man sneered, actually sneered, at his own daughter. 'I wanted to see firsthand how my own daughter is conspiring with Simon Trebarr and has been for so many years, since the death of my heir, Hedyn.'

'I did nothing of the sort and have only ever been a dutiful and devoted daughter to you.'

'Is that what you believe, daughter? And yet I find

you here on Trebarr land, with the lord of Trebarr himself.'

'And you know well the reason, Lord Bawden,' Simon interjected, sensing how upset Elowen was becoming. 'For it has been explained.'

'Damn you, Trebarr! 'The older man slammed his fist on his saddle. 'First you take away my son, and do not pretend what happened to him was an accident or that you had not managed to get my daughter to collude with your lies, as I know that Hedyn died by your own hands, Trebarr. And now you make my daughter your whore. I will not stand for this insult. No more, I tell you!'

God, but Simon had had enough of the man. He would not allow for him to continually disparage Elowen's good name. The intimacies they shared were between them alone, and her father had no right to call her such vile names.

'Enough!' Simon roared. 'It is I who will not stand for this. I shall not stand for your slanderous insults any longer, do you hear? Hedyn Bawden was a reckless and impulsive young man, much like his father, and he challenged me in much the same way as you have, regarding Elowen. But know that I have only ever treated your daughter with respect and care, and done nothing that would justify this threatening manner and on my own land!'

'Please…' Elowen implored in a whisper. 'Please take pity on my father and please do not listen to anything he has to say. He is all but a bitter old man.'

'This I know, but he insults both you and I greatly.'

'He does, yes, but please for my sake do not rise to him—do not allow him to trap you into showing your ire.'

'Very well, but only for your sake.'

'Thank you,' she muttered under her breath before turning her attention back to Breock Bawden. 'I shall ask once more, Father, why you should venture all this way out to Trebarr. I cannot fathom why you would come out in this fashion to halt my progress to my betrothed…my lord.'

All the puffed-up air seemed to go out of Breock Bawden in that instance. 'It is my boy…my heir,' the man said in a shaky voice. 'The babe is dead, as is your stepmother, Elowen.'

Chapter Thirteen

Elowen gasped and covered her open mouth with her hand as her eyes widened with shock and disbelief. 'Roesia and little Grifiud, dead? How…how did they die?'

'Does it matter how they died?' her father spat. 'Only that they're gone. They're gone, Elowen. Taken by a birthing malady.'

The sudden silence that had descended over them all was pierced by the muffled sound of a sob, which Elowen quickly realised had burst from her own lips. God, how awful. How tragic.

And it was then that she realised that it must be her father's mindless grief and anger that has propelled him to act in this reckless and threatening manner. Now that she looked on him again, she saw how hardened he seemed, how broken.

'I am sorry for your loss, my lord. To lose both Roesia and…' Her eyes filled with tears as she swallowed uncomfortably. 'To lose your heir…to lose the son you have craved for so long…little Grifiud.' She made a sign of the cross. 'I shall pray for both of them and for you.'

'I have no need for your prayers, daughter.' He scoffed with a slow shake of his head. 'What I need, however, is your loyalty and to prove what you said earlier by showing me how devoted and dutiful you are.'

Elowen frowned, failing to comprehend her father's meaning. She had never seen him like this, not even after her brother's death. Now he looked far more at a loss, far more unhinged. 'I do not know what you mean, my lord.'

'No. I do not suppose that a daughter of mine who has betrayed me, conspired against me and wounded me as you have, would now claim to misunderstand me as you seem to.'

She expelled a long, frustrated breath from her lips as Simon leant forward on his saddle and issued yet another warning to her father. 'While I, too, am sorry for the loss of your wife and your heir, Lord Bawden, I would refrain from speaking to Elowen in that manner. She has not conspired, betrayed or wounded you.'

Elowen was stunned. Not since Hedyn's death had someone stood up to her father on her behalf but also in Simon's case done so on equal footing, as one lord to another.

'Well, well, well, Lord Trebarr, you are quite the gallant hero here and it seems you were telling *some* truth, after all,' her father said through gritted teeth, with a sardonic bite. 'You do seem to take prodigious care of my daughter.'

His men laughed and it was then that Elowen took in both how many men her father had brought with him and how they were all dressed.

Dear God, what was her father about? What was the real reason he was here?

'You have still not answered why you have come here in this fashion, my lord, as you could have sent a missive to inform me of your sad news, and not with all these men as though you're about to do battle.'

'A missive, she says. Can you not tell why I am here, daughter?' Her father gave her a disdainful look before continuing. 'Retribution. For everything *he* has cost me. My son and heir, Hedyn, and now...*you*,' he bellowed, taking his sword out of its scabbard and pointing it at Simon.

She felt the blood drain from her face as she stared at her father in disbelief and then glanced at Simon and then back at her sire. God, but her father must be mad with grief after losing Roesia and the babe. That could be the only explanation for this precarious foolishness. His behaviour was completely irrational, as though nothing no longer mattered to him now that everything he'd once cared about had been taken away from him. And this unpredictability made her father far more dangerous than she'd ever have believed.

'No, my lord. Lord Trebarr did not cause Hedyn's death as you know. It was an accident.'

'Do you think that I should believe you, daughter, when I have come upon you alone with Trebarr and his men, conspiring against me?' He sneered. 'What I do know is that I should have done this five years ago. I should have challenged you, Trebarr, while your father was alive, and as the worthless spare you were at the time and with your father caring little about you, I would have had the satisfaction of gaining the vengeance I sought for the death of Hedyn.'

'Stop this, Father. Stop this madness now.'

Her father's nostrils flared as he shook his head. 'I demand that you stand aside, Elowen, while I take on

Trebarr and his pitiful handful of men,' her father said ominously. 'Did you not hear, girl? Come here to my side—the Bawden side, the right side. And once this is over I shall take you back to Bawden Manor and you may look after your young half sisters, or if you still want to go ahead with it then you may travel to your betrothed's, but it will be without the aid of Trebarr.'

'No, I think not. I do not need your escort to Stromley Castle and Lord Roger Prevnar as I have Lord Trebarr.'

'You defy *me*, girl?' He thumped his chest with a fist. 'Your father, your sire, your lord? Well, here I have proof now of your betrayal of me and your kin.'

'That is not true.'

'Is it not? Because I can tell you that you're not being devoted or dutiful now.'

Elowen could not take this any longer. The whole scene was reminiscent of the day her brother perished, except for the fact that her father was threatening more than just one man, and that Simon was now Lord Trebarr and not a *spare*... This whole situation was highly volatile and steeped in so much tension that could unravel at any time. 'Please stand down, my lord, think what you are doing. Think what you are saying.'

'I know precisely what I am saying, daughter.' Her father smirked. 'And I believe Trebarr also knows it, do you not?'

'What I know is that you are itching for a fight, Lord Bawden. But it is hardly a fair fight. You are threatening me on my land with around seventy of your men opposed to my ten and that's if you include my man steering the wagon.' Simon shook his head in disgust. 'Think what would happen if the people of Trebarr, the

Cornish Stannary, or even Edward the Black Prince, Prince of Wales himself would do when they find out of your misdemeanours. What would any of them do to you, your land and the good people of Bawden when they find out about your threats, your intimidation, your reckless behaviour, in coming here today and wanting to engage in combat with me and a handful of my men?'

'I. Do. Not. Care!' her father ground out through gritted teeth before addressing Elowen. 'As for you, daughter, I shall ask you one last time to stand aside so that you do not get hurt in the skirmish.'

But Elowen stilled her horse beside Simon's. She would not be going anywhere and certainly not to cross over and stand by her father. What he was doing was contemptable. It was dishonourable. And she would never again favour her father with her loyalty or her undeserved devotion and sense of duty. She owed him nothing—not if he wanted to hurt Simon. And in such an underhanded, treacherous manner when Simon Trebarr had been nothing but kind, considerate and had even given her shelter during the storms.

Simon shook his head. 'Do you hear what your lord has said, good men of Bawden? He declares that he does not care what happens to him for violating the Trebarr-Bawden truce, and for arriving on my lands to threaten me and my men. But what I ask you is whether you are also of the same mind as your lord? Do you also not care what happens to you, your children, your families? Do you truly want more bloodshed between our two noble houses? Because believe me, that is what shall continue for another generation if you do your lord's bidding and attack us today.' Simon leant forward and swept his gaze across the Bawden men who had gathered and rallied around her father. 'I ask you to think whether you would want to aim for a different path. A path that might offer you long-lasting peace, unity, stability and security between the Trebarrs and the Bawdens. Surely that is a far better goal and a far better alternative than the uncertainty offered by your lord.'

Elowen could hardly believe her eyes but sensed that Simon's rousing yet eloquent plea for peace and unity had made an impact on her father's men as they looked suitably impressed, as much as she was. But then she had always believed in him. She had always been impressed by Simon Trebarr and his many qualities.

'Do not listen to the upstart, Trebarr.' her father said. 'He is the enemy, *our enemy*, and speaks only to confuse, confound and distract you so that he can take advantage of all of us. But know this. The time for these discussions is now at an end. Do you hear? On my command, men of Bawden, you shall attack Trebarr. You shall attack his men.' He held his sword in the air and then swiped it down and roared. 'Charge!'

And yet none of Elowen's father's men moved an inch. They'd all seemingly hesitated, not knowing what to do. This seemed to incense her father even further as he became more and more angry, spitting and shouting at his men. And then it happened. In the blur of the mayhem and confusion of the moment, something in her father must have just snapped.

Her father grabbed a lance from one of his men and before she'd had any understanding of what he was about to do, charged at Simon before hurtling the lance in his direction, while Simon's attention was momentarily elsewhere.

'Look out!' The shout came from Sir Ranulf Gibbons or *Gibby*, as Simon called him, who pushed his horse forward and raced out, putting himself in front of Simon and the flying lance.

It happened so fast then. The lance swishing through the air before it made contact with Sir Ranulf. The sound of it impaling him with such force that it knocked him off his seat and onto the ground. The sudden eery silence that followed. A silence that was soon pierced by the noise of chaos and commotion.

Elowen could not move as she watched in horror while the poor man lay on the ground twitching until he stopped moving altogether. Simon screamed and shouted at his men while he dismounted and ran to his friend, who had, by virtue of putting himself in front of the lance, saved Simon's life.

And, oh, God, her father. Her father, who had caused all this madness.

Simon was bent over his friend's lifeless body before he stood and roared, his anger and rage dripping from every part of him. Elowen had never seen him like this; ruthless, intimidating, and every inch the seasoned and brutal warrior that he was, which he had unleashed. His shoulders squared, his jaw clenched and his chest pumped and holding his sword to his side. Even his march towards her father was formidable as it was fierce. Not one man would dare challenge him at that moment, not even her father, who suddenly looked as though all the fight had gone out of him.

* * *

Gibby was dead…

Simon could hardly contain the rage that was bubbling up inside him when he thought of his unwaveringly loyal friend, his boyhood friend who had selflessly given his life for Simon. The man was true and honourable and his death would not be in vain. Simon would have his vengeance. God, but this act would not go unpunished. It would not!

He marched up to Breock Bawden, who was sat upon his damn horse, and just when the man tried to strike him with his sword, he countered it with so much force that the sword flew out of the man's hand. Simon reached up and dragged the bastard down from his horse by the scruff of his chain mail and threw him to the ground, with the tip of his sword pointed at the man's black heart so swiftly, that neither Bawden nor his men had any chance to react.

Simon's chest rose and fell as he scowled down at the pathetic excuse of a man cowering in the mud. But through the silence with only the sound of his angry, ragged breath and the ringing in his ears, Simon could hear the sound of someone quietly sobbing behind him and knew instantly that it was Elowen. He closed his eyes for a moment, wanting to drown out that sound but he could not. And neither could he go through with it. He could not kill Elowen Bawden's father and in front of her very eyes. What manner of a man would that make him? The same as Breock Bawden. And what would Elowen think of him, if he went ahead and pushed his sword through the man's chest? He would lose any feeling, any regard, that she'd ever held for him. And he was not prepared to lose that. Despite the fact that Breock Bawden deserved such a fate. He still could not believe that he'd taken his friend's life. So quickly, so cruelly. Someone so full of life as Ranulf Gibbons, who had a wife, damn it, who had children.

Simon yanked the older man to his feet and pulled him around, holding on to him from behind with the dagger he'd pulled from his sword belt, drawn against his neck. 'Tell your men to stand down, Bawden. Not that you seem to have much hold, much sway, with them at this moment. Do it. Now!' he roared.

'Damn you to hell, Trebarr!'

'No, I rather think you're the one who's damned,' Simon said coldly. 'He was a good man, Ranulf Gibbons, the very best of men. And he certainly did not deserve to die in this manner.'

'Much like my boy, who did not deserve to fall to his death in that terrible manner he did, either. Broken and crushed against the cliffs, his limbs twisted and mangled.'

Simon swallowed down an emotion that he could not name. But God knew that it was enough. There had been too much of it; too much hatred, too much enmity, anger, aggression, hostility between their two great houses that had also led to death. Whether accidental or not, it mattered not. This could not continue; Simon wanted an end to it. No more.

'Listen to what I have to say, good men of Bawden. I demand that the wagon with all of Lady Elowen's belongings to be allowed to continue on its path to the coast. The rest of my men are to take Sir Ranulf's body back to his wife, or rather his widow now, in Trebarr, unencumbered. If any Bawden man dares to cause further trouble by provocation or further intimidation, you will have me to deal with. You will also retreat and leave my land while Lady Elowen and I shall make our progress to the coast without being followed…by anyone.' They would then board the *Morvoren* but Simon omitted this part.

His men did as Simon asked and started to move the wagon again and continued on its way, while his men crouched and lifted Gibby's body, carefully placing him on his horse before escorting him back to Trebarr.

'I cannot believe that you forced your men away,' Bawden hissed. 'But it rather leaves you and Elowen vulnerable now, does it not?'

'I'd rather doubt that you would want to be reacquainted with my sword, Bawden, but you should probably know that I'm also handy with this dagger,' Simon retorted in the man's ear. 'And just so we do not misunderstand each other, *my lord*, I have singlehandedly cut down far more men than the number you have brought onto my land today. I would hate to have to display my prowess right now, especially when I am this angry, so I suggest you take my word for it. And no, it does not in any manner leave either me or Elowen vulnerable.'

Simon pulled Breock Bawden against him as he addressed his men. 'Good men of Bawden, I had not wanted it to come to this. But know that you have been misled by your lord and brought to my land with no purpose other than to threaten and violate agreements made by the Trebarrs and the Bawdens, and I would wager that this has been done against your judgement. For no man of sound judgement would agree to this.'

Simon exhaled before continuing. 'The outcomes of which have been proved devastating with the murder of my friend and comrade, Sir Ranulf Gibbons. But I shall pardon each and every one of you for your part in this disastrous and unlawful campaign should you look the other way while I escort Lady Elowen, who has always been a true and dutiful daughter of Bawden's, as I am honour bound to do. This you will do, with your conscience intact, and with no reference to what Lord Bawden demands or accuses you of.'

With that, Simon pushed the older man to the ground before sprinting to his horse, mounting it in one fluid motion and catching the reins of Elowen's horse to race away.

They rode along the dirt pathway swiftly with Simon looking behind him inadvertently to assess whether or not they were being followed by Breock Bawden's men. But his more immediate problem was that despite being a competent horsewoman, Elowen was finding it difficult to keep up with him. He pulled the reins to slow his destrier and sidled up towards her.

'Give me your hand, Elowen. I want you to ride with me.'

'What? No, I am more than happy to carry on as we are.'

'But I am not. And despite the threats I made to your father's men, I cannot be certain that they will not come after us.' He reached across to her. 'Come, give me your hand.'

Elowen tentatively placed her hand in his as he clasped it tightly and gently pulled her towards his moving horse. He wrapped his arms around her waist and lifted her off her horse, drawing her across until she was sat on his lap. Letting go of the reins of her palfrey, he sped ahead.

'What about your horse?' she said, looking in the direction of the palfrey they had left behind.

'All of my cattle are trained well enough to get themselves back to the castle,' he murmured. 'We have more pressing matters to attend to. It seems that a few of your father's men have been cajoled into pursuing us, after all, especially since they know that we have splintered away from my men, who are returning back to Trebarr.'

'What are we to do?' Elowen said as she shifted on his lap, inadvertently rubbing her backside against him.

Dear God, but her body, its swoops, curves and softness as well as her alluring scent, wrapped around him.

What in heavens was the matter with him to dwell on the nearness of Elowen Bawden when a handful of her father's men were close to gaining on them?

'Worry not, my lady. I know this land like the back of my hand and can take us down to the coast to where the *Morvoren* is moored.'

Damn Breock Bawden, the belligerent old fool, for wreaking the havoc he had on this day, and damn Simon for being so affected by Elowen's being so close to him. And at such an importune moment.

They continued down the pathway that wavered and crisscrossed through craggy plains and long grass dotted around the landscape.

'My father's men are gaining on us, Simon,' she murmured, her breath tickling the side of his neck as he muttered an oath under his breath. His reaction was intolerable.

'I shall endeavour to get rid of them. Yah!' Simon

spurned his horse to go faster with the four or five Bawden riders not far behind. If he could get Elowen to reach his vessel, *The Morvoren*, before the Bawden men caught up with them, then they would have a chance of getting away. And with the number of men after them there was only one way that they would outsmart and outrun them. By going into the Trebarr coves and into the cavernous sea caves that Simon knew very well.

They descended the narrow pathway until they reached the sandy white beaches of Trebarr Cove and rode the length of it as fast as his powerful destrier could gallop. Reaching the mouth of the main sea caves, he dismounted and wrapped his hands around Elowen's waist, helping her down before untying the saddlebags. Simon then smacked the hind of his horse, prompting it to continue ahead, knowing his faithful stead would somehow find a way back to the castle, or at least he hoped so. God, but he would hate to lose him as well. Grabbing hold of Elowen's hand, he led her inside the sea cave.

'Where are we going, Simon?' Elowen panted.

'The perfect place where we shall finally lose your father's men. Now make haste, come.'

'You do not believe they would follow us?'

'They can attempt to but I doubt they will be able to keep abreast of our path, Elowen. It is a labyrinth and only someone who knows his way around even in the darkness will be able to guide us through.'

'And I take it that you are such a person?'

'Well, I do not wish to brag,' he said with a shrug.

'I rather believe that you do.' Simon sensed rather than saw her smile. 'But tell me whether there is a particular destination that your labyrinth will eventually lead us to or whether we shall have to turn back the way we came, once we have lost my father's men.'

'It connects to another cove, on the other side of the jutting cliff that we rode past. And a cove that should have an available fishing boat for us to row to *The Morvoren.*'

'That is a sound plan, Simon. I cannot fathom how easily you managed to form a new one after the disaster that we rode into earlier.'

'Ah, but that is part of being a warrior who is used to forming plans and strategies in battle that then have to be changed and adapted.'

'I see or rather I… I am unable to any longer, with the light fading here inside.'

'Do not worry, Elowen. I shall guide you and catch you, should you slip and fall.'

The deeper they went inside the cave, the darker and narrower it became, the walls dank and made from slippery, sharp rock, seeping seawater from tiny holes that pooled at their feet.

'I am sorry about…about my father and what he did, Simon. It was unforgivable.'

It was, but he did not want to think about it, otherwise Simon might turn back and seek the same retribution and vengeance that Breock Bawden had sought when he foolishly ventured to Trebarr. And in having the same desire to cause the man the same hurt, the same pain that he'd caused, made Simon realise the terrible grief that the older man must have experienced all these years in losing Hedyn, and only for it to repeat again so recently with the loss of his young wife and child. He realised what a heavy burden it must have been, even though Simon could never forgive Breock Bawden for taking the life of his friend, even if his aim had been meant for him.

'I know.'

Simon felt the bleak coldness from the caves sweep through him as he thought about poor Gibby. God, but what a mess. It was all too new and all too raw to think about what had happened and he was in no mood to do it yet. He would mourn the loss of Gibby but for now they needed to keep moving.

Once again, he thought about the man's wife and child and how they would never have expected of all the campaigns and battles that the man had faced it would be escorting Elowen Bawden to the Trebarr vessel that would be the cause of the beloved's death. It made him seethe with anger. Elowen might be suitably impressed with his new scheme but they had neither realised it, nor had there been much choice in the matter. Simon had to think of a way to outsmart Breock Bawden and the men who had decided to pursue them, just in case they were lying in wait for them. He had not told Elowen yet but once they got to the other entrance of the sea cave, they would have to wait until dusk had descended before they ventured out to sea, to avoid being discovered.

Being discovered...

A long-ago memory suddenly washed over him, one that he could recall as though it were yesterday, when he used to come to these very caves as a boy with Gibby and some of the other boys from Trebarr, and played and hid as children did when getting up to all kinds of mischief, while his brother Geoffrey would seek them out. Another was those warm summer days as he swam in the sea with Gibby until they reached a peculiar-shaped craggy rock that stuck out in the sea, which they named the Marauder's Point. They would climb up the steep rock and stand to survey the great expanse of sea around them and pretend that they were shipwrecked. Gibby had always been by Simon's side, as a squire, as a knight fighting together at many battles including Crecy, as a man and as a friend. And today he had thrown himself in harm's way and given his life for Simon's. It was all too much to take in, that his friend, his true brother and comrade, was no more. That he was gone. His life snatched so quickly, so effortlessly. Because he had put himself in front of the lance and Simon.

'This part of the cave suddenly becomes exceedingly narrow, Elowen, so we must try and pass through to the other side by shuffling through the gap on our side. However, be careful not to have any of the sharp edges of the rock wall cut into your flesh.'

'I shall try.'

They held hands as they moved through the narrowest of spaces on their sides. 'It seems you were not exaggerating when you said that this gap is so very narrow or that you knew these caves well.'

'I used to come here with Gibby and a few of the other boys in Trebarr when I was young.'

'You had known him a long time, then?'

'A very long time,' Simon muttered, not wanting to continue with this discourse but finding it oddly comforting talking about his friend whom he still could not believe was gone. 'His mother was my mother's lady and good friend. And after my mother's death, she looked out for me and treated me as though I was one of her children. I would never have known a mother's care if not for her. And now I have the task of telling her of her son's demise. As well as informing his wife and children.'

'God, how awful.'

'Not that remorse would bring him back. Nothing would.'

They continued through the narrow opening, drips of water coming through the damp rock that they were feeling with their hands along the way.

Finally, they got on the other side of the cave one and then the other. Simon blinked as the light from the entrance in the distance poured inside. He turned to assist Elowen down the uneven steps and caught her concerned eye.

'Again, I would say how sorry I am for everything. If you had not planned on escorting me here. If I had acquiesced and gone to my father's side as he demanded, then mayhap none of this would have happened.'

'That is a lot of *ifs*, Elowen,' he said flippantly, feeling none of it, wanting an end of this discourse.

'Yet, it is true.'

'No, it is not.' He sighed, dragging his hand through his hair as he guided her down closer to the entrance of the cave. 'It is no truer than for me to take the blame for your brother's death, Elowen.'

'Do you not see, Simon, that no matter what we do or what we say there will always remain this barrier between us, between our two families, that always somehow manages to lead to disaster?'

Simon did not respond. What could he add when he knew that the words she had uttered were nothing but the truth? The sooner he honoured the promise he made to Elowen Bawden and took her to Devonshire, the sooner he'd be done with this. The sooner they could part. For good.

Chapter Fourteen

A sombre mood had descended as the sun set over the horizon. Simon had hardly spoken a word to her, even when it was time to leave the relative sanctuary of the sea cave and pull out the small rowing boat that had been left in the mouth of the cave. Elowen had, however, understood his need for contemplation, knowing what he might be feeling after losing someone close to him. Someone who had obviously meant a great deal.

His true brother...not unlike her own brother.

The disbelief that they had actually gone, stripped from this earthly world, taken far too early and in the blink of an eye, was something that Elowen still found painful. And as they rowed towards the vessel waiting farther out to sea, she realised with a sad poignancy that it was yet another thing that they had in common. That unbearable loss.

Elowen sat silently in the rowing boat, welcoming the soothing noise of the waves lapping against the oars and reflected on that loss. She knew that everything that had come to pass today had been caused by her father. Her father, who had aimed all of his grief and anger at a man who had been steadfast in his care and kindness towards her. Indeed, he was the cause of Simon's loss now. God, but she would never comprehend the vicious spite and enmity that had always existed between the Bawdens and the Trebarrs but knew that it would always continue. She realised with a heavy heart the certainty of this. It would continue for generation after generation. Her father's outburst earlier and his terrible actions that led to the death of an innocent man made that a certainty in perpetuity.

She raised her head and peered at Simon, wondering whether he, too, was tired of it all. God, but when would all this bitterness, violence and hatred end?

Well, at least when she finally parted from Simon Trebarr, the hurt and pain of their attachment would also be at an end. As would all the pain and hurt that they had inadvertently caused their two families…

'Do you believe that my father's men would have quit the area by now?' she said, breaking the uncomfortable silence, hoping that the Bawden men would not wreak further havoc on Trebarr land.

'Yes, I believe so. It seems to me that your father's venom was mainly directly at me.'

'Yes, I agree,' she muttered.

'Even so, my men are far more superior to any of those in Bawden,' Simon stated because it was simply the truth. His men were superior, being not only seasoned warriors but far better organised as well.

'I know,' she said, hating the twinge of disloyalty that she felt towards her own kin. 'Yet, what they did today, especially my father, was both dishonourable and reprehensible.'

He nodded. 'Yes.'

She shifted uncomfortably, wondering what she should say to lessen his pain. 'You must be tired.'

'I thank you, but I am fine. In any case, we shall soon board *The Morvoren.*'

'*The Morvoren?*' Elowen had heard him mention the name of the Trebarr vessel earlier but it was only now that it registered with her. 'You named your cog ship *The Morvoren*?'

'I did.' His voice was flat and without infliction.

'Of all things, *The Morvoren*?' She leant forward and rested her elbows on her lap. 'May I ask why?'

For a moment she wondered whether he would answer as Simon continued to row the small boat farther and farther away from the coastline. His large arms clenching and flexing as he turned the oars smoothly through the water. Realising he was not intending to answer her, after all, Elowen turned her head and gazed at the inky sky with the pearlescent silver moon reflected in the deep waters of the sea.

'It was as good a name as any,' Simon said quietly at last, turning her attention back to him.

Elowen sank her teeth into her bottom lip to keep from asking more, knowing this nonchalance belied the reason why he might call his cog ship a name that he once used to call her in jest, when he wanted to taunt her. Not that she'd ever understood. Yet, she did not want to probe further. In his current pensive and forlorn mood, she did not want to voice her curiosity. And she certainly did not want to cause any discomfort, so she kept her musing to herself. And allowed the only noise between them to be the gentle lapping of the waves, as they were enveloped into yet another long moment of quiet contemplation. Again, her mind strayed to how this terrible day had unfolded, resulting in death and loss.

Simon had rowed the boat to the vessel in question, *The Morvoren*, which apparently had a beautifully carved bust of a sea maiden at the tip of the bow. Even the part of the large vessel, the hull, that was visible as the rowing boat gently lapped beside it, was a smooth wooden construction, the likes of which Elowen had never seen before.

A roped ladder had been thrown off the deck for them to climb up into the vessel. Elowen went first with Simon following after her and they both set foot on the cog ship one after the other. And after Simon's crew greeted their arrival by bowing and inclining their heads before getting off to see to their various duties, the captain of *The Morvoren* attended to them by escorting them to the sleeping quarters. The stern castle with a wooden covered roof had been arranged with all of Elowen's possessions stacked in one corner and a pallet and many bolsters, jewel-coloured cushions and soft fur blankets strewn across it.

'I trust that the stern castle is to your approval, my lady? My lord?'

The captain took a step back and swept his arms around the chamber. 'You can see that a small repast has been set fer yer, and all yer belongings have been boarded neatly over there.'

'I can… Thank you.' She smiled at the man, who inclined his head.

'Yes, thank you, Hamelin. That will be all for now.'

Elowen's stomach made a noise as she glanced at the

jug of wine with a handful of mugs, as well as trenchers of sweetmeats, breads, cold meats, cheese and potted fruit on top of a small trestle table. God, but she was hungry, having not had a morsel of food or a sip of drink since she had broken her fast that morn.

Yet, she needed to say something, anything, to take away that stark bleakness from his eyes.

'Again, I wish to say how sorry I am about…about everything that happened, Simon.'

'I thank you, my lady, but I wish you would not. None of it was your fault.'

She lifted her hand and cradled his jaw. 'But it was.'

'Must you do this, Elowen? Must you always take the blame for actions that are never your own?'

'Yet, in this case the fault does lie with me, Simon. Do you not see? That if you hadn't felt obligated to rescue me, if I hadn't been stranded with you in Trebarr Castle, if we did not start this…this attachment between us. If you had not felt that you had to escort me to my betrothed. If I had only gone to my father when he demanded I go to stand by his side, then…'

'Then you believe that Gibby might still be alive?' He dragged his fingers through his hair irritably. 'Hell's teeth, Elowen! How can you believe that you might somehow have affected anything that happened earlier? It's nonsense. And it is not how life works.'

'Yet, you know it is true in this case.'

'No, enough of this,' he whispered.

'But I…'

'Enough!' He then touched his lips to hers, his hand cradling her nape, drawing her closer. 'Hell's teeth, no more…please,' he murmured as he covered her mouth again, slanting his lips over hers. 'I do not want to talk of it,' he murmured against her lips as his nipped the corner. 'I want to forget,' he whispered as he kissed her again. 'Help me forget. Please… I need you.'

Elowen went on her tiptoes and dragged her arms around his neck, clinging on to him as he devoured her mouth. As he tangled her tongue with his. As she acquiesced to his need to make him forget. To make them both forget…everything.

His lips left hers as they trailed over her jaw, the shell of her ear, down the column of her neck, finding the spot that throbbed, sucking and nipping it gently. She moaned as he returned to her lips, their mouths meeting in a passionate, almost desperate dance of need and want. Would she ever tire of this all-consuming desire for Simon Trebarr? What in heavens was he doing to her?

'God, but what do you do to me, Elowen?' he murmured as he helped her out of her cloak and she obliged him by helping him out of his. He then shucked out of his gambeson and pulled his tunic over his head, throwing it on the floor with the rest of the clothing.

What she did to him…?

Simon moved his mouth lower again on a downward trail until he kissed and nipped around the edge of her neckline, eliciting yet another whimper from her lips. His clever fingers started to untie the lacing at the back of her dress as he continued to lick and suck on her tender flesh. He had unlaced the last long-ribboned ties holding her dress up and drew them apart in each hand. His hands then skimmed upwards on either side, settling on her shoulders, his fingers tugging the dress down, making it fall to the wooden floor.

Dear God…

'Simon…' she whispered, wanting him with an urgency that was making her head spin.

Elowen's shaky fingers went to work on the ties of his hose and he watched her, his eyes hooded, his breath coming in short, ragged pants. She pushed his hose down his hips, her eyes fixed onto his as they slipped down well-honed legs. Simon stepped out of them before he released her from her chemise. They then stood in front of each other, without a stitch of clothing between them, for a long moment. How was it possible for her to have this constant need for him? It was madness.

In one fluid motion Simon swooped Elowen into his arms and placed her in the middle of the pallet, his eyes glittering with desire and an emotion that she could not name. He crawled onto the pallet to where she lay, leant over her, his elbows on either side of her so that she was wrapped in his embrace, and he bent his head. He touched his lips to hers, parted her legs open with his knees, and then in one long motion, he thrust inside her, making her arch her back. For a moment he stilled, seemingly to catch his breath. The slick heat of their melded bodies made her groan as she leant up and slanted her lips over his, sliding her tongue inside his mouth. He held her there as his hands explored her body, his mouth following along the same trail. He took the sensitive tip of her breast into his mouth and sucked gently, making her cry out, as he plunged deeper inside her. His movements became frantic, slick and potent as he gently pushed them to their sides and then flipped them around again, so that now they were reversed. With Elowen atop, gasping in surprise and Simon beneath her, still joined and thrusting inside her until she felt that she was melting into him. Her head fell back as she felt him moving so deeply inside her. She became completely boneless. Undone. And she was sent hurtling over a precipice, crying out his name in a shudder as Simon also roared his release. Their mingled breaths came hard and fast. Their bodies were slick with heat and exertion. He rolled off Elowen, dropping a quick kiss on her lips and drew her into the crook of his arms as she nestled against him. Simon drew the coverlet over them, smiling faintly at her as she yawned, her eyelids heavy with exhaustion, and allowed slumber to take hold of her. Sated and at peace, Elowen slept in his arms while the cog ship rocked from side to side.

It was only a few hours later when Elowen's eyes fluttered open to find that she was still curled into Simon's side, her head resting on his chest, and his arm curled around her, enveloping her into his warmth. She blinked, looking up to find him studying her.

'Good morrow,' he murmured softly, touching his lips to hers.

'Oh, good morrow…' She blinked, noting the strips of light piercing through the wooden shutters. 'I had not expected to sleep for that long.'

'Yes, well, after everything that happened yesterday, it seems that we both fell into a deep slumber.' He smiled. 'You must be hungry. Shall I bring the trencher of food we left from last night? We can be decadent and break our fast here on the pallet.'

'Before we have our morning ablutions and change of clothing?' She chuckled lightly as she shook her head. 'So unrefined, my lord.'

'Just so. But I shall endeavour to do better and leave you to your morning ablutions, as I see to mine, which I might add is nothing more than cleansing in a bowl of clean water. But then again, we are on *The Morvoren* and fresh clean water is in short supply.'

'Ah, yes, *The Morvoren*. It is a handsome cog ship, Simon.'

He smiled and nodded. 'And sturdy too.'

'But I'm still intrigued by its name, despite the fact that you said it was *just as good a name as any.*'

'Ah, yes, because I used to call you by the same name? You believe that might be why I named the vessel that?'

'Was it?'

'You had my answer before, Elowen. It is just a name and calling a vessel after a sea maiden is quite common, I assure you. Now, allow me to get you some wine before you see to your ablutions.'

'My mistake.' She shrugged, taking the mug that he offered. 'And yes, I do recall that you used to call me Morvoren when I was a young maid. I remember how it annoyed me, mainly because I never understood why you did, believing that you meant it as an insult.'

'No, not an insult,' he muttered without expanding further. They descended into silence for a long moment as Simon took a sip of the wine he'd poured for both of them before speaking again. 'In truth, it was for a different reason altogether. But of course, when I discovered that the moniker annoyed you, that I had somehow penetrated through that ice maiden surface that you presented to the world, I purposely continued to call you that.'

'I remember it well. How you enjoyed mocking and taunting me whenever you had the opportunity.'

'I am ashamed to say that I did, if only to get a rise out of you, Elowen. You had such poise, such composure, even at such a tender age, that it made me want to shatter that illusion with anything at my disposal, so that I could peek beneath the surface and find the real maiden hidden underneath. All rather childish, all rather foolish, but then I was rather a foolish young man— nothing but a boy, actually.'

She raised a brow in surprise. 'I would never have said that about you.'

'Oh, I would.' He shook his head and shrugged at her. 'And I was rather foolish in the manner in which I spoke to you.'

'That could also be said of me for I always acted far too imperiously towards you.'

'Indeed, as well as being haughty. Yet, you were always so damn witty.'

'I do not know about that, my lord.' She chuckled softly. 'But tell me, did you peek beneath the surface, as you call it, and find the real maiden lurking beneath?'

'I certainly found something that always intrigued me about you, Elowen.' He leant over and curled one errant lock behind her ear. 'One of my most abiding memories of you was at a Stannary function that all the local lords as well as their families had been invited to, many, many years ago.'

'I remember it.'

'You were there, standing with your father and brother, with your back rigid and nose stuck in the air. But I remember watching in fascination as you tried desperately to capture the attention of your father. How you sought whatever affirmation, whatever approval, from him, but the man continually ignored you, so in the end you just gave up and stood there next to them, without saying another word.'

Yes, well, Elowen had always sought her father's approval and yet it had always remained elusive to her. It had always been out of her reach. Until yesterday, when she had decided after what he had done, that she no longer wanted it. She would never seek anything from him again. Not that that would change her decision to go through with the betrothal with Lord Roger Prevnar. She was needed at Stromley Castle, after all.

'My father had little time for me. He had only ever wanted an heir who would continue the Bawden name. But after yesterday, he is not fit to carry our illustrious name. In truth, I shall always be proud to be a Bawden, Simon, but never again would that be because it was also my father's name.'

Yes. They had this in common: their unfit sires.

Simon tossed the contents of the mug back and swiped his mouth with the back of his hand. 'But I remember as I watched you at the time, as you tried and failed to gain your father's notice all those years ago, thinking that I had seen a kindred spirit in you. Someone who shared my despair and anger at being disregarded and despised by my sire as well. It was freeing to acknowledge that. It was freeing to know that someone else knew of the same pain, the same humiliation. And that was certainly no illusion.'

'No, it was not,' she muttered quietly.

'So you see, while I assumed that by calling you a name that I might have annoyed you, that I might have got the better of you, I actually realised that I did no such thing. That what I found beneath the surface of your cool reserve was someone who was not that dissimilar to myself. Yet, I knew I was not meant to like you. I knew that you were of the enemy.'

'As I also knew of you.'

'Indeed, all that mocking and taunting hid the truth of my feelings, which I had always denied even to myself. That I actually liked you. That I always have, Elowen.'

She smiled as that familiar blush crept up her neck, spreading to her face. 'And I you. But apart from desiring to get the better of me, as you put it, why had you called me Morvoren?'

He sighed through his teeth before he answered. 'When I was but a young boy my nursemaid told me of the old Cornish legend of the sea maiden Zennor. You must know it.'

'Oh yes, the tale of a sea maiden who came out on land one day and captured the heart of a sailor. Did he not follow her out to sea, never to be seen again?'

'Indeed.' He nodded. 'Then one day, soon after learning about the beautiful sea maiden, I saw you, quite by accident and quite alone, coming out of the sea, after mayhap a swim with your clothes clinging to you and your hair wet and tousled and it struck me that you looked remarkably like what I imagined a sea maiden would look like.'

'Because of my messy wet hair and dripping wet attire?'

'No, it was because you always reminded me of Morvoren with your pale flaxen hair and that haughty look you always gave me whenever our paths crossed thereafter.' He shrugged. 'That was why I called you Morvoren from then on. Indeed, I believed at the time that you must have bewitched me.'

Elowen knew the truth of his words were laced with the same longing that she had always felt. All these years she wondered, despite everything, whether he had only seen her as an extension of her Bawden kin. Then she'd berated herself for even caring what a Trebarr might think. And yet, he had noticed, he had seen her, truly seen her, and had been drawn to her even when he knew he should not.

'In truth, you reminded me of the sea maiden of the legend of Zennor, who captured her sailor, as you also captured a part of me from that moment.'

She stared at him in amazement, unable to move, unable to speak, with tears stinging the backs of her eyes. Words failed her but they needed to be said. 'I do not know what to say.'

He smiled gently. 'I do not expect you to say anything. I just wanted you to know and now you do.'

And now you do...

But she was not certain that she did understand the reason why he had called a Trebarr vessel *The Morvoren*. And for some reason Elowen needed to know.

'So...' The words she wanted to say seemed to be stuck at the back of her throat. 'So...you named your cog ship after what you once used to call me, as some sort of reminder of that time?'

He nodded. 'I called my cog ship *The Morvoren* as a reminder of what I had once felt for you but.... But also, how I needed to conquer it.'

And then she understood, the confusion in her head

parted, bringing with it more clarity. 'Just as your cog ship would need to conquer the sea?'

His brows rose, as Simon seemingly had not thought she would have made such a connection. 'Yes, I suppose so, not that I made the same connection at the time.' He coughed, clearing his throat. 'As I said earlier, it was as good a name as any.'

Yet, from everything he had said, it seemed far more than just mere happenstance. Elowen was unnerved and amazed that Simon had put so much thought into naming his vessel after her or rather a name he used to call her. Because it had meant something to him—something quite profound. Mayhap it still did.

She had always believed that like her, he had fought to conquer his desire for her. And that it had been the same desire that she fought against. But had it always been more than that—for both of them? She was not certain. In truth, her head was all a muddle, which was not surprising after the events of the previous day.

She slowly turned her head and caught his eyes. 'There is one more thing that I wish to know, if you'd oblige me.'

Simon had moved to the trestle table to place some of the repast on offer onto a smaller trencher. He turned, carrying it and placing it on the pallet. 'Oh, and what is that?'

'I wondered whether you have, Simon?' she said, her heart hammering loudly in her chest. 'Whether you have conquered your feelings for me?' She took a shaky breath before she continued. 'Or…whether I still own a small part of you?'

Chapter Fifteen

Simon stared at Elowen for a moment, incredulous that she would even ask him such a thing. And what on earth was he to say? After all, the truth was something he did not want to address since he was afraid of what the answer might be. Or rather, what he knew the answer to be. He lifted his head and saw that she was also staring, also watching and noting every little movement he made.

'You do not need to answer,' she murmured, shaking her head. 'It's of no matter.'

Simon sighed in frustration as he sat down on the edge next to her. 'But to what purpose would you ask me this, Elowen? What would be the point of knowing such inanity? It would not serve at all.'

'Must it serve?' She shrugged. 'A purpose, that is?'

Yes, no. Damned if he knew. But one thing he did know was the idea of letting Elowen Bawden know the full extent of his feelings for her. Indeed, exposing the secrets of his heart was something that he feared gravely. For it brought him closer to being like his sire. A man whose love for a woman made him go mad with grief after her death and blamed her loss on an infant boy. A boy, an innocent child, for the love of God, who had to carry the shame of his father's censure, disfavour and dislike as he became a man. Simon refused to travel down the same path as him. He had made a solemn vow to himself when he became Lord Trebarr, that he would be different in every way to his damn father. And he would keep to that.

'You are to be wed soon, Elowen…' he murmured, unable to say more but hoping that he masked the bitterness from seeping in, knowing that it would not be long until he would have to give her up. And knowing that the closer that time came, the harder it would be for him to do it, despite also knowing that it would be for the best.

'You know the reasons I must continue on, Simon. The marriage must go ahead because the betrothal contracts have been signed, because I can do some good as chatelaine of Stromley Castle and because Lord Roger Prevnar needs me for his daughters much like my motherless sisters. As well as that after what my father did yesterday, I can never go back to Bawden Manor. I can never go back there again, knowing the destruction he caused.'

She moved closer to him, dragging the coverlet with her, pulling her glorious pale hair over to one side of her shoulder, letting it spill down to her waist. 'But none of that has anything to do with *us* and what we shared last night and all those nights at Trebarr Castle. I want you to know that they have been the happiest of my life. And I shall never forget them.'

Us… Simon had never believed that he could ever feel such a visceral emotion at hearing a word that tied him to Elowen Bawden but he did. He felt it keenly in the pit of his stomach, knowing, though, that it could not last. That it would be fleeting and would one day be gone altogether.

He cupped her jaw and lifted her chin and gazed into those warm brown eyes swimming with unshed tears. 'Oh, Elowen.' His voice was hoarse with emotion. 'It has been the same for me.'

'I also want you to know that what I…what I feel for you is beyond anything I have ever felt for another. And so yes, while it might not "serve any purpose" to know this or have it said, since it is futile, I still want you to know it.'

Simon was flummoxed with Elowen's heartfelt honesty and knew that he had to also share what he felt, however futile it might be. Because in truth, he was right, it served nothing other than prolonging the agony, once they parted for good.

'You ask me whether you still own a part of me, Elowen Bawden?' he murmured, taking a deep breath as he struggled to get out the words that needed to be said. 'Aye, you do. You always have and you always will.'

With that, he bent his head and claimed her lips, getting lost once more to the taste of this beautiful, vibrant woman, whom he cared about far more than he should. In truth, she owned far more than a *part of him*; she owned his whole heart. His body. His soul. And he suspected that that would always remain so, until he breathed his very last breath, not that it needed to be said. He deepened the kiss, eliciting a moan from her, as she pulled him down, down, down, back with her and onto the pallet where they once again came together. As once again they touched, explored, tasted. And as their bodies joined together in such breathless passion, it strengthened the words that they'd just confessed to one another, making it far more tangible, far more real.

God, but what was this woman doing to him? She was tying him up in knots and turning him inside out. Elowen Bawden was unlike any other woman he'd ever known and just as the previous night when she helped him forget the tragedy of losing his friend, by offering herself and giving him comfort, care and love, she was doing the same again now. She was showing in every way, with words and with her body, what she felt for him. This was one reason why he loved the woman with every part of his being. For her selflessness, her kindness, her sharp intellect and quick wit.

And he did. He loved her. But it could not be, could it?

Surely, Simon could not risk loving Elowen Bawden, and slowly turn into the man his father had once been. He vowed that he would never want...love. It was oppressive, suffocating and induced a grown man to madness. He could never allow himself to fall into that black precipice that caused nothing but pain and turn him into a loathsome, hate-filled person, as it did his father. So no, he could not love Elowen. He could not, despite the myriad tumultuous feelings he felt for her.

As they both reached the peak of their heightened pleasure, Simon wondered whether he had made a huge mistake in succumbing to his need for Elowen Bawden. For no matter how many times he had tried to keep at bay his mounting feelings for the woman, they still managed to threaten to consume him. It still managed to grow and become powerful despite all his denials.

There was nothing to it, he had to continue to fight

this; he had to resist falling in love with Elowen Bawden, just as he'd always resisted the ridiculous notion of courtly love. But as he lay on the pallet, in the aftermath of their intimacy, he wondered whether it was already too late. Whether he was already doomed to the same fate as his damned sire. Mayhap he was cut from the same cloth as him, after all. And that thought brought on a cold sweat of fear. One that he had no notion how to combat.

Enough...

His chest ached as he looked across at the woman nestled in his arms but Simon knew in that moment that he could no longer continue as he was. He could no longer allow himself to get even closer to Elowen Bawden. It was already far too difficult knowing that he would soon have to let her go and give her up to another man who would be bound to her. But to carry on while he was escorting the woman to her betrothed, brought Simon closer to disaster. He was not certain whether it was already too late. Whether he had already succumbed to love, but it no longer mattered. He would do all that he could to resist the woman and his feelings for her by putting distance between them, just as he'd intended when their party rode out of Trebarr the previous day. But it was the events of yesterday and the loss of Gibby that made him forget. Indeed, it was what made him seek to forget his loss in the luscious arms of Elowen Bawden in the first place. But now in the stark light of a new day, he could see his mistake quite clearly. And not once but several times since. Indeed, it was a disaster. Since it did not matter how often Elowen was beside him, how often they spoke, and how many times they shared so much of themselves, he was always left wanting more. And he could not risk that.

He pulled away and dragged his fingers through his hair. 'I must get to my men, my lady,' he muttered gruffly as he rose from the pallet and began to dress again. 'I have been away from my duties for too long.'

'I shall come with you, if you give me a moment.'

'No!' He turned to face Elowen and smiled a smile that did not quite reach his eyes. 'No, please stay in bed. And unless there is anything else, my lady, I shall bid you good morrow until later.'

Simon made a graceful bow and turned away from her, putting as much distance between him and Elowen as he could, as he opened the stern castle door and shut it behind him. He aimlessly strode across the wooden deck, greeted many of his own men as well as the rest of the crew of *The Morvoren*, until he reached the port side of the cog ship. He faced out towards the wide expanse of the sea and expelled a big lungful of air that he'd not realised he'd been holding on to.

He had been a fool to have spent this amount of time with a woman who stirred so much emotion in him, who made him feel things that he should not. God, but he should not have done a great many things with Elowen Bawden. He should not have become closer to her; he should not have become so invested in her and her life; he should not have come to care for her. He should certainly not have taken her to his bed again and again. And by God, he should not have fallen in love with her. All mistakes.

For Simon, it had not been just the enmity between the Trebarrs and Bawdens that should have kept them apart. Nor was it the chasm opening up between them after her father had taken the life of his good friend and comrade. It was that, in his moment of weakness, his moment of madness, he had opened up his heart to a woman who would bring him to his knees, who could make him forget everything that he stood for and who could, in truth, turn him into a stranger, into a man he no longer knew nor respected...someone like his own sire. He would not let that happen. And the quicker he ensconced Elowen with the man she would soon wed, the better, no matter how much the thought of her being with someone else pained him. She could never know how deeply he loved her because in the end he would still have to let her go. And in truth, the pain of losing her to another would have to be worth the pain of one day finding that he'd turned into someone else. Someone who used the act of loving another and made it into something nefarious, cruel and ugly. He would never be that person. Never...

Elowen stared at the closed door that Simon had just walked out from, as though she could will him back to her side. She could not comprehend the reason why he had suddenly got out of the pallet and left the small chamber. What had happened that made Simon leave? Was it what they had been discussing? It had to be.

The events of the previous day led to the intimacies that they shared, ending with their tangled limbs and breathless passion. And in that wonderful moment afterwards with their bodies sated and replete, when she felt at her most vulnerable, just when she felt secure, protected, cared for and wanted, Elowen made her confes-

sion about everything that she kept hidden in her heart
for so long. All that she had slowly come to realise about
herself. As well as everything that she felt for Simon.
That she loved him… And she did, with all of her heart.

Why had she revealed so much? Why had she allowed her curiosity to be voiced? Why had she asked
him whether she still owned a part of him? Dear God,
but the words just spilled from her lips. Thank the heavens that she had held her tongue regarding those three
revealing words that she still kept hidden inside. At
least she had not voiced that she was in love with him.
And now after the way that the man skulked out of the
chamber it was for the best that she never did. Indeed,
it was best that she kept those words to hersel. They
were redundant words, unnecessary since they truly
did not *serve a purpose*. In time it would all be forgotten. But for now, until Elowen reached Devonshire
and her betrothed, it would be for the best if she pre-
tended none of it had happened. It would be best to pretend that it was because of the events of the previous
day when she discovered that her infant brother and his
mother had perished, causing her father to do what he
did. That it had been his grief and despair that had led
him to the madness that he then unleashed, resulting in
death. Rather than the truth, which was that Elowen had
not only been attracted to Simon for a long, long time
but that the depth of her feelings had strengthened and
blossomed into love… A love so strong that it would
consume, overwhelm and ravage in the blaze of its intensity. A love that frightened her, a love she had never
sought, nor wanted.

God help her!

Indeed, it would be for the best if he never discovered this. Instead, she would pretend that they never had the discussion that they just had. And carry on until she reached her betrothed, as though nothing between them had shifted and changed forever. Since, in a very short time, she would never see Simon Trebarr again, in any case. Elowen might own a part of him, as he so eloquently said as he poured his heart to her, but he would never allow himself to love her fully. He had been honest with her there. And how could she risk the inevitable heartbreak that would then come? No, she was far safer to go to a man who wanted her as a mother for his small daughters if nothing else.

With the food on the pallet forgotten and her hunger abated, she got up, put the chamber to rights and began to get ready for the day, pushing all thought regarding Simon Trebarr away. She had much to get ready for and pining over a man, whom she would soon be forced to forget, would do her no good. She'd be far better served to think ahead now and get herself ready for her betrothed. And until she reached Devonshire, she would resort to treating Simon Trebarr as an acquaintance and as a friend. Someone who rescued her in the raging storms that ravaged the coast of Cornwall and gave her shelter in her moment of need. And that would have to suffice. It just had to.

However, as the day unravelled so did Elowen's resolve to keep away from Simon. Not that he sought her out nor even spoke to her more than necessary, beyond polite niceties. Indeed, he seemed far more distant with her since morning when he left the inner chamber of the stern castle. And it was for the best, she reminded herself. Nothing good would come of continuing this association with Simon and certainly not this attachment she had to him. She had to fight it; she must overcome her feelings. For all this constant longing would only continue to cause her heartache and pain. And Elowen had had enough of that.

She stared out to the sea, noting the outline of the coast, breathing in the sea air and letting the morning breeze, biting and cold, sweep through her. She hugged her cloak closer to herself and expelled a cold breath, wondering how matters would come to pass today, once they reached Roger Prevnar. She wondered what manner of man he was and hoped to God that he would have all the answers. That he might somehow be everything that she needed to forget Simon Trebarr once and for all.

She trained her eyes out to the sea, despite being able to hear the man whom her heart quickened for, somewhere on the wooden deck, speaking in a low voice to the vessel's crew. She closed her eyes tightly, knowing that even this was too much for her, presently. Elowen needed a moment alone, out here in the crisp open air, unencumbered by those feelings that tied her to Simon Trebarr. She shifted a little, moving away from where Simon was, judging by the low, husky voice. No, she needed more distance so that she could gather her thoughts and reflect on everything that had happened to her and come to terms with what she was about to embark on again. Marriage to a stranger, an older man. Just as her first husband had been. She moved along the edge of the side of the vessel, so that she might somehow blend into the background, so that she might become inconspicuous, unnoticed, invisible. Elowen continued until she was at the tip of the bow, the fore-end of the vessel. Here, it seemed a little quieter, a little more peaceful, with fewer hands and feet on deck.

The Morvoren sliced through the waves as it continued to bob up and down while it progressed through the sea. She looked down, her eyes catching sight of a carved wooden shape at the very tip of the bow as it skimmed below the surface a little and came back up. Instantly, she knew what it was—the Morvoren herself. It was indeed a beautiful wooden carving of a sea maiden. Yet, as Elowen stared at it, mesmerised by the evocative figure, there was something familiar about it; mayhap it was the shape of her face or the tilt of her head to the side, but it was as though she were looking at a figure of someone she had met before. With a sudden jolt she realised that the sea maiden had been fashioned to her liking, to Elowen's own visage. It was as though she had been used as inspiration for the vessel's namesake. And with this, she hardly needed further proof that the vessel that was carrying her to her betrothed was not only named after her, but that the figure of the sea maiden was the exact image of Elowen. She clasped her hands together and gasped, comprehending the significance of this. In truth, it was Simon who carried a piece of her with him. A visceral reminder of Elowen, even when he went out to sea.

Chapter Sixteen

Elowen maintained her distance from Simon Trebarr, even when *The Morvoren* came to dock in Bayard's Cove in the pretty Devonshire port of Dartmouth. The cog ship's sails in the Trebarr colours of gold, blue and green had been lowered, and a few deckhands jumped over onto the dockside to spring the lines and tie them up, mooring the vessel in the wharf.

Elowen watched as her belongings, stored inside large wooden chests, were carried one by one over the planks and then hurled onto a waiting wagon that would take her the remainder of the journey to the newly built Stromley Castle, the seat of Lord Prevnar, about a day's ride away north of Dartmouth.

She took a deep breath, knowing it was time to complete the last part of her travail, which she had started almost three weeks ago now. But with everything that had come to pass, it felt more like a lifetime ago now.

Without looking, she knew that Simon Trebarr had come to her side.

'May I escort you down, Lady Elowen?' he asked, clasping her hand and bending over it, in that gallant formal manner. But not before she had seen the dark circles beneath his eyes. He seemed just as tired and weary as she was.

'By all means, my lord.'

Elowen was aware of everything about Simon, as they descended the plank board in silence. From the way in which he gently held her hand in his, to the brush of his leg against hers as they walked closely together, to his scent—cool, clean and uniquely his, wrapping itself around her as it always did, making her crave him in a way that was now completely inappropriate.

'I have secured the use of a couple of private rooms in a nearby tavern, my lady. You may rest and take a meal for a short duration, while I can secure cattle for the last part of the journey, as well as a few other matters that I need to attend to before we embark to Stromley Castle,' he said as they stepped onto the pebbled pathway along the quayside.

'That is kind of you to think of my needs, my lord,' she said, hoping that Simon would turn and catch her eyes and acknowledge her beyond just the pleasantries. But alas, he did not. Elowen reminded herself that he was behaving as an escort should; that this was for the best, as nothing good would come from constantly craving more from one another. Not when there was nothing left between them.

He lifted her onto the wagon, his large hands lingering around her waist for far longer than need be. He stilled momentarily, breathing heavily and just as suddenly dropped his hands to his sides, clenching and unclenching them as though he was burned from the touch. He then took one step back and then another and then another.

'Until later, my lady,' he said in that irritatingly irk-some formal voice, before bowing gracefully despite his size and stature.

'I can hardly wait,' she hissed through gritted teeth, as she held on to her frayed temper.

And it was this that made Simon flick his head to catch her gaze, studying her briefly before looking away. She had obviously surprised him with her impulsive and petulant response. And no sooner had the words left her lips than she felt the heat of shame and regret of speaking to a man who deserved no such behaviour from her. Simon was the most caring and generous person she had ever known and without him, God knows where she would have been. And God knows if anyone would truly have cared about her—all except Simon Trebarr.

'I am sorry for my rudeness, my lord,' She said, rubbing her forehead. 'I believe that some rest could help restore my mood. And thank you again for thinking of me. Until later.'

He nodded and inclined his head before turning on his heel and moving in the opposite direction. Elowen watched him disappear into the bustling crowd at the quayside as the wagon began to move away. It went down a thoroughfare and turned a corner, rolling along the rocky pathway until it reached a tavern on the corner. The wagon entered a courtyard, where she met the proprietor of the tavern along with his wife, who was soon ushering Elowen inside a set of interconnecting chambers that had been reserved for her use. She ambled inside and sighed deeply, taking in the comfortably appointed chamber.

'Is der anythin' else that I may assist you with, me lady?' The tavern owner's wife bobbed a curtsey as she continued. 'I can send my new batch of hearty pottage and warm bread and butter to yer chamber, if yer should want it.'

Elowen smiled and nodded. 'That would be lovely. And may I ask for a warm bath to be brought up as well?'

The woman's bushy eyebrows shot up in surprise. 'Yes, me lady. I shall see to gettin' a bathtub which can be begged or borrowed for yer.'

She hoped that the woman would not need to beg for any such thing but kept that to herself. 'Thank you.'

'Pleasure, me lady, pleasure,' the older woman muttered, as she backed out of the chamber, bobbing another hasty curtsey as she left.

Elowen took off her cloak and her headdress, throwing them aside, and climbed onto the pallet and lay her head down on the soft pillow. She curled her body on her side and meant to close her eyes only for a short duration but must have fallen asleep, as she was awoken abruptly by the sound of knocking at the door. Bolting upright, she got up and opened the wooden door, admitting a kitchen maid to enter and bringing a tray with a small bowl of pottage, bread, knobs of butter and a small jug of ale with a couple of mugs. This was followed by a couple of young men carrying a large wooden bathtub inside the chamber with a half dozen maids hauling the hot water.

'You see to your dinner, me lady, while we see about getting your bath ready.' The tavern owner's wife followed her staff inside and set about directing the placing of the bath in front of the roaring fire and the clean cloth and small square of scented soap on a small chair beside the tub. The buckets of water were then thrown in, making the steam rise.

'Thank you,' Elowen murmured as she tucked into the surprisingly good pottage and spread a large dollop of creamy butter on the warm bread. 'And thank you also for the repast. It's quite delicious.'

'Yer welcome, me lady,' the older woman said with a single nod. 'Shall I send for one of the maids to assist yer with yer bath?'

'No, I thank you.' Elowen smiled. 'I shall see to it myself.'

'Verra good. The bathwater is piping hot but by the time you've 'ad yer food it should be just nice and tight. Oh, and the soap is made with local flowers and honey,' the older woman said, lathering the soap into the bathwater before setting it on top of the cloth. 'Well, if yer be wantin' nothin' else we shall see ourselves out, me lady.'

'Thank you again,' Elowen said as she ate a spoonful of pottage, dipping the crusts of the bread into the bowl and popping it into her mouth.

She continued to eat her meal, surprised that she had been so hungry. And after mopping up the last bit of pottage with her bread, she got up and started to get undressed and ready herself for the bath. After removing her stocking, chemise, tunic and dress, folding them over the small screen that had been set to keep in the heat, she tentatively dipped her toes into the steaming water scented with the rose-and-honey soap. She noted a handful of scattered rose petals that the tavern owner's wife must have strewn in and smiled at the lovely added touch.

After gauging the temperature of the water, Elowen stepped inside the bathtub and lowered herself down, submerging her body within the soothing bathwater. She tipped her head back against the edge of the tub and closed her eyes.

God, but this was so blissful…so calming. She allowed the warmth of the water to envelop her as she sighed in complete contentment for the first time that day…

Simon had had an exasperating time of it ever since the *The Morvoren* had docked in Bayard's Cove. He'd sent Elowen along to the tavern he'd arranged for her to stay at for a short time, so that he could go about acquiring a few horses for their small retinue, which he'd only just managed to do. He'd also a few other matters of business that he needed to attend to, and since they were now concluded he could finally turn his mind back to Elowen Bawden. And in particular, having to seek her out again, after avoiding her all day.

He strode inside the tavern courtyard, and after gaining the whereabouts of the chambers that Elowen was staying in, he continued on his way and without correcting the old woman's assertions that *his wife* had not needed the offer of a maid's assistance and some other inanity that he'd stopped listening to and bid her a good day.

He climbed up the stairway and opened the door to the main antechamber and walked inside before knocking on the door of the bedchamber. Yet, he heard nothing in response. He wondered whether Elowen was still vexed with him, after he had purposely kept his distance, not that he'd wanted her to notice. But the woman still managed to detect that that was what he'd been doing. Mayhap because he had made it far too obvious. Either way, this was not the manner in which he would want to part from Elowen Bawden. And knowing that, the only solution was to apologise. After all, he had no wish to cause her any distress.

He would just have to be far more prudent and careful as he would prefer matters between them to end with equanimity.

Equanimity? Hell's teeth, but their dealings had gone beyond anything that might be considered to be that. Besides, once they'd reached Stromley Castle it would cease to matter, in any case, since she would no longer be part of his life. And God, how the thought of Elowen no longer being part of his life cut him to the core.

He slowly opened the door and stepped inside, closing it behind him, noting how dimly the chamber was lit and how incredibly quiet it was. Mayhap Elowen was asleep on the pallet. It would certainly explain why she hadn't heard him knocking on the door. With these musings, he strode into the room, ducked under the panelled beam in the centre of the chamber and stilled. For there, beside the roaring fire in the hearth, was Elowen lying in a wooden bathtub, with her eyes closed, looking so peaceful and serene, it made his heart ache. By God, she was beautiful, with her pale flaxen hair plaited loosely and curled around one shoulder, her skin, wet, smooth and luminous and her mouth plump and so damn inviting. His eyes followed the delicate swoop of her neck, that expanse of skin across her slender shoulders and the curve of her breasts dipping beneath the water. Of their own volition, his feet moved closer and closer until he was standing in front of the tub.

Elowen's eyes suddenly flew open and widened in surprise, as she must have realised that she was not on her own. Quickly, she covered her breasts under the water and lifted her head. 'What do you think you are doing here, *my lord*?'

The disdainful inflection that had always grated was back in her voice as she *my lorded* him once again, not that he could blame her after he had also spoken to her with such forced formality. But what else was he to do? They could hardly carry on as they had been, as it would only cause far more hurt and heartache in the end. And he hadn't wanted to push away from Elowen Bawden intentionally but only as a way to remind them both of their positions and how they would soon part from one another. And yet, as he stared at her in that glorious state of undress, he could hardly remember why he had distanced himself from the woman in the first place. She would always be his undoing; she would always be his weakness.

'I… I apologise, my lady. I did not realise you were bathing,' he murmured, as he tamped down the unwanted stirrings of desire.

'Well, now you know, so if you don't mind turning around, or better still, leaving.'

'Come now, Elowen, there is no need to be prudish. Especially after all the intimacies we have shared,' he teased, noting how hoarse and ragged his own voice had become.

'Oh, of course, how could I forget?' she said sardonically through gritted teeth. 'In that case, look your fill, my lord. I wouldn't dream of denying you such diversions.'

Dear God, but Elowen Bawden was furious with him. Her eyes glinted with ire, flushed with so much heat and anger, she could burn him with one glare.

He did as she bid and turned around to face the wooden door instead. 'I just thought that since you seem to be without the aid of a maid, I might be of some assistance?'

'No, I thank you,' she said in a clipped tone. 'I have no need of your assistance.'

He raised a brow. 'Do I detect that you are somehow displeased with me, my lady?'

'What gave you that idea, my lord?'

'Since I cannot see your...your beautiful face, I must rely on the tone of your voice, which I have to admit is piqued. Are you angry with me, Elowen?' he uttered, turning slowly back around to face her.

'Did I give permission for your eyes to be turned in my direction again?' Her nostrils flared with indignation.

'You *are* angry with me.' He slowly moved towards her. 'Why?'

For a moment she didn't respond in words but with only a look of hurt in those pretty eyes.

'Why? You ask why?' Her voice rose as she spoke, laced with an annoyance that was somehow endearing. 'Well, mayhap there is a lot to be angry about. And mayhap I feel that I cannot share that with you.'

'But you can. You can share anything with me, Elowen.'

It was at that moment when Simon realised that he

was completely at this woman's mercy. When she was seemingly in despair, however much she tried to disguise it. He would give anything to take that look of hopelessness from her face.

'Not while I am trying to have a bath and ready myself for a man I will soon have to wed. And in any case, how can I share anything with you when we would soon part, never to see one another again?'

'Oh, Elowen.' Simon crouched beside the tub, close to her, and cupped her face, the pad of his thumb caressing her bottom lip. 'You need not wed Roger Prevnar. Not if you do not wish to.'

She pulled away and shook her head. 'How easily you say that, my lord. And yet, you forget that it is not so easy for me. I cannot go back and live with my father and I cannot renege on a marriage alliance that has already been agreed to. An alliance between the Bawdens and Roger Prevnar.'

In that moment he comprehended the difficulty that she must face, and had always faced, not only because she was a woman but a noble woman to be used and bartered for strategic alliances. In that of course, Elowen had this in common with Anaís Le Brunde Trebarr, who had been pulled apart from the man she'd loved to be forced into a marriage alliance with his brother Geoffrey.

He absently dipped his fingers into the warm water of the bath before he flicked his gaze back to her as she stared out in front, refusing to meet his eyes.

'I do not forget that it must be difficult for you, Elowen. I just wish there was more I could do. I wish I could be of more assistance to you.'

She shook her head and for the first time since he entered the chamber, her features softened as she finally looked at him. 'No, you have already done so much for me. More than even my own kin.'

Simon was gratified that the heat had gone out of Elowen's voice and that she no longer directed her anger and frustration at him.

'It was my pleasure, Elowen, as you must well know. I hope you also know that I would do anything for you.'

He could see that he had flummoxed her as she opened her mouth to say something but gave him a passive smile instead. She then stood up in the bath, with all the water sluicing off every curve and dip of her glorious body. 'It's time for me to get ready. Would you mind passing the towelling linen, my lord.'

He watched her for a moment, his jaw dropping a little. Swallowing uncomfortably, he reached for the warmed towel and handed it to her, watching her wrap it around her body.

'Allow me,' he murmured, looking up into those fathomless brown eyes that locked with his, before she blinked and nodded.

He curled his fingers around her waist and carried her out of the bath.

'Thank you,' she whispered breathlessly, as a different heat permeated her eyes. A heat that held a promise of want and need, matching the same heat coursing through his veins. 'It seems that I was in need…in need…

He dipped his head down as Elowen lifted her lips to meet his, silencing the reminder of her words. He groaned as he covered her mouth, tasting her deeply, knowing that he had failed yet again to resist the woman, as he had told himself to do again and again. God, but she could bring him to his knees with just a look. In truth, he had meant what he had said earlier; he would do anything for her. Anything at all.

She curled her arms around his neck, clinging on to him as her fingers plunged into the hair at his nape. He swooped down and lifted her into his arms, carrying her over to the bed, as he continued to plunder and devour her mouth. His hunger for her never abating. His need for her, a constant reminder. Elowen slid down his body, as both of them stared at one another, panting and catching their breath. He leant forward and pulled apart the linen towelling wrapped around her, making it fall to the ground in a heap at her feet. She smiled a small smile that could have belonged to a siren, a sea maiden—Morvoren herself—and stood naked before him. As always, Simon stood spellbound, watching her under hooded eyelids as she started to undress him so damn slowly, that he did not know whether he could take it much longer. Her fingers touched him as they peeled away his clothing, lingering all over his body, making him groan out loud. God, but he was unable to resist Elowen Bawden. As always. But he was also aware that this would be the last time they would come together, the last time that they would have this intimacy, this shared love…

He pushed that painful thought out of his head and returned her smile as she helped him undress the last item of clothing. And then she reached for his hand and took a step back, taking him with her, knowing that he would follow her anywhere and to any place.

'Would you get on the bed, my lord?' she said softly and getting on her tiptoes and kissing him on his neck, sucking on his pulse.

'After you, my lady,' he hissed.

They lay down together on the pallet and he covered her body, with his revelling in her smooth skin, her curves and her softness, in contrast to his own hardness. Emboldened with a shy confidence Elowen leant up and kissed him hard on the mouth, sliding her tongue inside his mouth, tangling with his. He loved this spirited side to her, and it was this fiery side that he'd been drawn to from the first moment he was aware of her all those years ago. And damn anyone to hell if they tried to tamp that side down and crush her spirit as both her first husband and her father had almost done. Simon would not allow it; he would not allow anyone to change Elowen.... But then a small voice reminded him that once she was married, he would not be able to prevent her husband from treating her however he liked. Simon would be powerless to do anything and would not be able to protect her, and could certainly not challenge any man who wished her harm...

He would not allow it. He would not allow her to be mistreated by anyone, especially not any other man. This he vowed on his oath as a knight, and as a lord. He should be the one to keep her safe. He should be the one to take care of her. The woman belonged with him as surely as he belonged with her.

Elowen moaned as he deepened the kiss, tasting her, consuming her, and pushed her knees apart and in one thrust he was deep inside her.

He was home...

'Open your eyes, sweetheart,' he murmured, bending down to kiss the tip of her nose. 'Look at me, Elowen.'

She opened her eyes, glittering with desire and need and wrapped her legs around him as he began to move inside her.

Reaching out, she cradled his jaw. 'I love you. I want you to always remember that, Simon, even when we will not be together. You will always be the keeper of my heart. Always.'

He had never wanted this. He had never desired Elowen Bawden's love but now that he heard those profound words spill from her lips, he savoured them above anything he had ever known.

Simon turned his head and kissed the palm of her hand. 'God, but I love you, woman. I love you. And I shall never stop loving you. Do you hear? Not until I breathe my last, my Morvoren.' He caught her gaze, wanting her to understand his feelings for her. Wanting her to know the depth of his love for her, in his very soul. He flipped them to the side, his movements becoming faster and frantic as he roared his release inside her.

Her legs were tangled with his; her arms were draped over him as their breathing returned back to normal. Simon held her in his arms, wanting to caress, wanting that nearness, that touch, and wanting to know and also not know that she felt the same as he did in the aftermath of their intimacy. And for the thousandth time that day, he wondered how the hell he was ever going to let her go.

I cannot do it... I cannot let her leave me.

He turned his head and pressed his lips to her forehead.

'Marry me, Elowen? he murmured, knowing this

was the only way he could keep her with him. And despite all his reservations and his fear, he meant to do just that—keep her with him. Simon did not want to lose her. Not to anyone.

Chapter Seventeen

Elowen blinked, wondering whether she had heard him correctly. Had Simon actually asked her to marry him? She could hardly believe it. And for a moment she could not form a response but allowed the feeling of surprise and elation to wash through her. Yet, with it came all their previous discourse, everything that they had divulged to one another, and Elowen knew then in her heart that however much she would want to spend the rest of her days with the man she loved, she could not do this to him. She would not take what he had to offer when it was not something he truly wanted just to suit her own needs and wants. That would be unfair to him and eventually to her as well.

'I do not know what to say, Simon,' she started slowly as she moved away to sit upright, taking the coverlet with her to hide her nakedness.

He looked at her and smiled. 'Say you will consent to be my wife, to be Lady Trebarr.'

'Me?' She shook her head slowly. 'A Bawden, to be Lady Trebarr? Surely that cannot be.'

'Of course, it can.' He covered her hand with his much larger one and gave it a squeeze. 'We can do as we wish.

We can be wed and be together, Elowen. Surely that is preferable than being wed to Roger Prevnar?'

'Preferable? My God, I would give anything to be with you. I love you, Simon. That is not what I mean at all. The enmity between our families is one thing, and yes, it would always remain as a reminder between us.'

'Not any longer. Not between us.'

'Mayhap not us but what about your people? What about Sir Ranulf Gibbons's family? His wife? His children?' She turned to face him, cupping his jaw with her hand. 'What would they think if you returned with me as your bride, a woman whose father murdered their husband, their father?'

'The Trebarr men who accompanied us would vouch for your disownment of your father. They would know that you stand with me, and with my Trebarr kin. Can you not see that a marriage alliance between us could bring about an end to all the hostilities between our two families? Once and for all.'

'That is now far too insurmountable for even us to achieve. It is not possible.'

'Anything can be possible, Elowen. We can overcome it. And must everything always come back to the differences between our families? Must everything constantly be reduced to whether we're either a Trebarr or a Bawden and where the line is drawn in the sand between us? Must you and I always be defined by our worthless sires? Because I will not have it, Elowen. Not any longer. I want you in my life. I want to be able to give you all the things you seek. I want to be able to give you my name, my protection…and my care.'

'Oh, Simon…you are the very best of men. And I

know you would do all that and more for me. But I cannot allow you to sacrifice your wants and needs for me.'

'What in blazes are you talking about?'

She sighed and absently played with a length of her hair. 'You forget that I know how you've never wanted to marry for love. That you never want to have a marriage that might be similar to the one that existed between your father and mother. And if you were honest with yourself, you'd know that that is still true.' The manner in which Simon grimaced and closed his eyes tightly confirmed the veracity in what Elowen was saying. She realised then that he was doing it again; he was rescuing her as he always had done. And this time from a marriage to Roger Prevnar, a man she did not truly want. But Elowen would not allow it. She would not allow Simon to make a decision that he might one day come to regret. 'And with what you and I feel about each other, you fear that a union between us would be the same.'

God, but she would never have believed that a love like theirs could ever hurt this much...

'I... I do not agree with your assertions,' he muttered, dragging his fingers through his hair uncomfortably.

'Even so, Simon.' She grabbed his hand and laced her fingers with his. 'I want you to know that you are nothing like your father. And you will never be like him.'

'You do not know that.'

'Oh, but I do.' She smiled faintly. 'For one, I know that you would never ever resort to blaming a helpless infant and refuse to love and care for that child, whatever the circumstances of his birth, and whatever you might be feeling. It is not in your nature to do that.'

'I do not know how you make such assumptions.'

'Because I know you, Simon. I know your character.' She smiled softly. 'You yourself said that we are not defined by our fathers and just as I'm nothing like mine, you, too, are not like yours. Just consider the manner in which you have cared for Anaís, giving her time and patience as she arrived in a new country and comprehending her heartache over a man she left behind in Brittany despite being your brother's widow. Also consider that you will soon take full responsibility of Sir Ranulf's widow and children. I see you, Simon. I see who you are. And you might be a shrewd and powerful lord but you are also fiercely protective and completely selfless. And because of that you will never be like your sire.'

For a moment Simon just stared at her in surprise, in shock. She could not tell but she sensed the difficulty he had in accepting her words as a tumult of emotions flashed across his eyes.

He then shook his head as though it would push away everything that she had stated. 'Hell and damnation, Elowen, let me take care of you!'

'I cannot accept,' she murmured as tears stung the backs of her eyes. 'I would rather have this handful of cherished moments that we have shared together than have you come to resent me one day.'

'Is that what you're afraid of?' He shot out of the pallet and began to dress. 'My constancy?'

'No, of course not. That is not what I meant,' she said, wondering how to make him understand. 'I know that you love me, Simon. As I love you.'

'Then what, Elowen?'

She got up and stilled him, pressing her lips to his, savouring this touch one last time, before reaching across for the scarf she had been embroidering back in Trebarr castle. 'I want to give you this as a token of my love for you. It is all I give, Simon.'

'But...' he muttered as she put a finger to his lips and shook her head.

'I cannot allow you to rescue me again,' she whispered. 'Not this time.'

Elowen moved past him, picking her attire up from the floor and striding behind the screen to dress. She heard Simon stay for a moment before moving across the chamber and leaving quietly, shutting the door behind him. With that, she sat on the wooden chair, covered her face in her hands and started sobbing as her heart shattered and broke.

It was many hours later, when Simon led Elowen's escort across the Devonshire countryside, that he allowed himself to reflect on the words that she had said to him earlier that day. God, but her rejection of his marriage offer had stung—in truth, it had hurt. And much of what she had uttered, especially regarding his father, kept turning around in his head. He tried to make sense of it all as well as going over what she had said regarding their attachment and feelings for one another. In particular, the fact that Elowen had fully comprehended his resistance to marry for love, knowing that he believed that it would make him similar to his damned sire. That it would make him weak. But did it? Elowen certainly did not think that he was anything like his father, nor that he would ever end up like him. And he had certainly never considered that since his character was so different to his late father's, then so would be the manner in which he approached any situations, including, God forbid, a tragedy. For a man who had faced many perils and arduous situations in his life as a warrior knight and leader of men and come through unscathed bar a scar or two, his fear of turning into someone as loathsome as his father was something that may not have been a possibility. He could see that now. After all, he had purposely done everything as differently as he could from his father, especially as Lord Trebarr, which meant that in loving Elowen he could still be the man that he always was. That he did not have to lose her. That in marriage to Elowen he was not just wanting to help protect her.

I cannot allow you to rescue me again. Not this time...

Elowen certainly believed that to be the reason for his offer of marriage and mayhap it had been initially, but not any longer. No. Simon wanted to be bound in marriage to Elowen Bawden because she stirred him in a manner that no other woman ever did. He wanted to be bound to her because he loved her and wanted to spend the rest of his life loving and caring for her.

And what a moment to realise this epiphany. Just as their convoy entered the inner bailey of Stromley Castle. Hell's teeth, but he needed to speak with Elowen and as soon as may be. He could not let her make the biggest mistake of her life, when she did not know that he wanted her desperately and not for any of the reasons she believed.

He dismounted from his horse and strode to the wagon to help her down.

'We need to talk, my lady,' he murmured in her ear as he held her hand and walked her over to the steps that led to the entrance of the hall, where a handful of men crowded around a tall, balding man with a grey beard wearing a long fur coat and a gold chain around his neck.

'Not now, my lord,' she hissed.

'It's important, Elowen,' he said as they continued to climb up the steps towards Roger Prevnar, towards a future where they'd be forced to part. Simon slowed their pace. 'You are wrong about us, and about the reason I offered to wed you,' he whispered softly. 'Don't you see? It is *you* who would be rescuing me, sweetheart. Not the other way around.'

Elowen stilled as she turned her head and gazed into his eyes, searching for something to validate his declaration, just as Roger Prevnar came tumbling down the last few steps to claim her hand from him, pulling her towards him.

'My Lady Elowen, I have been so desirous to meet you and here you are, finally, and after such a long wait. I would like to welcome you to your new home.'

This could not become Elowen's home. She did not belong here and belonged instead with him, in Trebarr. Simon had to do something, as he was running out of time.

'And my Lord Trebarr, may I extend my thanks for your escort of my betrothed. But I can take it from here on in.' Roger Prevnar gave him a cold smile 'You may of course join us at the banquet feast this eventide before you take your leave.'

Had the cur just dismissed him? Indeed, judging from the possessive glint in the man's eyes he had dismissed Simon since the man must have witnessed the short exchange between himself and Elowen. Hell's teeth!

'I thank you, Lord Prevnar. My men and I would welcome such a feast.'

The older man nodded before turning his attention to Elowen. 'Come, let us celebrate your arrival in the hall, then. And on the morrow, we shall be wed and I shall have you in my bed,' Roger Prevnar said loudly as the men around him roared with laughter.

Simon clenched his fists so tightly his knuckles paled and he could feel the sharp ridges of his nails biting into his skin. God, but the idea of the man going anywhere near a bed with Elowen revolted him.

Roger Prevnar kissed the back of her hand again and escorted her up the remainder of the steps. And just as they entered the hall, she turned and caught Simon's eyes from over her shoulder, and gave him a weak smile. Damn, but Simon had to do something and he had to do it soon. He had to get them both out of this place as soon as may be. He followed the party inside and watched at the entrance as Prevnar escorted Elowen up the dais at the back of the hall and sat her down beside him at the middle of a long trestle table. He motioned for the handful of Trebarr men with him to sit down at the nearest long table and sup with the rest of the gathered revellers. But all he could do was to keep his eyes peeled on Elowen, as she sat gracefully beside Prevnar and raised the goblet of wine that had been pressed into her hand, in a toast. The rest of the gathered people in the hall followed suit, toasting both Elowen and Prevnar on their forthcoming marriage. Everyone except

Simon. He sipped his wine, wondering exactly how he was going to get to have the necessary conversation with Elowen and convince her that he was in earnest with all that he had said. That he wanted her and that he wanted to marry her and not because of the reasons she had said that morn in the tavern.

Just then Elowen turned her head and their gazes locked from across the busy hall, and all those feelings of desperate need and want came flooding back. His chest ached just watching her and she tried and failed to smile. God, but how he loved the woman and how unbelievably foolish he had been to wait this long to realise that he could not live without her.

He tossed back the remainder of the wine and started to put together a plan in his head. A plan that had to work. Otherwise... No, he could not consider the possibility of a failure, and Simon Trebarr was nothing if not a great strategist. But as the evening drew on, Simon realised that he was not going to get an opportunity to speak with Elowen before he had to leave Stromley Castle. He had tried many times to gain access to her but each time it was somehow blocked and denied. So unless he was about to make a scene, he now had no choice other than to make his case to her as he took his leave.

And that time came soon at the end of the banquet, where Simon once again found himself on the steps outside the hall leading to the inner bailey. With his men behind him and their horses with the stable hands, Simon stood on the steps and bowed to Roger Prevnar and his men, who returned the formality, and then inclined his head to Elowen and held out his hand. She took it as he pulled her forward a step so that she was parted from Roger Prevnar for a moment.

'What are you doing, Simon?' she hissed from the corner of her mouth.

'I have to say something to you in private, Elowen,' he whispered as he bent his head over her hand.

'This is hardly the time.'

'This is the only time, sweetheart.'

'Simon...'

'Hush, Elowen, I must say this before I go.' He continued to clasp her hand. 'I want you to know that you were right when you said that I'm nothing like my father. The man was cruel and he was a brute to everyone around him and especially me. And I shall never be like him. Yet, you are also wrong, as I want to marry you because I love you desperately, not despite it.'

'But...'

'Listen to me carefully, Elowen,' he whispered quickly. 'You have until the morning before you're to wed Prevnar to think on it, but if you change your mind, my squire shall be waiting with a horse to bring you to me, just outside the castle walls. He shall be instructed to stay all morning.' He inclined his head once more before taking a step back and then turning on his heel and rushing down to mount his horse before leading the way out of Stromley Castle.

Elowen stood in a daze as she watched Simon and his men riding through the castle gates, leaving Stromley Castle for good. She found herself alone now in this strange castle with this strange older man whom she was meant to wed, with the words that Simon had uttered only moments ago running around her head.

'Come, my lady, my maiden daughters here will show you to your chambers. The chambers that you will only occupy just for one night.' The man leant closer, his stale breath making her feel a little ill. 'And let me say that I am pleasantly surprised by you. Yes, yes, you shall do very well, Elowen. I cannot wait until the morrow, when I can start to breed sons on you, God willing, and after so many daughters.'

Elowen tried to dismiss the man's alarming words, wanting to confirm at least one fact about Lord Roger Prevnar that her father had relayed to her. 'And do you have other daughters, my lord? Younger ones in need of a mother?'

'No,' The man said as he looked her up and down before running his long, spindly finger along her jawline and down her neck, making her stomach recoil from his touch. 'I believe you shall make me a good wife.'

He bowed in front of her, then turned away as he clicked his fingers for his maiden daughters to step forward to take her to her rooms. They walked in silence, crossing the bailey to another tower building, with her mind reeling.

God, but it seemed that once more her father had manipulated her to accept whatever terms he'd thought would entice Elowen to agree to a marriage to a revolting man who wanted to *breed sons on her.* And after his wife's death had wanted her back only to look after her motherless sisters. And while she loved her young sisters, Elowen could no longer do it. She could no longer be at her father's beck and call and she could no longer be a pawn to be used by him, or Lord Roger Prevnar. Or indeed any man.

Yet, there was only one man who wanted her for herself…

I love you desperately…

She followed the women inside the tower with Simon's words going around and around her head as she aimlessly climbed the spiral staircase, trying to process everything that they had said to one another that day.

I want to marry you because I love you…

Could it be true? Had Simon had such a change of heart? Had he come to the realisation that he would never be in danger of becoming like his sire and no longer had anything to fear, about being bound to the one he truly loved? And it was Elowen whom he loved, that she knew with absolute certainty. Yes, it seemed that he might have.

It is you who would be rescuing me, sweetheart. Not the other way around.

Simon had said those words to her knowing that her objection to his offer of marriage was that she did not want to be an obligation that he would one day come to resent. No, she had not wanted his offer to be another way in which he would come to save her.

Yet, by his own admission it was not that at all. He wanted her, he needed her. A surge of joy coursed through her as she grasped everything that he had said. And everything that it meant.

That he longed to be with her. That he wanted to be bound in marriage to her and that he would wait for her. If she would go to him…

Yet, here she was, walking within a castle belonging to a man who was not Simon. A man who made her skin crawl. A man whom she was supposed to pledge herself to. And at present, had no way of getting back to Simon. Ah, but of course, his squire. He had left his squire just outside the castle wall. Now all Elowen had to do was find a way to get there on the morrow.

'If you'll follow us through the antechamber, my lady, your appointed bedchamber is just inside,' one of the young women said as she opened the arched wooden door and ushered them all inside. 'And we shall stay with you, my lady. We shall stay in the antechamber until the morn, when we shall be delighted to ready you for the joyous day, of your marriage to Lord Prevnar.'

'Thank you.' Elowen followed the women inside the chamber and pasted a smile on her face, noting that her belongings, bar the wooden chest that contained the Bawden silver set as her marriage settlement, were there. Yet another reminder of why Roger Prevnar had wanted Elowen to be his wife—for the silver that she would bring to the marriage. As far as that chest was concerned, the man was welcome to it all, as long as he'd let her go to Simon. And if not, Elowen would have to find a way. And as she lay her head down for a moment on the large and exceedingly comfortable pallet, she thought about how she would accomplish everything that she needed to before drifting off to sleep.

Elowen woke with a jolt, coming up to a sitting position, her mind racing, realising that today was her wedding day. She got out of bed and started pacing up and down the length of the chamber, wondering how she was going to get herself out of the mess that she was in. And get her away from Stromley Castle so that she could be reunited with the man she loved.

The knock at the door halted her musing. She lifted her head and rubbed her eyes, annoyed at herself for how long she had slept. Elowen had meant to get up and formulate a plan a while ago.

'Lady Elowen? Are you awake? May we come in?'

The two women from last night, Roger Prevnar's daughters, had come to help her ready herself for her *joyous day.*

'Yes, of course, come in.'

'Good morrow, my lady.' The two young women came storming inside, bearing a tray with soft, warm honeyed bread, cheese, apples, sliced cold meats and a small jar pot of honey. While the other brought forth a jug and a handful of mugs. Behind them a handful of serving maids followed them inside, bringing large bowls filled with warm water infused with rose petals, and another carrying a large basket filled with dried and fresh flowers.

'And a good morrow to you...all.'

'Oh, my lady, we hope you slept well!'

'Yes, I thank you.' Elowen nervously wrung her hands together as the women began to place their offerings around the chamber and then turned to face her.

'It is time to ready you, my lady, for this great day,' one of the young women said with a smile.

Yes, her joyful day...

What was she to do? The only thing for now was to get ready and then find an opportunity to make her escape from this unfolding nightmare. Elowen allowed the women to lead her by the hand and begin to use the warm scented water on her skin, and then dress her into her finest dress made of green velvet, with a square neckline trimmed in silver and gold embroidery, that she brought from Bawden. She nibbled on a bit of bread, unable to stomach much else as the women then set about to arrange her hair. Her hair, which she'd always hated because of the strange unusual colour because it made her so different, so uncommon. It was what Simon had used to tease her about when they had first met many, many years ago, but had since told her how much he loved her hair, as it was an example of how unique and rare she was.

Simon…

Simon, who was kind, passionate, loyal and had the most generous heart. Simon, whom she loved. Simon, whom her heart ached for as she wondered whether it was all too late, whether she would see him again. What if she did not get away? What if she failed in her endeavour to get to him and never saw him? No, she could not allow herself to think like that.

She exhaled slowly, trying to calm herself, watching the young women hover about her like busy bees as they threaded silver and gold thread into her hair and then finally placed a beautiful floral garland on her head. For a moment she felt a pang of regret that she would be deceiving them, after they had looked after her and taken so much care of her. But she pushed those musings away, knowing that she did not have the time for any regrets.

The time was nigh. Elowen was ready, she had to be. She took one final deep breath and followed the women through the hallway and down the spiral staircase as they made their way to the bailey. Here, Elowen was surrounded by many of the villagers who had come to pay their respects and give their well wishes. An intense dread mounted in the pit of her stomach as Elowen made her way through the inner bailey and in through a stone archway that led to the outer bailey with the procession of people following her behind, clapping and cheering. Her heart beat quickly against her chest, making her take swift gulps of air.

Elowen had to do it now. She had to make her escape. Otherwise, it would be too late the closer they got to the chapel where Roger Prevnar would be waiting for her. And as they strolled near the castle gate, she did just that. She hiked up her skirts and dashed through the stone gatehouse, surprising the guards who did not react quickly enough. She ran as fast as she could, reaching the outside gates, not caring of the shouts of people calling her back or that any of Roger Prevnar's guards might be in pursuit of her. It mattered not. She had to find Simon's squire. She ran across the opening on the edge of the demesne land outside the castle gates, looking in every direction, when she spotted him.

Elowen continued to run as she heard cries of people calling her name behind her. Reaching the squire, who was now sat on his horse, she grabbed his hand and mounted the horse Simon had left for her and pulled the reins to get away. She had done it; she had gotten out of the castle. Now all that was left was for her to get to Simon and hope to God that none of Roger Prevnar's guards or retainers would follow her and fetch her back.

It was many hours later that Elowen finally could breathe a sigh of relief after losing the handful of men who had followed her out from Stromley Castle. Yes, the relief that she would soon be reunited with Simon was palpable and made her feel like anything was a possibility now. Happiness, love and a future with Simon Trebarr. She rode through the pathway that entered the small woodland on the edge of Dartmouth Harbour and saw him. The man she loved, the man who made her heart soar.

'I was beginning to think that you might not come, my Morvoren,' he murmured, helping her down from the horse, his hands lingering around her waist.

'I wanted to come to you from the moment you left.'

'But you needed time.' He curled his lips into that smile that made her stomach flip over itself.

'Yes, I needed time, but I needed you more, Simon.' She reached out and cupped his jaw. 'I believe I might always need you, want you, love you.'

'Then it is a good thing that you will now be mine, Elowen, as I shall be yours.'

'Yes,' she whispered, unable to say more.

'Yes,' he echoed as he knelt in front of her and presented her with the emerald ring of Trebarr that he wore on his finger. 'This will have to do for now my lady. And you look beautiful, by the by. A beautiful bride. One whom I hope would also say yes to being mine, my love, my life.'

Tears sprang into her eyes. 'Yes,' she repeated, as no other words could possibly be needed. 'Yes.'

He slipped the ring onto her finger and lifted her in his arms, swinging her around. 'I love you, Elowen Bawden, soon to be Trebarr.'

'And I you, Simon Trebarr, soon to be wed to a Bawden.'

It seemed that today was to be her wedding date, after all. And indeed, it was a joyful day. A very joyful day. Simon smiled at her as they sealed their unusual vows there in the middle of the woodland with a kiss that held the promise of their life together. A life pledged in love and togetherness.

Epilogue

Three months later

Lady Elowen Bawden Trebarr stood beside her husband, Lord Trebarr, on the edge of the cliff as they watched *The Morvoren* sail away from Cornwall with Lady Anaís Le Brunde Trebarr aboard. Her young friend was returning to Brittany and back to the love of her life, Sir Gregor Bartele.

Elowen hoped that this happy event would bring forth the marriage between Anaís and the man whom she had given her heart to…much like Elowen herself.

She slipped her hand into Simon's and squeezed gently. 'I think it very good of you to let *The Morvoren* take Anaís back to Brittany.'

'How could I not, when I wish for her to have what we have?' He lifted her hand and kissed the back of it.

Indeed, they had more than Elowen could ever have believed possible. More than she had ever allowed herself to dream. Yet, it had been hard fought for and hard won. Their love, their union and the coming together of two houses that had always detested and mistrusted each other was one that defied all the odds…and heavens above, it had been worth it!

Her betrothed, Roger Prevnar, had initially been in-candescent with rage after Elowen had run away on the morn she was supposed to wed him. But once again, Simon had used his immeasurable talent in diplomacy to ease the man's sense of outrage and softened his bruised pride by letting him keep all the Bawden dowry, by adding more silver to it from the Trebarr coffers. This went some way to abate the loss of making Elowen his wife after learning that she had already wed Lord Tre-barr by the Bishop of Cornwall himself in any case. The man was prudent enough to know that it was better to accept the situation rather than engage in a protracted and bitter conflict with the Trebarrs.

Elowen had managed to negotiate an arrangement of her own with her father, Breock Bawden. With many who were now vocal with their resentment and appre-hensive of her father as overlord, he had been forced to begrudgingly make reparations to Sir Ranulf 'Gibby' Gibbons's widow and made a large settlement on his young daughters. As well as this he also named Elowen as his heir, upon his death, a promissory oath that was scribed and signed by both parties in front of all his men in Bawden.

And as for Elowen and Simon, their love went from strength to strength.

After all, Elowen couldn't be happier than being wed to a man who loved her, cared for her and made her heart soar, as Simon did. Well, except for one other thing…

'Yes, we are indeed blessed to have what we have,' she murmured, placing her hand absently on her stom-ach, knowing that they were soon to be blessed in more ways than one. 'And with something else that we might soon have.'

Simon's head snapped around. His eyes wide with surprise, his lips curling into a slow smile. 'Truly?'

'Truly,' she chuckled, her eyes filling with tears.

He placed his hand over hers on her stomach. 'God above, Elowen, you make me the happiest of men.'

'As do you, Simon.'

He picked her up in his arms and kissed her full on the mouth. 'Always, my love. Always.'

* * * * *

*If you enjoyed this story
then you're going to love
Melissa Oliver and Ella Matthews's
Brothers and Rivals duet*

Her Warrior's Surprise Return
by Ella Matthews

The Knight's Substitute Bride
by Melissa Oliver

*And be sure to read Melissa Oliver's
Protectors of the Crown miniseries*

A Defiant Maiden's Knight
A Stolen Knight's Kiss
Her Unforgettable Knight

HARLEQUIN
Reader Service

Enjoyed your book?

Try the perfect subscription for Romance readers and get more great books like this delivered right to your door.

See why over 10+ million readers have tried Harlequin Reader Service.

Start with a Free Welcome Collection with free books and a gift—valued over $20.

Choose any series in print or ebook. See website for details and order today:

TryReaderService.com/subscriptions